Fractured Reflections

Bekka Scott

Published by Bekka Scott, 2024.

This is a work of fiction. Similarities to real people, places, or events are entirely coincidental.

FRACTURED REFLECTIONS

First edition. October 8, 2024.

Copyright © 2024 Bekka Scott.

ISBN: 979-8227502087

Written by Bekka Scott.

For all the parts of me and you that no one else understands. You are seen, you are valued, and you are loved.

ACKNOWLEDGMENTS My husband and children, thank you for believing in my wild journey, even when I didn't believe in myself.

Chapter 1

Arthur Hall slouched at his desk, the usual office noise fading into a low buzz in the background. His computer screen flickered, each flash making his heart race. His eyes darted across the screen—he wasn't sure what he was looking for, but whatever it was, it felt close, lurking in the numbers he couldn't quite make out. The overhead lights buzzed, casting a cold, sharp light on the mess of papers in front of him. He reached for one, its edges curling up as if it had been left there too long.

Arthur blinked, trying to pull his mind back to the task at hand, but the numbers on the screen twisted and blurred, like they were trying to slip away. Something was wrong. Something in those numbers, in the data, was hiding from him. His hands trembled as he typed, his mind racing, wondering if he'd already missed something important.

He couldn't shake the feeling—something or someone was watching him.

Arthur's phone buzzed on the desk, breaking the uneasy silence he'd wrapped himself in. His hand shot out, knocking a pen to the floor in his rush to grab it. His fingers hesitated over the screen when he saw the name—Claire. His throat tightened, and for a moment, he didn't move, just stared at the phone as if it might explode. Then, with shaky fingers, he accepted the call and brought it to his ear.

"Arthur," Claire's voice came through, calm but with an edge that made his stomach twist. "We need to talk."

His eyes flicked around the office, scanning for anyone who might overhear. His voice dropped to a whisper. "Claire."

"Are you alright?" she asked, her tone sharp but laced with something softer, something that almost made him feel guilty. "You've missed our last two appointments. You promised, Arthur."

He swallowed, forcing himself to speak as the words clung to his tongue. "I know. I've been... busy."

The office buzzed around him, phones ringing, keyboards clacking, but it all seemed distant, like he was in his own bubble of tension. He looked down at the mess of papers on his desk, trying to focus on anything other than the knot forming in his chest.

"Is that the truth?" Her question has a cutting edge due to having had too many similar conversations. "Or is it one of your shadows speaking?"

"No, Claire, it's me," he insists, fighting to keep his voice level to project the image of calm he so desperately clings to. "Just me."

"Arthur, I'm scared." Claire's words hit him like a cold slap, cutting through the routine and shattering the fragile illusion he'd built.

He squeezed his eyes shut, finding solace in the darkness that enveloped him. "I'm managing, Claire," he said quietly, each word an effort to push through the heaviness in his chest. "J—just trust me a little longer."

"Managing?" Her voice cracked, trembling with frustration, pain, and something deeper—fear. "You call this managing? You're shutting everyone out! You're slipping away, Arthur. From me. From yourself. From reality."

The word hung between them like a thick cloud. Reality. He didn't even know what that was anymore. It felt like a distant memory, something he could see but not quite touch. "I've got to go," he said, his voice hollow. "Work. I... I'll call you later."

"Arthur, don't hang up, please—"

But he pressed the button, cutting her off. The silence that followed was deafening. He stared at the phone, still in his hand, as if it might ring again. But it didn't. Claire's voice lingered in the stillness, her words echoing in his head long after the line went dead.

He let out a shaky breath and tried to focus on the screen in front of him. The numbers swam, refusing to settle into anything that made sense. His hands shook as he reached for the keyboard, the tremor a physical reminder of the chaos inside him.

Arthur was holding on, but just barely.

The phone call hung in the air, like a shadow clinging to the corners of Arthur's mind. Claire's voice still echoed in his head—her fear, her plea. The usual office sounds buzzed around him—the soft click of keyboards, distant chatter—but it all felt distant, like he was watching it through glass.

"Arthur!" Gary's voice jolted him back to the present. He looked up to see his coworker leaning against his desk, all smiles and easygoing charm. "Any big plans for the weekend?"

Arthur forced a weak smile, trying to mask the storm churning inside. "No, nothing special. Just some quiet time at home."

Gary chuckled, completely unaware of the weight Arthur was carrying. "You need to get out, man. Weather's gonna be perfect! Great for a hike or even a barbecue. You know, relax a bit."

Arthur nodded, though his mind had already drifted away. His eyes fell on a random file on his desk, the numbers blurring like static, offering no distraction from the suffocating thoughts. Gary kept talking—something about a community event—but Arthur wasn't really listening.

Inside his head, the chaos grew louder. The whispers were there again, a constant hum beneath his thoughts, pulling him deeper into his own spiraling fears. His mind felt fractured, like there were too many voices battling for control, each one louder than the last. He clenched his fists under the desk, trying to steady himself, but it was no use.

I'm not strong enough for this.

The thought wrapped around him, tightening like a noose. He imagined himself as a puppet, his strings pulled by some unseen force, ready to snap at the slightest wrong move.

"Arthur? You alright?" Gary's voice cut through the haze, pulling him back for a moment.

"Yeah, fine," Arthur managed, though the lie felt heavy in his mouth. "Just... tired."

Gary gave him a friendly pat on the shoulder. The touch, meant to be reassuring, sent a jolt of panic through him, like his whole facade might crack open if anyone looked too closely.

"Alright, mate. Let me know if you need anything," Gary said, already turning away, his attention caught by another coworker's loud greeting.

Arthur nodded, though Gary was already gone. Alone again at his desk, Arthur felt the weight of it all crashing back down. The numbers on the screen blurred once more, the noise in his head growing louder, and he wondered just how much longer he could keep it all from unraveling.

Arthur sat alone again, shutting his eyes tight, trying to will away the chaos swirling inside his head. He imagined the turmoil in his mind as a stormy sea, wild waves crashing against each other, pulling him in different directions. His thoughts were the waves, uncontrollable, smashing into him with relentless force. Somewhere in that storm, he was fighting—fighting to stay afloat, to keep control.

Every breath he took felt like a victory, every beat of his heart a reminder that he was still here, still holding on. "Just maintain," he whispered to himself, his voice barely audible. It was his mantra, his lifeline. "Maintain."

Outside, the office buzzed along, coworkers moving, talking, and laughing, completely unaware of the battle raging inside Arthur Hall. He was at war with himself, and no one else could see it.

His trembling fingers hovered over the keyboard. He typed, but each keystroke felt wrong, shaky. The words on the screen blurred, twisting into shapes he didn't recognize. He wasn't sure if they made any sense anymore. His breath grew shallow, each inhale feeding the knot of anxiety tightening in his chest.

"Control," he muttered, the word a desperate plea to the parts of himself that felt like strangers. In the back of his mind there were voices—whispers—trying to pull him deeper into the shadows. They weren't loud, but they were persistent, each one wanting to take over, to decide for him, to drown out the little bit of sanity he had left.

But then, through the noise in his head, something else crept in. A memory, faint but sharp enough to make him pause. He could see it—sunlight pouring into a small kitchen, warm and golden. Laughter filled the air, light and carefree. For a brief moment, Arthur was pulled back to that time, to that place, where life felt simple. Where he didn't feel broken.

In the memory, Claire was standing there, her hair glowing in the sunlight, making her look almost angelic. She was humming a tune, one that wrapped around them, tying that moment together like a fragile thread. "You're off-key," Arthur had teased her back then, and she'd laughed—a sound so pure and full of joy it had made the room feel brighter.

"Perfection is overrated," she had joked, her eyes sparkling with mischief. That's how he liked to remember her—carefree, untouched by the darkness that now seemed to cling to everything. In that moment, they had felt invincible, like nothing could ever go wrong.

The outside world had seemed so far away, just a murmur in the distance.

But as fast as the memory surfaced, it vanished, leaving Arthur alone again in the cold, fluorescent light of the office. The warmth, the laughter—it was all gone, replaced by the harsh reality of the present. That world he remembered, that perfect moment, felt like something that had slipped through his fingers, piece by piece, until there was nothing left.

Arthur blinked hard, trying to shake off the memory, but it lingered like a shadow. He stared at the report on his computer screen, forcing his focus back to the task at hand. The black letters blurred, then sharpened, as he began typing again, each word a way to keep himself grounded.

With every keystroke, he tried to rebuild the walls around him, closing himself off from the storm that threatened to pull him under.

Arthur sits in his chair, blending into the background of the bustling office like a shadow no one notices. Phones ring, keyboards click, but his attention flits between his flickering computer screen and the pile of papers scattered on his desk.

He keeps his gaze low, avoiding eye contact, shrinking into himself like he can disappear if he just stays small enough. His shoulders hunch forward, as if he's trying to protect himself from something, though no one around him seems to notice. The air feels thick, filled with the weight of questions he can't, or won't, answer.

A soft vibration from his phone cuts through the noise. Arthur reaches for it, his hand calm on the surface, though everything inside him is fraying. Again. Claire's name flashes on the screen, a reminder of the life he's slowly unraveling from, thread by thread, one lie at a time.

"Arthur?" Claire's voice comes through, the concern in it unmistakable. "Don't hang up, seriously. We really need to talk about last night."

He can envision her restless steps in their dimly lit bedroom, clutching the phone as if it's the sole anchor keeping her from drifting away. The image tightens a knot of guilt in his chest, but he pushes it away.

"Claire, please, I am working. Nothing happened," he says quietly, the words barely escaping his lips. The lie comes easy. "I was just tired."

"Arthur, you were talking to someone who wasn't there," Claire presses, her voice trembling but firm. "Please, you have to get help before—"

"I'm handling it," Arthur interrupts, his voice sharp, like he's cutting the conversation short before it can go anywhere dangerous. It's a lie he whispers to himself as much as to anyone else. Admitting he's not in control would mean letting everything inside him spill out, and that's a risk he's not ready to take.

"Arthur, please—" She starts again, but he's already hung up, cutting off her voice, her concern, her fear, all of it. The silence that follows is heavy, a void where her words still echo in his mind.

He drops the phone back onto his desk, where it lands softly among the papers and clutter. Around him, the office moves on, oblivious. The buzz overhead fits with the lights casting a sterile glow on the rows of cubicles. Colleagues shuffle past, lost in their own worlds, as the clock ticks relentlessly. People keep talking, typing, going about their day, completely oblivious to the fractures lurking beneath the facade. No one sees the way Arthur is crumbling from the inside out.

He breathes in the sterile office air, each breath an effort to calm the shaking inside him. The day ahead feels like an endless stretch of hours, and he knows he has to keep walking through it carefully. If he slips, if he lets his guard down, they'll all see it—the fragile state of his mind, the chaos he's barely holding back.

Gary's shadow stretches across Arthur's cluttered desk, cutting a dark line through the messy papers and half-drunk coffee cups. Gary leans in, wearing that same easy smile he always does—bright and carefree, like nothing in the world could ever bother him.

"Hey, Arthur," Gary says, his voice light, almost too casual. "A few of us are going out for lunch. Mexican place down the street. You coming?"

Arthur looks up briefly, his eyes flickering away just as quickly. "Thanks, but I've got to finish this report." His fingers hover over the keyboard, not quite typing. The words come out smooth, but it's a lie—one he tells so often, it feels like second nature now.

Gary chuckles, patting Arthur's shoulder in that friendly way of his. "Come on, mate. The work'll still be here when you get back."

Arthur flinches ever so slightly at the contact but hides it. "I really can't," he mumbles, his voice low, like he's hoping Gary won't push any further.

Gary sighs, stepping back. "Alright, no pressure." He drifts away, joining the others, who are laughing and chatting as they leave—like a group of birds flying off, leaving Arthur grounded and alone.

The door closes behind them, and the office falls into a dull, almost eerie silence. Arthur's heartbeat echoes in his ears, loud and fast. The quiet isn't comforting, though—it's suffocating. A stillness that leaves too much space for the voices to creep in.

"Pathetic," one of them sneers in his head, the word slithering through his thoughts. "Can't even go to lunch like a normal person."

"Everyone sees right through you," the same one hisses, cold and sharp. "They know you're not okay."

Arthur swallows, his throat tight, trying to block them out. "Stop," he whispers, barely audible, his fingers shaking as they rest on the keyboard. But the voices don't stop. They never do.

"Making excuses again?" Another voice chimes in, its tone mocking. "You can't keep this up."

"Shut up," Arthur mutters under his breath, typing random words just to drown them out, to feel like he's doing something, anything, to keep them at bay.

The voices swell, overlapping now, their taunts becoming a cruel chorus in his mind. "You're falling apart, Arthur. Losing control. Everyone knows it."

He presses his palms into his eyes, hard enough to see stars bursting behind his eyelids. The world feels like it's tilting, spinning, and he's barely holding on. He focuses on the feel of the cool desk under his hands, the steady ticking of the wall clock—something, anything, to anchor him in reality.

"Get it together," Arthur whispers to himself, teeth clenched. "You have to keep it together."

But deep down, he knows the truth. He's slipping—slower now, but slipping all the same. The voices won't stop, and the chaos inside him is growing, a storm that he's no longer sure he can outrun.

For a brief moment, everything is still. The storm inside Arthur's mind quiets, like the eye of a hurricane. But he knows better than to trust the calm—it never lasts. Soon enough, the voices stir again, each one clawing at the edges of his thoughts, fighting to break free from the cage of his mind.

"Let me take control," one whispers, its voice smooth and dangerous, like silk sliding over a blade. "I can fix this, make everything disappear."

"No," Arthur breathes, barely audible, but firm. He knows what happens when he lets go, when he gives them even an inch. Chaos. Destruction.

"You're too weak," another voice sneers, sharp as glass. "You can't even make a decision."

Arthur squeezes his eyes shut. "Enough," he mutters, but it's more of a plea than a command. The word feels foreign, his own voice unfamiliar, as if it belongs to someone else. His chair scrapes loudly as he stands, sudden and awkward, trying to shake free of the rising panic.

"Arthur? You alright?" The question comes from across the room, distant, detached.

He nods quickly, a stiff, jerky motion, afraid that speaking might open the floodgates. He forces himself to sit, fingers hovering over the keyboard as if work will save him, as if the numbers and figures on the screen can anchor him to reality. But the whispers are still there, gnawing at his sanity, relentless.

The ticking of the clock grows louder, matching the frantic beat of his heart. Just as the voices rise again, he senses her before he hears her—Ms. Thompson, moving with practiced grace, clipboard tucked neatly under one arm.

"Arthur," she calls, her voice clear, slicing through the fog in his head. "A moment?"

His heart stutters, and for a second, everything feels too sharp, too real. He forces himself to meet her eyes, but only for a second. Something about the way she stands there, calm and composed, feels like an omen.

"Of course," he manages, voice tight and strained. He rises from his desk and follows her to the quiet of her office, every step stiff and mechanical, as if he's walking through molasses.

"Your recent reports," she says, flipping through the papers on her clipboard, "they've been outstanding. Really impressive."

Outstanding. The word lands like a stone in his chest. It should make him feel proud, but it doesn't. Instead, it feels like a spotlight has been thrown on him, and all the cracks in his armor are suddenly visible. Inside his mind, the voices jostle, fighting for control—some desperate to take the credit, others to run.

"Thank you," he replies, the words hollow. The relief he expected doesn't come. Instead, there's only a sinking feeling, as if the ground is slipping out from under him.

Ms. Thompson smiles warmly. "Keep up the good work. We're noticing your dedication."

Noticing. That's the last thing he wants. People noticing means they'll start asking questions. He nods quickly and slips out of the room, back to his desk, back to the relative safety of the cubicles and the noise of the office.

The hours drag by, each one heavier than the last. Finally, as the sun sets and long shadows creep across the floor, the workday ends. Arthur shuts down his computer, the hum of the office machinery dying down with it. His co-workers offer him passing nods and polite smiles, but he barely registers them. He's already halfway out the door.

The elevator ride down is suffocating, the fluorescent lights flickering as if they, too, are fighting the darkness. But when the doors open and he steps into the cool evening air, Arthur feels something loosen inside him, something small but vital.

It's a short walk to his apartment, the city buzzing around him, indifferent to the war inside his head. Once inside, he locks the door, the sound of the bolt sliding home bringing a sense of fragile peace. For a moment, he just stands there, breathing in the quiet, letting the solitude wash over him. There's a note on the table: *'I took a late shift; see you in the morning; I love you, Claire.'*

"Good. Safe," he whispers to himself, the word a small comfort in the empty room. The shadows here know him—they've seen his worst, and they don't judge.

Arthur sinks into his armchair, the familiar cushions cradling his exhausted body. The voices inside were quiet, retreating to the corners of his mind, content to lurk in the background for now. Tonight, he is alone—truly alone—and it's enough.

For now, the chaos is kept at bay. For now, he is in control.

Chapter 2

Arthur's mind stirs slowly, like something heavy being pulled up from the bottom of a deep, dark ocean. He blinks a few times, but nothing makes sense. The room around him is blurry, just a hazy mix of dark shapes and strange colors that don't fit together. Everything feels wrong—like he's still trapped in some strange dream, and nothing feels safe or familiar.

His breathing comes fast, sharp, and too loud in the eerie silence, as though even the act of taking air feels unnatural. When he tries to sit up, the world spins violently, like the ground is slipping out from under him. The room seems to stretch out, walls too far away, too cold, with shadows creeping longer with every flicker of dim light. His heart pounds hard, each beat echoing in his ears, and that's when he notices it.

A smell—sharp and metallic. It fills the air, heavy and overwhelming. It doesn't belong here, but it's everywhere. He can't tell what it is, but the scent wraps around him like a warning, sending chills crawling up his back.

Something is wrong. Very wrong.

Arthur tries to move, but something heavy pins him down. He shifts, struggling to get up, but his body feels wrong, weighed down by an invisible force. His hands—they feel strange, sticky, like something's covering them. Slowly, he lifts them toward the faint light. When he sees them, his heart nearly stops.

His hands are covered in blood. Dark, thick, wet and shiny, it clings to his fingers like a second skin, almost unreal. His mind stumbles over the sight, like it's trying to catch up to what's right in front of him but keeps missing.

Blood. But is it his? Or someone else's?

His thoughts jump from one piece to another, fragments of memories that don't make sense. He tries to remember, to grab onto something solid, but nothing comes. The blood on his hands feels thick and cold now, smearing across his palms and under his fingernails. It's everywhere, dark and damning.

A chill runs through his body as his eyes drift down to his clothes. His shirt—something he wore just like any other day—now has streaks of red all over it. The blood stands out against the fabric, each stain looking like an accusation. The more he stares, the more it feels like the stains are alive, pointing fingers at him.

Arthur's pulse races, pounding so hard in his ears it blocks out everything else. His hands begin to shake, uncontrollably now. Droplets of blood fall to the floor, stringy with soft, wet sounds, louder than they should be in the dead silence of the room. Time seems to stretch out, every second feeling impossibly long.

A scream tries to rise in his chest, but it gets stuck in his throat, raw and painful, unable to come out. His mind spins, racing for answers that aren't there. Everything feels like a blur—confusion, fear, and an overwhelming sense of dread. He searches frantically for some memory, anything that can explain the chaos surrounding him, but there's nothing. Only an empty, terrifying silence where the truth should be.

The walls feel like they're closing in, the shadows stretching and creeping toward him, as if they're alive. It's all too real. Too much to handle.

"This can't be real," Arthur thinks, his mind grasping for some kind of escape. The thought is weak, almost useless, like trying to hold back a tidal wave with a paper shield. The blood on his hands and clothes—so vivid, so accusing—seems to mock him. His life was never like this. It was simple, routine, nothing out of the ordinary. And now? Now, it's like he's trapped in a nightmare, only it's too clear, too solid to be a dream.

His heart races, thudding hard against his chest, each beat like a fist banging on a door that won't open. The blood—none of it belongs to him. It's someone else's story, written in red streaks on his hands, but he doesn't know how it got there. There's no memory of what happened, no clear picture of the moment that this nightmare began. His throat tightens, panic rising up inside him, a wave that he can't stop. His mind is screaming for answers, but there's nothing to calm the storm that's building in his head.

"Think, Arthur, just think," he whispers into the empty room, but his voice is shaky, barely a whisper. The sound feels strange, like it's coming from someone else, as if he's not really here. He feels disconnected, like he's watching himself from the outside, a stranger to his own life, trapped in a scene that doesn't make sense.

Questions start to swirl in his mind, filling the silence with fear and confusion. They loom over him like dark storm clouds, but he can't grasp any answers. What happened? What has he done? Or worse—what was done to him?

The shadows stretch across the room, swallowing the dim light, creeping closer with each passing second. They feel alive, almost like they're closing in on him, and Arthur can't look away from the blood on his clothes. His body is frozen, paralyzed by shock, unable to do anything but sit there. The red stains scream at him, accusing him of something too horrible to understand. The air feels thick, heavy, like the room itself is holding him captive, trapping him in this nightmare.

His mind is a mess, thoughts splintering apart. The memories—the lost hours—taunt him, mocking him with their absence. What happened during that time? What did he do? The dread gnaws at him, filling the empty spaces where answers should be, suffocating him with the unknown.

Arthur feels himself slipping away, his sense of self cracking under the weight of it all. He was always the quiet one, the man who went unnoticed, blending into the background. Just Arthur Hall. Just ordinary. But now? Now he's not sure of anything. The image of himself in his mind is shattered, replaced by something darker, something he doesn't recognize. And the blood—it feels like more than a mistake. What if this isn't just some horrible accident? What if the blood on his hands tells a truth he's too afraid to admit?

Doubt coils around him, tightening with every breath. Maybe he's not as innocent as he thought. Maybe there's something lurking inside him, something he's kept buried for years, that has finally come to the surface.

He fights it, struggling to hold on to the person he believes he is—or was—but it's no use. His thoughts are scattered, flying in every direction like leaves in a storm. And one question rises above the chaos, echoing in his mind: *Who is Arthur Hall now?*

TIME DRIFTS AWAY FROM Arthur like sand slipping through his fingers, disappearing without him even noticing. He sits there, frozen, stuck in a silence that feels louder than anything he's ever heard. Everything around him feels off—like he's not supposed to be here. The room is strange, unfamiliar, and the outside world? That's so distant, it might as well be a dream. His old life, whatever it was, feels blurry, like a memory that's slowly fading away with each breath.

But he knows he can't just sit there forever. The horror in front of him is too much, and the need to escape it pulls him out of his chair. It's like something else is controlling him, pushing him to move. The blood—it needs to be cleaned. It has to be gone.

Arthur stumbles toward the bathroom, barely feeling his feet hit the floor. He feels detached, like he's not really in his own body, just watching from the outside. He turns on the faucet, and the sound of the water seems so loud, almost deafening. He starts scrubbing his hands, rubbing at the blood, but it won't come off. It sticks to him, stubborn, as if it's part of him now. The sink turns red, and no matter how hard he tries, he can't make it go away, can't get it all off.

Then, through the chaos in his mind, he hears a sound—a hum. At first, it's barely there, but then it cuts through everything. The TV. He hadn't even realized it was on, but now it's the only thing keeping him tethered to reality. Trembling, he turns to look at the screen.

A news anchor fills the screen, her face serious and grim. Her voice is calm, but the words she's saying hit him like a punch. "A brutal murder shocks the city tonight," she reports, her tone heavy with the weight of it all. "The community is reeling from the violent attack."

Arthur freezes, his hands still dripping red water. The images on the screen shift—flashing sirens, yellow police tape flapping in the wind. His stomach turns as he hears the details: someone's life was taken, in the most brutal way. The body was found in an alley, the wounds so precise, so deliberate, that even the toughest cops are shaken. Arthur's breath catches in his throat, the room suddenly feeling too small, too tight.

"No," he whispers, his voice cracking. He wants to turn away, to look anywhere but at the TV, but he can't. His eyes are glued to the screen, his heartbeat thudding in his ears. "It can't be," he mutters, but doubt is already creeping in, eating away at him. It gnaws at the edges of his mind, whispering that maybe, just maybe, this is all connected in a way he doesn't want to believe.

His hands—still covered in red. His clothes—streaked with stains. His mind—completely blank. The murder on the news feels too close, too real. Arthur's heart races, thoughts spiraling out of control. This can't be connected, it's just not possible.

But then, something dark stirs in the back of his mind, a whisper of doubt that creeps in like a shadow. What if it's not a coincidence?

His pulse speeds up, fear crawling through his veins. He's always been just Arthur Hall—an ordinary guy, invisible in the grand scheme of things. Filing reports at work, blending into the background, small talk that never led anywhere. But the blood on his hands tells a different story. The fear gnawing at him suggests something much, much worse.

"Coincidence," he says aloud, his voice trembling. "It has to be." But even as he speaks the words, they feel weak, hollow. Uncertainty presses down on him, his mind spinning, trying to make sense of it all. It's like trying to put together a puzzle with pieces missing crucial pieces he can't find.

The images flashing on the screen, the blood staining his skin—what if he's not the man he thought he was?

"Arthur Hall doesn't do these things," he whispers to the empty room, clinging to the words as if they can somehow save him. He repeats it, over and over, like a prayer. Like it can protect him from the truth that's lurking just beyond his reach. But the doubt—it's there. It sinks its claws deeper, making him question everything. What if he's wrong?

His eyes flick back to the TV screen. The anchor's voice seems far away now, the words slow and muffled, as if the world is closing in around him. Each sentence feels heavy, like stones dropping into a pool, sending ripples of fear through his entire body.

"Arthur Hall goes unnoticed," he mutters again, but his voice is weaker now, less certain. His throat tightens, his mouth dry, tongue sticking to the roof of his mouth. Unseen. Unremarkable. That's who he's supposed to be.

But with every glance at his bloodstained hands, with every beat of his racing heart, that version of himself slips further and further away.

But the images on the screen won't let Arthur rest. The faces of the victim's family flash across his mind—eyes wide with pain, hands shaking, gripping each other as though they might disappear. A strange feeling takes hold in his chest, something deep and unsettling. Guilt? Recognition?

The sensation tightens, coiling like ice around his heart. *No,* he tells himself. *It's not possible.* Not him. Not Arthur Hall, the man who blends into the background, who stays quiet and out of the way. The man whose biggest act of rebellion was sneaking a few extra sugar packets from the office break room.

"Paranoia," he mutters to himself, his voice barely more than a whisper. He looks up, catching his reflection in the darkened window. Hollow eyes stare back at him, tired and worn. Eyes that have skimmed spreadsheets, filed reports, and counted down the minutes until the end of the workday. *These* aren't the eyes of a murderer. They can't be.

But the question gnaws at him, an unspoken shadow looming larger with every passing second: *If not him... then who?*

His heart thunders in his chest, pounding so hard he wonders if it's trying to escape. He presses his palm against the table, the only thing anchoring him to the moment. The wood feels solid beneath his hand, but when he pulls it away, his fingers stick, catching on something wet. He stares down, his stomach lurching.

His hands—still red, still smeared. They don't feel like his own.

The air thickens around him, pressing down like a weight, and the room seems to shrink. The sharp smell of iron is everywhere now—too strong, too overwhelming. It fills his nose, clogs his throat, clings to his skin. He can taste it—metallic, bitter—like pennies dissolving on his tongue, and no matter how hard he swallows, the taste won't go away.

Arthur's pulse quickens, panic creeping into every corner of his mind. The blood on his hands, the suffocating smell, the faces on the screen—it all feels too real, too close. Each breath comes quicker, shallower, as if the room itself is closing in, trapping him in this nightmare.

The silence in the room presses against Arthur, heavy and alive, pulsing in time with the relentless pounding of his heart. *Think. Think!* His mind commands, but his own voice feels distant, swallowed by the eerie quiet. His thoughts whirl like a storm, crashing and scattering before he can catch hold of anything solid.

He squeezes his eyes shut, desperate to pull together the pieces of whatever happened tonight. There has to be *something*—a clue, a memory—anything to make sense of this nightmare. But every time he gets close, his mind slips, like trying to hold on to ice. A blurry glimpse of streetlights. Maybe. Footsteps echoing. Were they his? Or someone else's? A conversation—no, more like muffled voices, warped and distant, as though underwater.

Nothing fits. The pieces of the night feel jumbled, as if someone tossed them into a black hole and left him fumbling in the dark. It's a puzzle with no picture to guide him, just random fragments that refuse to align. The harder he tries to remember, the more the evening fades away, leaving only the crushing weight of dread in its place.

Frustration tightens in Arthur's chest, his pulse quickening, frustration coiling tighter and tighter. Each attempt to focus is like chasing a shadow—just when he thinks he's getting close, it slips away. There's something inside him, lurking at the edges of his mind. He can't explain it, but it feels dark, ominous, growing stronger with every passing second. Like a cold shadow where warmth should be.

He runs a trembling hand through his hair, yanking at the strands as if pulling hard enough will force the truth out. But nothing comes, only the emptiness, the unknown.

"*Focus*," he whispers, but it's useless. Trying to focus is like trying to hold sand—it slips through his fingers no matter how hard he clenches.

Suddenly, he shoots to his feet, too quickly. The room spins violently around him, the colors blurring together like a smeared painting. He reaches out, grabbing the back of the chair with white-knuckled hands, trying to steady himself. His breaths come fast, shallow, each one feeling like a fight—like he's drowning, unable to break free from the suffocating weight of everything unknown. His head throbs, his vision tilting with each pulse.

Outside, the city hums, oblivious to the chaos unraveling inside Arthur. The distant wail of a siren slices through the night air, the sound sharp and eerie, sending a shiver down his spine. It's the cry of something gone horribly wrong. Just like him. Just like this.

Arthur drops back to his bed, shakes his head, hoping to shake off the fear that's digging in, cold and relentless. But no matter how hard he tries, the dread sticks to him like a second skin, wrapping around his chest and squeezing.

"*Remember*," he mutters, his voice barely a whisper, cracking in the stillness. "*You have to remember.*" The darkness around him offers nothing in return. No clues, no answers. Just silence. Just the reflection of a man he doesn't know anymore, a man who feels like he's standing on the edge of something terrible. He feels it—the abyss pulling at him, deep and endless, threatening to swallow him whole.

His pulse quickens, hammering against his ribs as his eyes sweep the room. Every shadow seems to shift, hiding something, but he doesn't know what. Then his gaze lands on it—a smear, just a streak of red on the bedside table. Blood. His blood? Someone else's? His stomach churns violently. It shouldn't be there.

Clean it, a voice whispers inside him. His own? Or something darker? He can't tell anymore. The urge to scrub it away, to erase the evidence, takes over, stronger than his panic, stronger than his fear. Before he knows it, his hands are moving, shaking as he grabs the nearest cloth.

He scrambles to wipe the blood away, his hands frantic, scrubbing harder and harder at the table. The red smear spreads, staining the cloth, but no matter how much he rubs, it's still there, glaring at him, a mark of something he can't escape. The faster he cleans, the more desperate his movements become. His breath comes in shallow gasps, the room closing in on him as the silence presses down.

Each stroke of the cloth feels like an admission of guilt, like he's confessing to something he doesn't even understand. The sound of fabric against wood scrapes through the quiet, louder and louder, until it feels like the only thing left in the room is that terrible sound. It fills his ears, growing until it's all he can hear—until the scream trapped inside him rises, clawing at his throat, threatening to rip free.

THE SHARP, BITING SCENT of bleach clogs Arthur's nose, burning his throat with every shallow breath. His hands move in frantic strokes, wiping down surfaces as though he can scrub away the fear clawing at his chest. His grip tightens around the rag, knuckles white, as if cleaning is the only thing tethering him to reality. He can't stop. He *won't* stop. But the more he wipes, the more the panic builds, until every stroke feels more like a frantic plea for escape.

In his mind, he's trying to piece together what happened, replaying the night over and over. But the memories are blocked,

locked behind a heavy door that refuses to open no matter how hard he bangs against it. His hands falter, the rag slipping from his grasp.

"Nothing," he growls, throwing another stained rag into the pile already sitting in the corner. "There's nothing." No answers. No clues. Just a haze of confusion, thick and suffocating.

Then a knock. Quiet at first, barely a sound, but it cuts through the silence of the room like a blade slicing flesh. Arthur freezes, his bloodied hand hanging in the air, breath caught in his throat. His heart slams against his chest, the pounding almost louder than the knock itself.

Then it comes again. Louder this time. Insistent.

Who's there? The thought sticks in his mind, cold and unwelcome, but his mouth stays shut, throat dry and tight. He doesn't dare speak. His body goes rigid, every nerve on edge. The knock echoes through the room again, like a countdown, each one pulling him closer to the edge of something terrible.

He glances at the door, the space between him and it growing heavier with each second. Is it the police? A neighbor? Someone who knows what's inside? His mind races, running through every terrifying possibility.

Arthur inches toward the door, his steps slow, deliberate, each one heavy with dread. His heart beats wildly, his pulse so loud he can barely hear the next knock. This time, it feels more urgent.

Whoever it is—*they're not leaving.*

Arthur stands frozen, just inches from the door, breath trapped tight in his chest. Every second stretches painfully, the silence almost too much to bear. His eyes flick toward the peephole, but his feet won't budge. Fear has anchored him in place, as if any movement might give him away.

Can't let them see. Can't let them know.

The knocking shifts, growing louder, heavier, more demanding. Each thud shakes him to his core, rattling his nerves like a drumbeat signaling the end. His pulse pounds in his ears, the rhythmic thudding syncing with the relentless knock. Sweat beads on his forehead, trickling down his neck, but he doesn't dare move to wipe it away. His mind whirls, thoughts crashing into one another in a chaotic scramble.

Run. Hide. Fight.

Every instinct screams a different command, pulling him in every direction. But his body refuses to obey any of them. He's paralyzed, standing on the brink of something terrible, unable to take a step forward—or back.

The knocks grow more frantic, almost angry. Whoever's on the other side knows he's here, waiting, hoping they'll just go away.

Please. Just go away.

He doesn't say it out loud, but the words are there, repeating over and over in his mind like a desperate prayer. His heart hammers against his rib cage, the weight of his fear pressing down, making it harder to breathe.

And then, without warning, the knocking stops. The sudden silence is deafening, leaving Arthur standing in the void, trembling. His breath escapes in a sharp, uneven rush, a sound too loud in the eerie quiet. Was he imagining the knocking? Surely not. He's still here. Still standing.

Safe, he tells himself, but the word feels hollow. Fragile. As if the slightest sound might shatter it.

Arthur counts his heartbeats, each one a victory. Each one a reminder that he's still alive. But the quiet is unnerving, unnatural. He knows better than to trust it. Safety is a lie, an illusion that can be torn away in an instant.

He doesn't dare move. Doesn't dare breathe too loudly. The darkness presses in around him, thick and suffocating, like it's waiting—waiting for the perfect moment to strike.

Arthur stumbles back into motion the moment silence grips his apartment again. His hands, still slick with thick and dark blood, tremble as he twists the faucet. Crimson spirals swirl down the drain, vanishing into the black void below. The water burns his skin, but it's the guilt that scorches deeper, like a fire searing through his very bones. He scrubs his hands frantically, each movement more desperate than the last.

"Clean... clean... it has to be clean," he mutters under his breath, a shaky chant to drown out the chaos inside his head.

His clothes—stained with evidence of something horrible—are ripped off and thrown into a heap on the bathroom floor. The fabric sticks to his fingers for a moment, as if accusing him of something he can't remember. He shoves the bundle into the washing machine, the whirr of the cycle deafening in the small apartment. Fresh clothes replace the bloodied ones, clinging to him like armor, but they can't protect him from the storm raging inside.

Arthur catches his reflection in the mirror and freezes. The man staring back is a stranger. His eyes are hollow, his face pale and stretched tight, like someone else is wearing his skin. The Arthur who once lived here, who blended into the background of everyday life, is gone—replaced by something broken, something dangerous.

A voice breaks the silence, jarring him back to reality. The TV flickers on, a breaking news report cutting through the quiet dread that's suffocating the room. His attention snaps to the screen as the anchor speaks in solemn tones.

"...a brutal crime scene, leaving investigators shaken..."

Arthur's heart stutters. The camera zooms in on a street blocked off with yellow tape, flashing police lights casting an eerie glow. He stares, transfixed, as the words crawl across the bottom of the screen.

Brutal... heinous... no suspects...

The words pound in his skull, each one hitting harder than the last. He takes a step closer to the TV, hand reaching out as if he can somehow stop the news from existing, from being real. But the images on the screen are a mirror of the chaos in his mind—flashes of blood, fear, and the gnawing feeling that something terrible has happened.

"...the victim remains unidentified, and authorities urge the public to stay vigilant."

Vigilant. The word ricochets around his brain, mocking him. He shakes his head, trying to shove away the creeping suspicion worming its way into his thoughts.

"Paranoid... it's just paranoia," he whispers, barely louder than the hum of the washing machine. But the tightness in his chest doesn't loosen. His heart hammers, and the more he tells himself it's nothing, the more it feels like *something.*

His gaze flicks back to the TV, the camera now focused on the grim faces of bystanders. People in the background move slowly, like shadows, carrying the weight of some unspoken horror. He imagines they're looking for someone—maybe someone like him.

"No... it can't be," Arthur mutters, shaking his head harder now. The denials feel weaker with every repetition, as if the truth is just waiting to swallow him whole.

"Arthur Hall doesn't do this," he whispers, clinging to his name like a shield, like it might protect him from the truth. "Arthur Hall is nobody. Just a man."

But the blood on his hands, the gnawing feeling in his gut—it all says otherwise. His name, his past, his ordinary life—it's slipping away, leaving only questions, fear, and the terrifying possibility that he's not who he thought he was.

Arthur's vision swims with flashing images—blood on a knife, glass shards scattered across the floor, and the still form of a woman whose face he can't see. The horrific snapshots burn themselves into his mind, each one sharper, more vivid than the last. But are they real? Or just fragments of a nightmare he can't shake?

"Could I...?" he whispers, the question hanging in the air, incomplete, suffocating. The doubt wraps around him like a vice, tightening with each passing second, gnawing at the edges of his sanity. He grips the armrest with white-knuckled intensity, as if he can somehow force the truth out by sheer will.

"Remember, damn it! For fuck's sake, remember!" His own voice is harsh, the desperation in it echoing off the walls, but his memory remains a dark, tangled mess. Every time he reaches for a clue, it slithers away, just out of reach, leaving him stranded in the maze of his mind.

The news report drones on in the background, a haunting soundtrack to his unraveling. He glances back at the screen, but the words barely register anymore—just noise, a blur of flashing lights and solemn faces. The line between what's real and what isn't has begun to dissolve, melting into a shapeless fog. Is this his life? Or someone else's nightmare?

Arthur's hands twitch restlessly, tapping out an uneven rhythm on the couch. His breathing grows rapid, shallow—each breath a sharp gasp like he's suffocating in his own skin. The images, those awful images, blur together in his mind, twisting into something grotesque, something too terrible to comprehend.

"I didn't... I couldn't..." But the more he tries to convince himself, the less certain he feels. Every corner of his mind is haunted by doubt, an insidious voice whispering, *What if you did?*

With a sudden jerk, Arthur stumbles to his feet, the room spinning as if the ground beneath him is unstable. His heart pounds violently, like a drumbeat inside his chest, each thud a reminder that something is terribly, horribly wrong.

A cold presence lingers at the edge of his thoughts, something lurking just out of sight. It feels both alien and achingly familiar, like a ghost from his past come to reclaim him. The weight of it presses down, the air thick with unspoken horrors.

"Come on," he pleads with himself, his voice cracking under the strain. "Remember. You have to remember." But the memories slither away, coiling into the dark corners of his mind, refusing to show themselves.

The more Arthur tries to grasp at them, the further they slip from his reach, leaving him standing on the edge of a terrifying abyss. All he can feel is the overwhelming sense that something monstrous is waiting in the shadows. And it's closing in.

Arthur stands frozen, his heart hammering in his chest as a low, eerie chuckle echoes through his mind. It's not his laugh, but it shakes him to his core, a sinister sound that clings to him like a second skin. Then, a flash of steel—sharp, cold, unforgiving—cuts through the haze. Somewhere, a scream pierces the air, but it's faint, distant, like it's coming from underwater. The noise swirls around him, a whirlpool of fear and confusion threatening to drag him under.

He shuts his eyes, plunging headfirst into the darkness within. His mind is like a storm, each wave of memory crashing against him, but none of them clear. They come in flashes—glimpses of faces, the smell of blood, the sting of cold metal in his hand. It's all fragmented, disjointed, a puzzle where none of the pieces fit.

"Impossible," he whispers to himself, but even as the word leaves his lips, it feels wrong, false. The doubt gnaws at him, an unrelenting force that refuses to let go. Inside his head, voices scream for attention, each one pulling him in a different direction. One tells him he couldn't have done it, while another accuses him outright, dragging him deeper into the abyss.

His mind has become a battleground, each thought ricocheting like a bullet, leaving wounds that bleed doubt. The stickiness of his hands is gone—scrubbed clean—but the sensation lingers. His skin crawls with the memory of blood, as if it's still there, seeping through the cracks of his sanity.

A cold sweat breaks out across his forehead, despite the suffocating warmth of the room. Arthur rises suddenly, his movements jerky, unsteady. He paces back and forth, each step frantic, like he's trying to outrun something, but there's no escape. His eyes catch his reflection in the window, and what he sees stops him cold.

The man staring back at him is a ghost. Hollow-eyed, pale, on the verge of losing control. His own reflection taunts him, daring him to remember, to face what he's done—or didn't do. His breath quickens, panic rising like a tide.

"Think, damn it!" he hisses at his reflection, the words bouncing off the walls, echoing back at him. But thinking is dangerous. Every time he tries, he finds himself walking down a twisted path where memories lurk like predators, waiting to pounce. Each step feels like it might be the last, like one wrong move will send him spiraling into a pit he can't climb out of.

And yet, he can't stop. He has to know. He has to remember.

Arthur stares at the TV, the news anchor's voice fading until it's nothing but a distant hum, like a storm far off on the horizon. The quiet that follows is deafening, filling the room with the sound of his own racing thoughts. There's a pattern, something lurking beneath the surface, but no matter how hard he tries, he can't grasp it.

Then, a dog barks—a sharp, jarring sound that cuts through the silence like a gunshot. Arthur jumps, his heart slamming against his chest, pounding harder and harder like it's trying to break free. The fear that had been bubbling under the surface now hardens, a sick weight that drops into his stomach.

He stands frozen by the window, the cold from outside creeping through the glass and wrapping around him like a cold, suffocating blanket. His mind is racing, thoughts crashing into one another, but one thing stands out, sharp and undeniable: he can't run from this anymore. The truth is right there, lingering in the shadows, whispering his name.

"Could I have done it?" The question slips out of his mouth, barely a whisper, but it hangs in the air, heavy and terrifying. His lips tremble as he says it, because deep down, he knows—he's the monster in this story. He's the one standing in the middle of a blood-soaked nightmare that his mind refuses to fully uncover.

His heart hammers harder, louder, almost drowning out his thoughts. The blood on his clothes—it's not his. The sticky, dark stains aren't just some fluke, some accident. They're proof. They tell a story he's too scared to remember. Panic rises in his throat, a beast clawing at his insides, making it impossible to breathe, to think.

"Focus," he rasps, his voice shaking as he tries to pull himself together. He needs to remember. He needs to know what happened. But every time he tries to grab hold of his memories, they slip away like smoke through his fingers. The harder he reaches, the further they pull back, leaving him lost in a maze of uncertainty.

"Damn it, there's nothing," Arthur mutters, his voice raw and desperate. He's trapped, drowning in the emptiness of his own mind. But the blood doesn't lie. It's right there, soaked into his clothes, smeared across his hands, like a brutal confession written in red.

His breaths come fast and shallow, panic tightening around him like a noose. The walls feel like they're closing in, pushing him toward the edge of sanity. He's stuck, teetering on the brink, with no way out.

"Think!" he shouts, his voice cracking, but it's no use. The memories are locked away, hidden behind a thick fog that won't lift. He's left standing in the dark, blind to the truth, but painfully aware that whatever lies buried in his mind is worse than anything he could have imagined.

Arthur jerks into motion, his movements frantic, as if time itself is chasing him down. Every tick of the clock feels like the breath of a predator on the back of his neck. He's out of time. He has to do something—now—before it all slips away.

The blood is everywhere, smeared across his hands, splattered on his shirt, clinging to him like it belongs there. He stares down at his hands, fingers trembling, staring at the red that clung to his skin, that has dried into the lines of his skin, lodged under his fingernails. It's like it's mocking him—taunting him with memories he can't reach.

"Clean," he whispers, his voice cracking. The word sounds like a prayer. Clean it, and maybe everything will be okay. Maybe the panic will stop, maybe his mind will clear.

With unsteady legs, he stumbles toward the bathroom, his heart pounding so hard it's almost painful. He twists the faucet, water pouring out in a rush, clear and cold—a harsh contrast to the blood on his hands. He scrubs hard, rubbing until his skin feels raw, watching as the water swirls down the drain, turning pink, then red, then clear again.

But no matter how much he scrubs, the guilt is still there, burning into him, seeping into his bones. The blood may wash off, but the feeling doesn't.

"Out, out, damned spot," he mutters, a crazed laugh slipping out. It's a line from some play—something he barely remembers seeing years ago, back when things were normal. Back when his life wasn't this dark, twisted mess.

And then— the knock, again.

A sound so simple, yet it shatters the fragile calm he's been trying to hold onto. His heart stops for a split second, his hands freezing in the water as droplets of bloodied water fall to the floor.

Knock, knock. Louder this time, more insistent.

Panic flares up inside him, sharp and all-consuming. He needs to run, to hide, to do something, but he's trapped. There's nowhere to go. No way to escape whatever's on the other side of that door.

His breath catches in his throat.

"Who... who is it?" he calls out, his voice shaky, barely audible over the pounding in his chest.

No response. Just another knock, louder. It rattles through the apartment, vibrating the walls, and Arthur feels like he's going to shatter right along with them.

He swallows hard, hands still dripping water onto the floor. "Keep it together, Arthur," he whispers to himself, barely able to hear his own voice over the sound of his own panic. "You didn't do anything. You're innocent. You have to be."

But the blood on his hands tells a different story, and the silence behind the door only makes it worse.

But doubt latches on, squeezing tighter with each passing second, its grip suffocating. Arthur dries his hands on the towel, smearing streaks of red across the white fabric—a surrender, a grim reminder of something he doesn't want to face, but too late to fix.

Knock, knock, knock. Another set of thuds, as sharp and terrifying as gunshots.

"I'm coming," he lies, voice barely louder than a whisper, trembling with fear. He's not ready. He's stalling, trying to put together the pieces of who he's supposed to be, of who he thinks he should be in this moment.

Step by step, he moves toward the door. His feet feel lighter, like he's being pulled forward by invisible strings, like a puppet in someone else's twisted game. Each step sounds louder than the last, even though he's trying to be quiet. The apartment is so silent that every breath, every movement, feels like a scream. His heart pounds in his chest, every beat threatening to drown out any rational thought.

His hand trembles as it reaches for the doorknob. This moment, this door—it feels like everything hinges on it. His past, his future, all balanced on the edge of what lies on the other side. The air feels heavier, charged with dread.

"Please," he whispers, barely able to form the words. "Please, let me be wrong."

Arthur's breath comes in short bursts as he twists the faucet, watching cold water splash into the sink. The blood swirls away in pale pink streams, fading into nothingness. He scrubs his hands again and again, desperately trying to wash away the stains—and the memories. But no matter how much he scrubs, the images won't come back, just the feeling of horror lurking beneath the surface.

He looks up at the mirror, and the face staring back at him is a stranger's. His eyes are hollow, wide with panic, and his skin is pale, almost ghostly. He barely recognizes himself. Each time the blood fades from his hands, it feels like the evidence is washing away, the proof of something terrible slipping through his fingers.

Grabbing a towel, Arthur dries his hands, ignoring the red streaks it leaves behind. He folds it quickly, hiding the stains, pretending they're not there. His hands shake as he pulls on clean clothes. They hang loose on his body, like a disguise—clothes for a version of himself that no longer fits, a role he's unsure of. Is he innocent? Guilty? Or something worse?

The knocking continues, louder now, more urgent. Arthur swallows hard, standing frozen, knowing that whatever waits for him on the other side will either unravel the lie he's been living or confirm his worst fears.

Silence falls around Arthur like a heavy blanket, smothering him, save for the faint hum of the TV in the living room. It calls to him, offering the illusion of normalcy—something to cling to. He moves toward it slowly, every step careful, as though the very air might shatter around him. The soft carpet beneath his feet swallows the sound of his movements, but inside, his heart pounds louder with each second.

The screen flickers, casting an eerie glow as it shows scenes from the city—headlines, blurred images, and somber voices. The anchor's voice drones on, but a few words cut through the haze in Arthur's mind: "Gruesome," "unprecedented," and "murder."

His stomach clenches. A pixelated body lies under a tarp, an outline on the pavement, and Arthur's breath catches. No names yet, just rumors and a chilling image of death.

A cold unease slithers into his chest. He forces his gaze away from the TV, focusing instead on the small, mundane things in the room—the crooked curtains, the coffee mug on the table. He needs these details, anything to ground him, to keep him from being swallowed by the darkness creeping into his thoughts.

But the more he tries to steady himself, the harder it gets. Doubt wraps tighter around him, squeezing his mind like a vice. The blood on his hands may be gone, but its ghost lingers, and with it, the weight of suspicion that clings to his very skin.

Arthur paces, his bare feet thudding on the floor like a drumbeat of his rising panic. The ticking clock on the wall feels like it's speeding up, each second louder, accusing. Tick. Tick. Tick.

Blood flashes in his mind, those red streaks that stained his hands. His breathing grows shallow, his lungs burning with each inhale. He scratches at his palms, though the skin is clean. Still, they itch, as if the blood hasn't truly washed away.

"Just a coincidence," he mutters, barely audible, but the words feel thin, useless. His thoughts slip like sand through his fingers, spiraling deeper into memories he can't reach. Whispers of something darker swirl in the pit of his mind, and no matter how hard he tries to push them away, they persist.

He stops in front of a mirror, staring into it. The face staring back at him is familiar, but it doesn't feel like his. His eyes are wide, darting, filled with the chaos boiling inside. His reflection wavers, and for a moment, it's like he's staring at someone else. Someone dangerous.

"Stop it!" Arthur snaps at his reflection, his voice shaky. "You're not real."

But the doubt gnaws at him, tearing apart any last shred of certainty. He turns away, the weight of fear thick in the air, hanging like a foul smell, clinging to him, following him wherever he goes.

Bang, bang, bang. A knock cuts through the silence like a thunderclap. Arthur's heart skips a beat, panic shooting through him like an electric shock. He freezes, unable to move, the sound ringing in his ears. No one should be here. No one.

Sweat beads on his forehead, cold and slick as it trickles down his temple. His mind races, a whirlwind of blood, news reports, and the sensation of his hands scrubbed raw. It all points to something he refuses to face, but the truth claws at him, forcing its way to the surface.

"Who's there?" His voice sounds strange, distant, like it doesn't belong to him.

Silence.

Arthur's hand hovers over the doorknob, shaking. The cold metal feels like ice under his fingers, and he recoils slightly, fear gripping him. Every instinct tells him not to open the door. To run. But there's nowhere to run to.

"Think, Arthur, think," he mutters, but his mind is a jigsaw puzzle with pieces missing. Every thought is jagged, sharp, cutting deeper into his sanity.

The news, the blood, the itch on his skin—it all leads to one chilling possibility. And now, standing here, the realization hits him like a sledgehammer: He might be the monster they're talking about.

Dread gnaws at Arthur's insides, twisting tighter with every passing second. It isn't just a fleeting thought—it's a weight, heavy and suffocating, sinking deeper into his bones. He feels it with every breath, solid and undeniable. The truth, the one he's been avoiding, is waiting just beyond the edge of his consciousness, lurking in the shadows like a predator ready to pounce. He can't hide much longer.

His mind might be playing tricks on him, memories slipping through his fingers like sand, but somewhere in the darkness of his thoughts, the truth is hiding. And when it finally shows itself, Arthur knows it won't be kind.

He moves through his apartment like a man in a trance, every step slower than the last. His fingers graze the cold doorknob, hesitation clawing at him. Does he even want to see what's out there? His pulse quickens, the silence around him pressing in as he pulls the door open with a slow creak.

Nothing.

The hallway stretches out, empty, barren—too quiet. Arthur's heart thunders in his chest as he steps into the threshold, peering down the long corridor. No one. Not a sound. Just the hum of fluorescent lights and the soft groan of the building settling.

He swallows hard, scanning left and right. Still, no one. The oppressive silence makes him dizzy. He's alone. Or is he?

A shiver crawls down his spine as he quickly retreats back into his apartment, slamming the door shut behind him. His breath comes in shallow gasps as he locks the door, as if that flimsy bolt could keep out whatever was lurking just out of sight. But even here, in the supposed safety of his apartment, Arthur feels exposed—watched.

His eyes dart around the room, but it's just his cluttered, darkened space. Nothing out of place. No sign of anything, or anyone. But that feeling won't leave him. The dread, the sickening certainty that something is wrong, clings to him like a second skin.

He forces himself to walk to the bed, each step heavier than the last. Maybe sleep will help. Maybe, if he can just close his eyes, he can escape for a little while, push away the creeping fear that threatens to consume him. But he knows deep down, sleep is a false promise. There is no real escape. Not from this. Not from himself.

Arthur collapses onto the mattress, the springs creaking beneath him. He pulls the covers up tight, but the bed feels cold, too cold. His mind spins, thoughts colliding—images of places he can't quite remember, faces that seem familiar but twisted with fear and anger. Something is clawing its way to the surface of his memory, something dark and terrible.

He squeezes his eyes shut, willing the thoughts away, but the whispers in his head grow louder. The truth is closing in, a nightmare he can't outrun. It's there, waiting in the shadows, waiting to be uncovered. And when it comes, it will tear everything apart.

The silence in the apartment feels alive, pressing down on him. Arthur curls into himself, desperately trying to find comfort, but the dread won't let him go. His breath catches in his throat, and for a moment, he thinks he hears something—a faint shuffle, like footsteps just beyond his door.

He freezes.

But then, silence again.

Just his imagination. Or was it?

Arthur pulls the covers tighter around himself, praying for sleep that won't come, knowing that the truth, whatever it is, is coming for him. And when it does, there will be no more running.

Chapter 3

A rthur's heart slams in his chest as the radio blares, tearing apart the stillness of his bedroom. The harsh beeping of the alarm morphs into a cold, detached voice. It speaks of another murder—describing blood splashed across the city like some twisted piece of art.

His eyes fly open, breath catching in his throat. The early light of dawn spills through the blinds, casting jagged shadows that stretch across the walls like creeping phantoms. Panic seizes him as he jolts upright, the sheets clinging to him like a suffocating second skin, drenched in cold sweat.

"Another victim found..." The voice continues, flat and emotionless. "...in what appears to be a series of connected murders."

The words hit him like a punch to the gut. His stomach churns, bile rising in his throat. A string of murders—how many now? Five? Six? He's lost track, but this one, this report feels different. Too close. Too real.

Arthur's mind races. He struggles to untangle himself from the sheets, his hands shaking. His fingers tremble, slick with sweat, as he fumbles to shut off the radio, but the voice keeps going, detailing gruesome facts with a clinical detachment that makes his skin crawl.

The images flash in his mind—blood, bodies, the feeling of something horrible lurking just out of reach. He squeezes his eyes shut, but the words from the radio claw their way in, burying themselves in his brain.

"Related homicides."

His breath comes fast and shallow. His pulse thunders in his ears, louder than the news report, louder than the thoughts screaming in his head. It's too much. Too many coincidences. Too many pieces falling into place. His hands won't stop shaking.

He stumbles out of bed, nearly tripping over the tangled sheets, the weight of dread pressing down on him. The air in the room feels thick, suffocating. The shadows on the walls seem to stretch closer, like they know something he doesn't, whispering secrets he can't remember.

"God, no... not again," he whispers, but the fear curls tighter around him, an iron grip squeezing the life out of him. He can't shake the thought—what if he's connected? What if this latest murder is more than just a news story? What if it's a part of something buried deep inside him, something he can't control or understand?

He staggers toward the window, throwing it open, desperate for air. The cool breeze does nothing to calm him. It feels like the city itself is holding its breath, waiting for the next piece of the puzzle to fall into place.

But Arthur knows—whatever it is, it's coming for him. And he can't escape it.

Arthur's mouth floods with a bitter metallic taste, fear clawing its way up his throat like bile. He fumbles with the radio, fingers shaking as he finally silences the voice that shattered his fragile sense of peace. The room falls into a heavy silence, but the news report still echoes in his mind, every word slamming into him like a hammer. His breath comes fast, too fast, shallow gasps that feel like he's suffocating under the weight of dread pressing on his chest.

He runs trembling hands through his graying hair, desperate to remember, to claw back the pieces of last night. But it's all a blur, slippery and fractured, teasing him with flashes that make no sense. There was an alley, thick with fog. Rain hit his face like needles. And somewhere, a song—a lullaby—soft and haunting, both strange and heartbreakingly familiar.

He forces himself out of bed, his bare feet hitting the cold floor, pacing like a trapped animal. His reflection in the mirror catches his eye—a ghost staring back at him, eyes sunken with exhaustion and fear. His skin feels tight, buzzing with panic. He can't shake the flashes of memory, or the feeling that something—*something bad*—happened in that alley. But he can't be sure. Did he...? Could he have...?

"No!" Arthur's voice cracks in the stillness, cutting off the thought before it can spiral into the terror he can feel lurking at the edges of his mind. But the doubt is there now, a dark seed planted deep in his gut, spreading its roots into every corner of his brain.

"Think," he mutters, his voice barely above a whisper. "What did you do last night?"

But no answer comes. His mind is a mess of tangled images, half-formed scenes, each one darker than the last. It's like a maze in his head, twisting and turning, every path leading to another dead end. Panic tightens its grip on him as the hours he can't account for loom over him like a black cloud.

His eyes drift to the clock on the nightstand, the glowing red numbers ticking away, counting the hours he's lost—hours he can't remember. Hours where *anything* could have happened. The thought slams into him with the force of a punch to the gut.

What if...what if he was there? What if he did something terrible? His heart races, pounding in his chest so hard he feels lightheaded. The world around him seems to blur, reality warping as the sickening possibility settles over him like a heavy fog.

Arthur Hall, the quiet man with a simple life, could he be something worse? Something dangerous? The thought wraps around him, tight like a noose, choking him with a truth he's not ready to face.

The room, once familiar, now feels strange and alien—like a stage set for something terrible. And Arthur, standing in the center of it all, feels the terrifying pull of the unknown, the awful question gnawing at his soul: What if he's not as innocent as he believes? What if he's already crossed a line, and there's no coming back?

ARTHUR'S FINGERS FLY across the keyboard, tapping with a frantic rhythm that fills the silence of his small, cluttered study. The harsh glow of the computer screen bathes his face in cold light, casting shadows over the lines etched into his forehead. Sweat beads at his temples as he sifts through page after page of news reports and crime scene photos, his eyes darting from one headline to the next.

Each article feels like a puzzle piece, and with every click, Arthur searches for a connection, something to make sense of the gnawing dread that has taken hold of him. The screen flickers, showing images of dark alleyways, splattered blood, and police tape, but no matter how much he stares, the memories still slip away, just out of reach.

His heart pounds as he scrolls faster, the tension in his chest tightening like a vice. Each news story feels like a slap in the face, each crime scene photo a jolt to his already frayed nerves. A cold chill runs down his spine as his mind races, trying to piece together the nights he can't remember. The articles blur before his eyes, words like "unidentified" and "brutal" stand out like jagged shards of glass in the otherwise mundane text.

Arthur wipes the sweat from his brow, his hands trembling as they return to the keyboard. His fingers hesitate for a moment, hovering over the keys, before resuming their relentless search. His breath comes faster, more ragged, as the gravity of what he's looking at begins to sink in.

The police reports, the witness statements—they're all here, laid bare in front of him, each one pulling him deeper into the darkness. And in that darkness, he feels something stirring, something he's been trying to keep buried. The more he reads, the more his fear takes root, winding tighter around him, suffocating him with the possibility that he's not just a curious onlooker—he might be part of this nightmare.

His vision swims, the images on the screen melding into a sickening mosaic of violence and blood. Arthur's chest tightens as the undeniable thought creeps in. Could he have been there? Could his hands be stained with the very blood he's looking at? The idea hits him like a punch to the gut, leaving him gasping for air.

He slams the keyboard in frustration, the clatter of the keys a brief, angry outburst that punctuates the suffocating silence around him. His hands, now clammy and trembling, hover over the mouse, torn between the urge to dig deeper and the fear of what he might find. The room feels like it's closing in on him, the walls inching closer as the weight of his doubts crushes down on him.

With one final click, Arthur opens another news article, the headline glaring at him like a silent accusation. His heart hammers against his ribs as he reads the words, his mind spinning. Every crime feels like a mirror reflecting back the horrors lurking in his subconscious.

His breath comes in shallow bursts now, as the overwhelming need to know the truth battles against the terror of what that truth might be. The study that once felt like a sanctuary now feels like a cage, trapping him in a nightmare that refuses to release him.

Arthur's eyes flicker to the door, to the outside world where Claire sleeps peacefully, unaware of the storm raging inside him. But there's no peace for him—not until he finds the answer that's gnawing at his soul. The computer screen flashes with another headline, and his fingers start tapping again, more desperate this time. Somewhere in this sea of information lies the truth, and Arthur is ready to tear through every lie, every fear, to find it—no matter the cost.

Arthur stares at the reports sprawled before him, each gruesome detail like a punch to the gut. Crime scenes, victim profiles, dates, and methods—all of it spread out in front of him like pieces of a macabre puzzle only he seems desperate enough to solve. His hands shake as he pins photographs to the cork board , red string stretching from one crime scene to another. The tangled web of connections casts long, eerie shadows across the room, each thread leading back to one haunting question: how is he involved?

His heart pounds with each click of the mouse, the sound a jagged heartbeat that pulses in the room's uneasy silence. He's not sure where his paranoia ends, and reality begins.

One moment, he's a bystander. The next, he wonders if he's the one responsible for the very horror he's tracking. He can't shake the images flashing in his mind—rain-slicked streets, the distant wail of a siren, blood pooling on cold concrete. The memories are fractured, slipping through his grasp, and yet they cling to him like a nightmare he can't wake from.

Arthur's mind races as he cross-references articles with the dates and times etched in his own fuzzy memory. Witness reports, weather data, autopsy results—it's all there, but the pieces don't fit together. Not yet. His stomach churns with fear and doubt. Could he be blacking out, losing hours, doing things he can't even comprehend?

A chill runs through him, as though someone's walked across his grave. His fingers dig into the table as the swirling chaos in his mind reaches a fever pitch.

"Am I the hunter or the hunted?" he mutters, his voice barely a whisper.

His thoughts break apart like glass under pressure, paranoia creeping in, seeping through the cracks of his resolve. Every logical path he follows seems to twist back on itself, forming a labyrinth of terror he can't escape.

Arthur looks around the room, half expecting to see some twisted version of himself lurking in the shadows, blood on his hands, a smirk on his face. But there's nothing there, just the heavy silence pressing down on him and the evidence staring back at him like a ghost he can't shake.

He rubs his temples, feeling the headache growing, and slumps back in his chair. The weight of his own thoughts feels unbearable, but he can't stop now. He's too close—too close to something he doesn't even fully understand.

"Paranoid," he whispers, unsure if he's condemning himself or just grasping for a lifeline in the madness. The word feels hollow, offering no comfort. He forces his eyes open, his mind spinning, as he dives back into the reports.

Then he's there, standing in front of the yellow police tape, a silent barrier that separates him from the truth. The crime scene feels all too familiar, like a bad dream he's had over and over. The smell of blood clings to the air, and the damp pavement sticks to his shoes with each step. His heart races, and though the police officers move with certainty, Arthur feels lost in his own mind, trapped in a fog of doubt and fear.

He steps over the tape, the weight of the place heavy on his chest. He shouldn't know this place, but he does. His pulse quickens, his thoughts swirling faster as he tries to make sense of it. Was he here before? Is this just another twisted nightmare? The questions tear at him, each one more maddening than the last.

"Excuse me," Arthur calls to a nearby officer, his voice barely steady. "I might have seen something."

The officer turns, raising an eyebrow.

"And why are you just saying this now?" His voice is laced with suspicion, but Arthur has no good answer. His throat tightens, the words dying in his mouth. Anything he says will sound crazy, even to him.

"I—" he stammers, feeling the weight of his uncertainty crush him. He's met with a dismissive wave, the officer turning his back on Arthur without another word. The rejection is like a slap to the face, but Arthur can't let it stop him. He needs to know. He *has* to know.

He starts circling the block, scanning every alley, every corner, hoping to find a way inside. But every door is locked, every alley blocked off. He's trapped outside, cut off from the truth that feels so close he can almost taste it. The frustration builds, the tension in his chest tightening like a noose.

Arthur glances back at the crowd, hoping to spot someone who can help. Most of them are just curious onlookers, whispering among themselves, content to watch the tragedy unfold from a safe distance. But then he sees her—a woman standing near the alley, her eyes wide and bloodshot, her face pale. She looks like she hasn't slept in days, her hands trembling as she watches the crime scene unfold. Her window overlooks the alley where the body was found.

Arthur feels a jolt of recognition. She's seen something. Maybe she's the key. Without hesitation, he pushes through the crowd, his heart thundering in his chest as he approaches her. His voice is low, urgent, as he leans in.

"What did you see?" he asks, the words coming out sharper than he intended.

The woman's eyes flicker with fear, her lips parting, but she doesn't speak right away. She hesitates, her gaze darting from Arthur to the scene behind him. He can see the terror in her eyes, the same terror that's been gnawing at him for days.

"I don't know," she whispers, her voice barely audible. "I don't know what I saw."

But Arthur isn't buying it.

Arthur approaches the woman carefully, his voice low but insistent.

"Miss," he begins, taking a step toward her. "I saw you talking to the police earlier. Did you see anything last night?"

The words hit her like a physical blow. She recoils, eyes widening as if his question is laced with poison.

"I told them everything already," she snaps, pulling her coat tighter around her trembling frame. "Just leave me alone."

But Arthur can't walk away. The desperation creeps into his voice, betraying the fragile calm he's struggling to maintain.

"Please," he implores, his throat dry as his heart pounds. "I just want to understand. I need to know what happened."

The woman shakes her head, a broken shudder escaping her lips. She crosses her arms, clutching them around herself as if to ward off the memories—or perhaps the truth she's too terrified to confront.

"No more questions," she whispers, her voice barely audible. "I can't. I won't."

Arthur steps back, watching helplessly as the last shred of hope slips away, leaving him standing in the cold, unanswered. The woman's guarded expression, her refusal to speak, slams a door in his face, and all he's left with is the growing suspicion that the truth he's chasing might be too monstrous for him to bear.

The sun sinks lower in the sky, casting jagged shadows across the crime scene. Arthur stands frozen as darkness settles over him, the questions gnawing at him, unanswered. Each one weighs heavier than the last, crushing him under the unbearable weight of uncertainty. As the last traces of daylight disappear, Arthur turns and walks away, the dusk swallowing him whole.

ARTHUR'S FINGERS MOVE frantically across the keyboard, the clacking of the keys a frantic staccato that fills the otherwise empty office. Numbers blur before his eyes, spreadsheets turning into indecipherable messes of data that he can't focus on. He stares at the screen, but his mind is consumed by something far darker—the string of murders that now seem to crawl under his skin.

He hasn't slept in days. Maybe more. His bloodshot eyes flicker to the clock, the minute hand ticking away with cruel precision. His coworkers keep their distance, their sideways glances filled with concern—no one wants to get too close to a man unraveling at the seams. They've noticed the tremor in his hands, the coffee-stained mug he clutches like a lifeline, the dark circles that seem to grow deeper each day.

The office is empty now. Everyone has gone home. But Arthur is still here, tethered to his desk by an invisible force, unable to tear himself away from the haunting pull of the investigation. He clicks open the latest news article about the murders, skimming over the same grisly details he's read a dozen times. But this time, something catches his eye—a comment buried beneath the article.

A user claims they saw something on the night of the last murder, something the police missed. Arthur's heart skips a beat, his breath quickening as he clicks the link in the comment. It opens to a site with blurry surveillance footage and grainy photos, a compilation of potential sightings from that night.

And then he sees it.

Among the pixelated faces and shadowy figures, a person steps into frame. They're wearing a coat—*his* coat. A coat with a distinctive tear along the hemline, one he's never bothered to fix. Arthur's blood runs cold. His heart slams in his chest as he leans closer to the screen. The footage is blurry, but the tear is unmistakable. The figure is moving with purpose, heading toward the alley where the body was found, just hours before the murder.

His breath catches in his throat. The room seems to close in around him as if the walls are suffocating him.

"No..." The word escapes his lips, barely more than a hoarse whisper.

Panic clutches at his chest, his hands trembling as the realization sinks in. The figure in the footage—it looks like him.

Arthur stumbles back from his desk, his legs unsteady. The cold glow of the computer screen casts his reflection in eerie light, revealing a face pale with terror. He stares at the coat draped over his chair. Slowly, he reaches for it, fingers brushing the torn hem as dread seeps into his bones. The rip is identical to the one in the footage.

His head spins, the room warping around him as the panic rises in his throat. Could this be another blackout? Another gap in his memory? He tries to remember where he was that night, but the hours blur together, a jumbled mess of confusion.

"Focus," he mutters, but the word sounds desperate, hollow. He can't make sense of it. How could he be involved? How could he not know?

His eyes dart back to the computer screen, to the figure in the footage—the figure that might be him. The timestamp confirms it: whoever this person is, they were at the scene. His mind races, piecing together the terrifying possibility that he's been chasing a killer, only to find the evidence pointing back at him.

Arthur grabs his coat, slipping it on as if putting on the weight of his own guilt. The fabric feels heavy, suffocating, as the tear along the hemline seems to accuse him of a crime he can't remember committing. His pulse pounds in his ears as he stumbles toward the door. He has to find out. He has to know if he's the monster lurking in the shadows, or if his mind is playing twisted tricks on him.

But as he steps into the cold night air, one question burns in his chest: if he's the one responsible for the murders, how many more will there be before he can stop himself?

ARTHUR'S HAND TREMBLES violently as he fumbles with the key, his heart hammering so hard it feels like it might burst. The key scrapes the metal, and finally, with a click, the door swings open to the darkened hallway of his apartment. Shadows cling to the walls like they've been waiting for him, lurking in the corners. He steps inside, but the familiar scent of lavender and lemon fails to calm the suffocating dread wrapping tight around his chest.

"Arthur?" Claire's voice drifts from the kitchen. It's soft, but there's something off—worry hiding beneath it, like she can already sense the weight he's carrying.

He finds her by the sink, the glow from the under-cabinet lights casting a soft halo around her, but there's no comfort in it. Her eyes meet his, wide with concern, searching for an explanation.

"I'm glad you're home, I haven't seen you in days. Oh, Arthur, you look pale," she says, her voice shaky. "Haunted."

"Haunted," Arthur repeats, his voice barely a whisper. He's trying to hold it together, but his composure is slipping, cracking. "Claire, something happened today... I saw something—something that makes me think I might be involved."

Her face goes white. "Involved? Involved in what?"

"The murders," he blurts out. His throat is dry, and every word is like choking on glass. "Someone saw me—someone who thinks I was there."

Claire grips the counter, her knuckles white. "No... no, you can't be serious. This can't be happening. Arthur, you're not a killer. You know that."

But he can see it—the flicker of fear, the hesitation in her eyes. Doubt. She doesn't want to believe it, but a seed has been planted, and it's growing, fast. He wants to reassure her, to tell her it's all a mistake, but his own uncertainty gnaws at him.

"I have to find out," Arthur says, his voice cracking. "I need to know for sure."

"No!" Claire steps forward, grabbing his arm, her nails digging in. "Please, let it go. Let the police figure this out. You're driving yourself mad, Arthur!"

He wants to listen, to collapse into her arms and let go of this nightmare, but the pull is too strong. He's in too deep, and the darkness inside him won't let him rest.

"I can't," he whispers, his gaze distant, as though staring into the abyss that's swallowed his life whole. "I need answers."

Claire lets her hand fall away, her eyes full of a fear she can't hide anymore. "I'm scared for you. For what you might find. Or worse... for what might find you."

The silence that follows is thick with dread, a heaviness that presses down on them both. Arthur turns away, retreating back into his own private hell, the weight of her words clinging to him like a warning.

Later, long after the last traces of daylight have disappeared, Arthur sits alone at the kitchen table, papers and photographs scattered across it like debris from an explosion. The faint blue glow of his laptop bathes his face in ghostly light, the same articles, the same blurry crime scene images replaying in his head over and over. There's no clarity, only more questions. And those questions are eating him alive.

The phone rings, loud and sudden, slicing through the silence. Arthur's hand hovers over the receiver, heart pounding. He hesitates. His fingers shake. Then, almost without thinking, he picks it up.

"Mr. Hall," a voice says, low, cold, and too calm. "We need to talk. It's about your investigation."

Arthur freezes, his blood turning to ice. The voice on the other end is smooth, but there's a sinister undertone—something threatening just beneath the surface.

"Wh—Who is this?" Arthur demands, his voice barely above a whisper, his throat constricted by terror.

The line crackles, and then the caller hangs up. The dead air hums in his ear, leaving Arthur alone with the suffocating knowledge that he isn't the only one digging. Someone—or something—is watching him.

He slams the phone down, heart racing, a sickening feeling twisting in his gut. The search for answers has led him into the dark, and now, something in that darkness is coming for him.

Rain begins to patter against the window, soft at first, then harder, louder, until it's drumming against the glass, matching the chaotic storm of thoughts in Arthur's head. He stands at the window, staring out into the night, watching his reflection flicker in the glass. He's a ghost—a shadow of the man he used to be. The call keeps echoing in his mind. His heart won't stop pounding.

"Who am I?" Arthur whispers, staring into his own eyes in the glass. He doesn't know anymore. Is he innocent, or is there something darker lurking inside him, waiting to surface? The truth feels closer than ever, but with it comes a rising terror.

He turns from the window, grabbing his coat, its familiar weight now a burden. The streets call to him, pulling him deeper into the heart of the city where shadows linger and secrets rot.

He walks through the rain-soaked streets, his steps quick and uneven, his pulse loud in his ears. The world around him feels unreal, like a dream, or maybe a nightmare. Then, in a dark alley ahead, he spots a figure. A woman. Her eyes are fixed on him.

Arthur's breath hitches. He steps closer, heart racing. "Can I help you?" he calls out, his voice faltering.

The woman looks around nervously, then leans toward him, her voice a whisper barely audible above the rain.

"You're looking for answers. But some things... once you find them, they change you forever."

Arthur's pulse races. "What do you know?"

She steps back, her eyes full of something unreadable, something cold. "Beware the truth, Mr. Hall. It might just be the end of you."

Before he can ask another question, she vanishes into the rain, leaving Arthur standing in the alley, drenched and trembling. He can still hear her words in his head, haunting him.

But it doesn't matter. He's too far in to turn back now.

With a growing sense of dread, Arthur plunges further into the night, chasing after shadows that always seem just out of reach, and the truth that's tearing his life apart one piece at a time.

Chapter 4

Arthur's fingers drummed nervously against his pant leg, an erratic beat that seemed to clash with the relentless ticking of the clock. The sound grated against his nerves, each tick louder than the last, reminding him that time was running out. Soon, he would have to speak. He would have to try to put the madness inside his head into words.

The waiting room was dull and lifeless, gray walls closing in on him, shadows gathering in the corners like they had nowhere else to go. The sterile scent of antiseptic hung in the air, clashing with the musty odor of old books that lined the shelves. The odd combination only added to the chaos in Arthur's mind, like his thoughts were battling between order and the spiraling disorder he couldn't seem to control. His breath came out in quick, shallow bursts, barely louder than the ticking that filled the suffocating silence.

"Arthur Hall?"

The voice cut through the room like a knife, yanking him from his tangled thoughts. He jerked his head up, eyes darting to the door. There she was—the assistant—standing in the doorway, backlit by the soft glow from the office beyond. Her figure blurred slightly in his vision as his pulse quickened. Numbly, he nodded and stood up, his legs shaky like they might give out any second. The act of rising from the chair felt monumental, like a step toward unraveling the last thread of control he had left.

He followed her down the narrow hallway, the muted hum of fluorescent lights buzzing above. He felt like a ghost trailing behind, his presence barely noticed, barely real. The assistant's footsteps echoed softly, but Arthur's felt heavier, like each step was dragging him further into something he wasn't sure he could escape. The dim light flickered on the walls, casting eerie shadows that danced and twisted, as if the very air around him was unsure what shape to take.

As they passed by closed doors, muffled voices seeped through, secrets and private lives spilling out in whispers Arthur could barely hear. People dealing with their own demons behind those doors, people like him—yet he felt like an outsider. They were whole, he was not. He was a broken man, trying to piece together the parts of himself he no longer recognized.

Soft music floats through the hallway, the gentle melody tugging at Arthur's frayed nerves. For a brief moment, the sad tune feels like a blanket, wrapping around him, offering a fleeting sense of comfort. But it can't hold back the storm of dread building inside him. His footsteps, muffled by the thick carpet, make no sound, as if the world is shrinking, closing in, until there's nothing left but the narrow path ahead. Each step carries him closer to Dr. Turner's office—the place where the answers might lie, or where he might lose himself completely.

Finally, the assistant stopped in front of a door. She gestured for him to enter; her expression neutral, almost cold. The nameplate gleams in the dim light, stark and unwelcoming. It feels less like a simple door and more like an unmovable wall he has to break through. Arthur swallows hard, his mouth dry. His fingers twitch at his side as he pulls in a deep breath, steadying himself for what's next. A shiver runs down his spine. His thoughts swirl, a chaotic mess he can't control. What if this is the moment he uncovers something he's not ready to face?

The quiet buzz of the clock filled the room, but it was drowned out by the frantic beating of Arthur's heart. The door shuts behind him with a soft, hollow click, locking him into the quiet of Dr. Turner's office. The room feels small and closed off, the walls lined with books, like silent witnesses to the countless souls who have poured their hearts out in this very spot. His eyes flicker over the room, settling on the chair where he's expected to sit. The fabric is worn, a testament to the many who have sat there, lost in their own pain, searching for peace.

He sinks into the seat, the cushion giving slightly under his weight. His hands rest in his lap, fingers fidgeting with the hem of his jacket. The steady ticking of a clock on the wall fills the silence, each second marking time as if counting down to some unseen reckoning. His eyes dart to the diplomas framed on the wall, proof of Dr. Turner's expertise, but they offer no comfort. A small potted plant sits on the windowsill, its leaves stretching toward the weak light, a fragile thing fighting for life in the gloom.

The air shifts as Dr. Turner steps into the room. Arthur tenses. She glides in, her movements calm, as if she's done this a thousand times before. There's a quiet strength about her, an aura that seems to still the panic rising inside him. Her face softens with a small, reassuring smile that cuts through the tension like a warm breeze. Arthur feels a flicker of hope, like maybe, just maybe, she can help him untangle the mess inside his head.

"Arthur," she says gently, her voice soothing, "it's so good to see you." She reaches out her hand, her grip firm but gentle. The contact lasts only a second, but it grounds him. For a moment, he's not drowning. He can breathe. But the relief is fleeting. The real work is about to begin, and Arthur knows there's no turning back.

"Thank you for seeing me, Dr. Turner." Arthur's voice is tight, the words thick and rough as they leave his throat, like he's hanging onto something solid in a world that feels like it's slipping away.

Dr. Turner offers him a small, calming smile as she settles into her chair, crossing her legs and folding her hands neatly.

"Of course, Arthur. You've been carrying something heavy, haven't you? What brings you here today? How can I help you find your way through the storm you're in?"

Her words cut straight to the heart of it, and Arthur feels the weight of the question press down on him like a boulder. He knew this moment would come. That he'd have to dig deep into the chaos swirling inside. He sits there, staring at the carpet, the seconds stretching on, like they're mocking him. There's no easy way to say it. He feels his fingers twisting together, knuckles turning white with the pressure, his pulse thundering in his temples. The silence grows louder, heavier.

He takes a shaky breath, his chest tight, his throat dry. The room feels smaller now. Claustrophobic. Every inch of him wants to bolt, but the gravity of his confession pins him to the chair. He opens his mouth, but the words almost fail him, caught in his throat like they don't want to come out.

"I... I've been... I lose time." His voice is barely audible, cracking under the strain of saying it out loud.

Arthur blinks, and for a moment, the room seems to shift, shadows moving at the edge of his vision.

"There are others inside me," he adds, his voice trembling. The confession hangs in the air, thick and unnerving, like a dark secret breaking free after years of being buried.

Dr. Turner leans in slightly, her eyes locked onto his, not breaking away. There's a depth in her gaze—serious but compassionate. She picks up her notepad, but her focus is entirely on him, as though every word matters.

"Can you tell me more about this missing time? When did you start noticing it?"

Arthur's mind races, trying to grasp the tangled mess of memories. He's drowning in the fragments, unsure of what's real anymore.

"It was gradual at first," he whispers, his voice barely a breath. "Like small cracks in a window. But then it started happening more often. I'd wake up and... hours were gone. Days, sometimes. I'm there, but I'm not. Like I'm trapped inside, watching someone else live my life. And then, I come back."

Dr. Turner's face remains calm, but there's a quiet intensity in her eyes. "Who do you become during these times, Arthur? Do you know?"

Arthur swallows hard. His heart hammers in his chest, a sick feeling swirling in his gut. His voice is so low it's almost a whisper. "I don't know. Fragments... parts of me that shouldn't exist. People I could've been, maybe. I don't know who they are. They're just... not me."

Dr. Turner nods slowly, not interrupting, letting the silence settle around them before she speaks again. "And these others," she says carefully, "do they have names? Histories?"

Arthur hesitates. His mouth is dry, his mind racing. A chill runs through him as he says, "Sometimes... they talk to me. They feel... real. More real than I'd like to admit." He closes his eyes, voice dropping lower. "It's like they want to take over. And I'm afraid one day... I won't come back."

Arthur's confession escapes his lips like a secret he's kept buried for too long. "Yes," he says, his voice trembling, a shiver crawling down his spine. "They're as real as anyone else."

Dr. Turner doesn't flinch. She leans in slightly, her calm eyes steady as she speaks.

"Understanding them is the first step, Arthur. Together, we'll uncover each piece, no matter how deeply buried."

Her words are a lifeline, but Arthur feels the edges of his reality starting to blur. The office—the bookshelves, the soft lamp—seems to fade, transforming into something darker, an arena where his battle isn't just within his mind but out in the open. Dr. Turner sits across from him, unyielding, her unwavering presence the only thing holding him together as the cracks begin to show.

His breath quickens, and images start to flash in his head, bright and overwhelming. A younger version of himself—just a boy, wide-eyed and scared—flickers into view.

Shadows loom over him, cold and formless, suffocating the air. He can almost smell the sterile sting of antiseptic, a scent that mixes horribly with the dread he feels crawling up his spine. A small, pitiful whimper echoes through the scene—a sound he recognizes as his own. His heart races, his skin prickling with fear, and the room in his mind begins to shrink, closing in like the walls are pressing him into the past.

Dr. Turner's voice cuts through the chaos like a lifeline. "Arthur," she says softly but firmly, "you're safe. Here, with me."

The words pull him back just enough. He's in the office again, in the chair, the ground beneath him solid. His chest rises and falls in shallow breaths, but his eyes glisten with tears that haven't fallen yet. He nods, gripping the arms of the chair like it's the only thing keeping him grounded. His past might haunt him, might have left scars deep inside, but at this moment, he's not drowning in it.

"Abuse can fracture even the strongest minds," Dr. Turner continues, her voice low, her hand gently extended toward him. "But those fractures don't have to define you. Healing is possible."

Arthur's hands tremble, reaching towards her but pulling back just before making contact. He's still wary, still unsure, but her understanding smile doesn't falter. There's no judgment—only the promise that he isn't alone in this.

Dr. Turner shifts gears, her tone shifting to something soft, yet with a purpose.

"Let's try something," she suggests. "Imagine a space where you can communicate with the others inside. What do they need? What are they afraid of?"

Arthur closes his eyes, the room fading as his mind unfolds. In the darkness, a space appears—doorways leading to the identities that live within him. He stands there for a moment, hesitating, but then steps forward, feeling the subtle shift in the air. He can sense them—the parts of himself that aren't him.

Arthur's fingers gripped the chair, knuckles whitening, the soft leather grounding him in the present even as his mind slipped further into the abyss of his fractured self. The weight of Edmund's years pressed on him like an anvil, suffocating yet full of a strange clarity that only comes with time. His breath quickened, and the room seemed to darken around him, shadows growing long and cold as if they were stretching from the distant past to consume him.

"Edmund is... old," Arthur muttered, his voice barely above a whisper, like he was speaking the words to himself for the first time. "He carries wisdom, but he's lost so much to time."

A shiver ran down his spine, and suddenly it wasn't just age that he felt—it was loneliness, the kind that seeped into the bones. The room around him faded, replaced by a colder, older world. He could feel Edmund's memories creeping in - war, loss, regret. The scent of earth after rain, the clink of medals long forgotten. It all washed over Arthur like a wave, threatening to drown him in someone else's life. But it wasn't someone else. It was *him*—another part of himself, buried deep and long forgotten.

"Arthur," Dr. Turner's voice broke through the haze like a flashlight cutting through fog. He snapped back, eyes darting to her steady gaze. "What about Samuel?" she asked, her voice gentle but firm, her presence the only thing keeping him anchored to reality.

Arthur's heart skipped. He could already feel Samuel stirring, that deep-rooted fear tightening around his chest like a vice. "Samuel..." His throat constricted. The name alone carried with it a cold sweat. "He's young, so young... and he's scared. Always hiding."

"Let's try to reach him together," Dr. Turner suggested. Her voice was calm, soothing, but the room felt like it was closing in, walls shrinking, suffocating. Arthur's breathing turned shallow. The shadows were growing again, darker, closer. Samuel's fear was infectious, like a blanket of dread thrown over everything.

"Samuel!" Arthur called out, his voice trembling, almost pleading. Silence. Then, faintly, from somewhere deep within his mind, a small, fragile voice echoed back.

"Safe... safe here..."

A chill settled in the room, and Arthur could feel it—the fear. The fear of being seen. The fear of being hurt. Samuel's fortress wasn't made of walls, it was built from every insult, every failure, every moment of terror.

Dr. Turner leaned in, her voice steady and firm, slicing through the silence. "Arthur, look at those fears. Don't run from them. *Face* them."

Arthur swallowed hard. His whole body was trembling now, but he nodded. His mind's eye wandered into Samuel's space, into the dark, lonely corner where Samuel crouched, hiding from the world. Arthur stood before him, seeing himself reflected in Samuel's fearful eyes. They were the same—two parts of a broken whole.

"Confronting them isn't weakness," Arthur whispered to himself, his voice gaining strength. "It's the only way to take back control." He wasn't sure if he was talking to Samuel or himself anymore.

Dr. Turner nodded, her calm presence a lifeline in the storm. "Exactly. You're stronger than you think, Arthur. Each part of you has a role, but none of them are greater than *you*. You are the one in control."

As the session dragged on, Arthur felt the weight of his different selves pulling him in every direction—Victor, the cold, calculating force within him; Samuel, the frightened child; Edmund, the weary old soul. The room felt heavier, the air thick with the tension of his fractured mind trying to stitch itself back together.

"Victor," Arthur says slowly, his voice gaining strength, "he thrives on power. Control." The name alone sends a shiver down his spine but speaking it out loud is the first step. "He's the storm that's always brewing inside me."

Dr. Turner's pen pauses on her notepad, her eyes never leaving his face. "Understanding Victor's role will help you take back the power he holds. Balance, Arthur. That's what we're working toward."

The session stretches on as Arthur continues to navigate the labyrinth of his mind. Each word feels like lifting a weight off his chest, each revelation bringing him closer to the truth. It's slow, painful, but there's progress. He can feel it.

Dr. Turner's voice is calm but firm as the session nears its end. "This journey won't be easy," she admits, her gaze steady, "but every step forward is a victory. You're not alone in this. We'll walk it together."

When Dr. Turner finally spoke again, it was to guide him toward something even darker. "And now... let's talk to Victor."

Arthur's stomach clenched at the mention of Victor. He didn't even need to summon him—Victor was always there, lurking in the darkest corners of his mind, waiting for a chance to take control. His hands curled into fists, his nails digging into his palms. He could feel the cold presence of Victor, like a shadow growing ever closer, ready to swallow him whole.

"I know you're here, Victor," Arthur choked out, his voice barely steady. "Why are you here?"

The room seemed to freeze over, an invisible chill creeping up Arthur's spine. Victor didn't speak in words, but his presence was enough—an oppressive weight, a silent promise of violence. Arthur's chest tightened, his heart racing as if Victor was drawing all the air out of the room.

Dr. Turner leaned in, her voice cutting through the tension like a blade. "Remember, Arthur, he's just a part of you. He doesn't define you. You have the power to face him. You're in control."

Sweat dripped down Arthur's face, and for a second, he thought he might lose himself to Victor. But then Dr. Turner's words echoed again in his mind: *You're in control.* He took a deep breath, summoning every bit of courage he had left. Victor's power was born from his trauma, his pain. But it didn't have to rule him.

"What are you protecting me from?" Arthur finally asked, his voice stronger now, his gaze no longer avoiding the shadows.

The shift was immediate. The tension in the room seemed to ease, if only slightly, as though the very act of questioning Victor had weakened his grip. Arthur could almost *feel* Victor pulling back, not defeated, but acknowledged.

Dr. Turner smiled; her eyes filled with something like pride. "That's it, Arthur. It's not about eliminating your identities; it's about understanding them. You're doing exactly what you need to."

Arthur stands slowly, his body heavy but his mind a little clearer, the pieces of his fragmented world starting to settle. As he steps out of the office, the weight of everything hasn't disappeared, but it feels more balanced—like he can finally carry it.

A fragile hope blooms in his chest, something small but real, as he walks out into the daylight. The world beyond the office feels less overwhelming, and for the first time in a long while, Arthur has a sense that he's not entirely lost. He's beginning to find his way.

As the session came to an end, Arthur felt like he had survived a battle—bloodless, but exhausting all the same. When he stood to leave, the weight of his fractured selves was still there, but lighter, as if the act of facing them had started to shift the balance.

Dr. Turner's final words echoed in his mind as he left the office, stepping into the cold hallway: "This is just the beginning, Arthur. But every step forward is a victory."

Arthur walked into the bustling city outside, the noise and chaos of the streets a jarring contrast to the internal battles he had just faced. But with every step, he felt a little stronger. The shadows of Victor, Samuel, Edmund—they were still there, but for the first time in years, Arthur felt like he could see a way forward.

He wasn't just surviving anymore. He was *fighting*.

Chapter 5

Arthur's eyes snap open in the dark, heart pounding, a cold sweat clinging to his skin. The walls of his apartment close in on him, but they aren't the same. For a moment, the familiar surroundings blur, and all he can see are the cracked, decaying walls of a different place—a place he thought he'd left behind.

The memory drags him under like a riptide.

The paint, yellowed and peeling, flakes off in brittle strips, curling like dead skin. The once-white walls are now an eerie mix of rot and neglect, streaked with grime. Each corner of the old house feels alive in the worst way, its decaying structure breathing around him. Arthur crouches under the dining table, knees drawn to his chest, his fingers gripping the splintered wood as if holding on might save him.

The table groans under the weight of time, the legs barely supporting the broken top. But it's the only thing between him and whatever lurks in the house—whatever is coming for him.

Dust dances in thin, silvery beams of light that filter through cracks in the boarded-up windows. For a brief, surreal moment, it almost looks peaceful, the soft glow giving the air a strange, ethereal quality. But Arthur knows better. There's no peace here. Only dread. The kind that crawls up your spine and whispers in your ear, telling you that you're not safe, that you never will be.

He holds his breath, listening.

It's quiet—too quiet.

A muffled sound, like footsteps, echoes through the floorboards. Heavy. Deliberate.

Arthur presses himself deeper under the table, as if he can somehow disappear into the cracked tile beneath him. His heart slams against his rib cage, the rhythm too fast, too loud. He knows he shouldn't move. Shouldn't even breathe. But the need to know, to see, gnaws at him.

Slowly, he leans to the side, peering out from beneath the tablecloth's edge.

Shadows shift across the walls, dark figures moving just out of sight. His chest tightens as he strains to see more, but the light barely reaches beyond the confines of his hiding place. The footsteps grow louder, closer. They aren't in his imagination. Something—or someone—is coming.

He presses his face against the cool tile, trying to disappear. The dust clogs his throat, makes his eyes sting, but he dares not move. He bites down hard on his lower lip, forcing the whimper back down into his chest, where it burns with the pressure.

The creak of the front door. The slam of it closing.

And then... silence.

Arthur waits, every second stretching into eternity, until finally, the suffocating quiet breaks.

The table jolts—just slightly, but enough to send a splinter of wood into his hand. He gasps, a sharp, involuntary breath. And that's when he knows. It knows he's here.

"Useless! You're both useless!" His father's voice tears through the silence, ripping it apart like a blade through flesh. The words hit Arthur like stones, each one making him flinch. His back presses tighter against the wall, knees pulled so close to his chest they might crush him. If only he could disappear into the darkness beneath the table, into a place where his father's words couldn't reach him. But there's no escape.

"Just stop yelling! Please, stop!" His mother's voice cracks. It's broken, desperate, like she's already lost the fight but doesn't know how to quit. Her words fall apart as soon as they leave her mouth, mixing with the shouting to fill the crumbling house with a sickening tension that never goes away.

Arthur hears everything from his hiding spot—the sound of his mother's pleading, his father's rage boiling over, the dull thud of something heavy hitting the wall. Through the gap between the wall and the floor, Arthur watches, wide-eyed, as a bottle flies through the air, smashing against the living room wall. Glass explodes, sparkling in the dirty light like fake jewels. For a second, it's almost beautiful, until the sharp edges rain down on the filthy floor.

The house reeks of old booze, sweat, and something worse, something Arthur can't name but feels deep in his gut. It's the smell of hopelessness, of regrets that cling to everything in the room, making it hard to breathe. He's used to it, though. He's been trapped in it for as long as he can remember.

"Look at what you made me do!" his father bellows, louder now, angrier. Arthur's heart pounds, each beat echoing in his chest like a drum. He knows what's coming next. He always knows.

The heavy thud of footsteps pounds through the house as his father storms through the hall. His mother's sobs follow, weak and full of a sadness that makes Arthur's stomach twist. He curls tighter into himself, his body stiff with fear. His father is getting closer.

Arthur holds his breath, praying he'll stay unnoticed, that he'll be forgotten. But the house has a way of trapping him, holding him in place. He hears the floor creak just outside the door, and his muscles tense. This is his life—an endless game of hide-and-seek in a house that smells like violence and broken dreams.

Through the shattered glass, his father's shadow looms larger, and the screaming grows louder. Arthur's tiny sanctuary beneath the table feels smaller with each passing second. His eyes squeeze shut, and for a moment, he pretends he's somewhere else, anywhere else, but the sound of his father's rage yanks him back to reality.

He can't escape. Not yet.

"Look! I said, look what you made me do!" his father's roar crashes through the house, louder than thunder. The sound is sharp, stabbing the air like a knife. Arthur freezes under the table, heart pounding in his chest, every word hitting him like a fist. His father's voice is filled with rage, each syllable a barb sinking into the heavy silence.

His mother doesn't answer with words, just a sound—a soft, broken sob that echoes through the room, low and shaky. It cuts deep, a sound Arthur feels all the way to his bones. It's a kind of sadness too big for him to understand, but he feels it every time she cries. The sadness isn't new. It's always been there, lurking in the walls of this house, and it's sinking into him, becoming part of who he is.

The doors slam, glass shatters—his father's anger has no end. Every crash makes Arthur flinch, his small body curling tighter, muscles tense as if waiting for the next hit. His memories are littered with these sounds, these violent moments that feel like they'll never stop. It's always the same—a cruel show where Arthur is the only audience, forced to watch the endless chaos unfold.

He barely breathes, terrified that even the smallest noise will give him away. His breaths come quick, shallow, each one a whisper, a plea to stay invisible. His mind pulls him into a dark corner, far from the yelling and the fear, but it's no use. The screams still reach him, chasing him even in the safety of his imagination.

Arthur's eyes, wide with fear, stay locked on the scene in front of him. His father, towering, furious, smashing whatever he can grab. His mother, crumpled and crying, too tired to fight back anymore.

It's a nightmare that feels as real as the cold floor beneath him, a nightmare that never seems to end.

As the shouting grows louder, rising to a deafening pitch, Arthur sinks deeper into his hiding spot, shrinking into himself, praying it will stop. But it never does. The yelling, the violence—it's all he's ever known, and there's no escape from it. Not here.

Then the explosion happens. A fist crashes into soft flesh, and Arthur is sent flying across the living room, his small body hitting the worn-out carpet hard. Pain explodes in his chest, making him gasp for air, but he doesn't scream. He's learned not to. Screaming only makes it worse. Silence is his only shield now, his only way to survive.

His mother stands over him, her face twisted in rage. Her eyes, bloodshot and wild, lock onto him with a hatred that cuts deeper than any punch. She leans down, her words like poison, each one tearing at him.

"Worthless," she hisses, her breath reeking of alcohol, "just like your father."

Arthur doesn't fight back. He doesn't even cry. He just curls into himself, trying to make his small frame disappear, to make himself so small they'll forget he exists. His heart races in his chest, his mind racing, but his body stays still, as if the tiniest movement could make it all worse.

The blows come faster now—kicks, punches—each one driving the breath out of him, each one a reminder of how powerless he is. His father's heavy footsteps thud closer, and Arthur knows it's not over yet. It never is.

In that moment, as the storm of violence crashes around him, Arthur clings to one small hope buried deep inside—a flicker of defiance, a tiny spark of something stronger. It's barely there, hidden under layers of fear and pain, but it exists. Someday, somehow, he'll escape this house. He'll rise above the misery and the cruelty. But for now, all he can do is survive.

Arthur curls up tighter, pulling his knees to his chest, trying to shrink himself into nothing. His body feels like it's folding in on itself, like an armadillo hiding from danger, bracing for what's coming. He knows it's coming. The heavy footsteps of his father get louder, each one a warning, making the old floorboards groan under his weight. Arthur's heart races in his chest as if it's trying to escape before the next blow.

And then it hits—a hard kick straight into his stomach. The pain explodes through him, sharp and crushing, making him gasp, but no sound comes out. The air rushes from his lungs, leaving him struggling to breathe. His world narrows to that pain, but worse than the pain is the fear. It's like a cold, heavy weight pressing down on him, paralyzing him. His father and mother aren't just people—they're monsters in his life, ruling over him, his suffering their cruel game. He is nothing but prey, a sacrifice in their hands.

For a moment, the violence stops. The yelling fades, the hits pause, as if his parents are tired of the game, at least for now. Arthur's body shakes, but his mind snaps into survival mode. He knows this is his chance. His heart pounds as he scrambles, moving fast, sliding through the furniture like a ghost. He's silent, desperate to escape before they realize he's gone.

He finds his refuge, a small, hidden alcove behind the old curtains. Dust swirls in the dim light seeping through the cracked window, but to Arthur, this cramped space is a haven. It's not much, just a few feet, but here, fists can't reach him. Words can't slice into him. He curls up, pulling his legs in tight, hugging himself as if that can hold him together. His eyes squeeze shut, trying to stop the tears from spilling over. This corner is his fortress, the shadows his shield.

For a fleeting second, Arthur imagines he's safe. In this tiny space, he builds an invisible wall around him, and for just a heartbeat, he lets himself believe he's somewhere else. But he knows better. The house groans, and the quiet outside isn't real—it's like a predator catching its breath before pouncing again. Arthur doesn't move. He stays as still as a statue, waiting for the next explosion of anger, the next hit to come. He knows it will. It always does.

But in the darkest corners of his mind, something stirs. It's faint, like the flicker of a match in a storm, but it's there—something that hasn't been snuffed out by the violence. A small spark of defiance. Maybe hope. Deep down, part of him still dreams that one day he will escape. One day, he'll be free from the nightmare, rising from the ruins of this life.

As Arthur's breath steadies, the world around him seems to fade. He sinks deeper into his mind, building another place, a place where the pain can't follow. In that space, he imagines someone there with him, a friend he's made up in his mind, out of sheer desperation.

"Edmund," he whispers softly, barely moving his lips. The name feels like a shield, a small bit of magic to hold back the darkness.

In his mind, Edmund appears—an old man with kind eyes and a gentle smile. He sits beside Arthur in the alcove, his presence warm, calming. They sit together in silence, backs against the cold wall, hiding from the world outside.

"Tell me about the world beyond," Arthur pleads, his voice shaky, craving stories that will take him far away from this place, even if just in his imagination.

Edmund begins to speak, his voice soft and soothing. He talks of rolling green fields, blue skies, and laughter. A world where the sun shines, and where kindness heals instead of hurts. As Arthur listens, he can almost feel it—the warmth on his skin, the wind in his hair. It's like the nightmare fades for a moment, replaced by a fragile sense of peace. In this world Edmund weaves, Arthur is safe.

But even here, in the safety of his mind, reality pushes its way in. The house creaks again, a warning that the quiet won't last. His parents' voices rise and fall, like a storm building again. Edmund's voice grows faint, his presence flickering like a candle about to go out.

"Don't leave," Arthur begs, his voice barely louder than a whisper. His heart pounds louder, the fear creeping back in. The walls he built in his mind are crumbling, the fantasy slipping away as the danger outside creeps closer. He clings to the last traces of his imagined friend, but he knows—sooner or later, the real world will crash back in. And when it does, he'll have to face the storm once more.

Arthur trembles as the blows rain down, the line between the real world and his mind blurring. Each strike chips away at his grip on his imaginary refuge, and the voice of his comfort—Edmund—begins to fade. What was once a shield now feels thin, fragile. The world inside his head crumbles like sand slipping through his fingers.

"Be strong, Arthur," Edmund's voice echoes, faint and distant. It feels like it's coming from somewhere far away, a whisper carried across time. "I'm still here."

Something stirs deep inside Arthur as the old, familiar fear starts to shift. He feels it—something new, something strong—rising from the cracks in his mind where Edmund's fading comfort used to be. It's no longer just a dream or a ghost. Edmund isn't just an escape now; he's becoming something more, something Arthur needs to survive. A part of him, a protector made of the very fear he's lived through.

"Edmund," Arthur says again, but this time it's not a whisper. It's a call, a declaration, pulling strength from within himself. The pain, the fear—it's all there—but now, so is something else. Something harder. The imaginary friend he clung to as a child is transforming, no longer just a fantasy but a shield, something solid within him. His eyes, once wide and full of tears, harden with resolve. Edmund, the guardian born in his mind, is no longer a soft comfort. He's the armor Arthur needs to endure.

The house groans as a door slams, shaking the walls. Dust floats through thin beams of light slicing through the broken windows. The house is empty now, but the echoes of the violence hang in the air. The ticking of the old clock on the mantel is the only sound left, ticking in time with Arthur's racing heart.

Time drags on, hours feeling like days. There's nothing left in the house—just empty rooms and empty cupboards. He searches the pantry and finds nothing but old cans, their labels long gone. He picks at a crust of bread, scraping off the mold, chewing slowly as hunger gnaws at him from the inside. The cold of the house seeps into his bones, and he wraps his arms around his knees, holding himself together in the silence.

Night falls, bringing with it the shadows. They creep up the walls, twisting into shapes that make Arthur's heart pound in his chest. He shivers, not from the cold but from something else—the darkness outside reflecting the darkness growing inside him.

"Samuel?" Arthur's voice is barely a whisper, a name that feels strange on his lips. It isn't Edmund he calls now but something different, something new. The shadows seem to shift, and from the corners of the room, a figure begins to form, hazy and indistinct, but real in its own way. Samuel—another ghost from Arthur's mind—takes shape.

"Arthur," Samuel's voice trembles, weak, but clear. "Don't let them see you. Don't let anyone see you."

Samuel's face is twisted in fear, his hollow eyes full of dread. His body is hunched over, like he's trying to fold into himself, to disappear completely. Arthur watches, seeing in Samuel what he's always felt—the desperate need to hide, to vanish from a world that only brings pain. Samuel isn't a protector like Edmund was. He's a reflection of Arthur's deepest fear—being seen, being hurt.

"Hide with me," Samuel says, retreating into the darkness, his form melting into the shadows that blanket the room. His hand, outstretched and ghostly, beckons Arthur to follow, to join him in the safety of the dark where no one can hurt him.

Arthur feels the pull. It would be so easy to give in, to hide in the shadows where no one could find him, where the pain could never reach him. In the darkness, in the hidden corners of his mind, maybe he could finally find peace. Maybe he could disappear completely, just like Samuel.

"Come, Arthur," Samuel whispers, his voice soft, like mist in the air. "Here, no one will ever hurt you again."

Arthur's breath comes shallow, each inhale pulling him deeper into the abyss that Samuel offers. The world around him fades, the sharp edges of reality blurring and softening. The harsh light, the slamming doors, the pain—all of it begins to disappear, replaced by a heavy, comforting darkness. Samuel, the embodiment of Arthur's fear, promises safety in the shadows, a place where no one can touch him.

And Arthur lets go. He sinks further into the darkness, slipping away from the world that has only ever hurt him. Samuel's hand, cold but reassuring, leads him deeper into the shadows, into the fortress of fear where no one else can enter. Arthur disappears, swallowed by the blackness Samuel calls home, a place where the pain finally stops.

In the quiet, in the dark, Arthur closes his eyes. And in that moment, he is gone.

ARTHUR WALKED THE CROWDED city streets like a man adrift in a sea of bodies, his shoulders hunched as though he carried the weight of the world on his back. People brushed past him, their lives loud and hurried, while Arthur moved through it all like a

FRACTURED REFLECTIONS

73

ghost—there, but unseen. His steps faltered as though an invisible tug-of-war waged inside him, his mind at war with itself.

"Walk tall," Edmund growled, his voice low but demanding, cutting through the noise of street vendors and honking cars. "Show them who owns these streets."

Arthur's fingers twitched, his hands shaking slightly despite his best efforts to seem normal. He tugged at the cuffs of his sleeves, smoothing fabric that wasn't wrinkled. His breath came in short, shallow bursts, as if the very air around him was too thick to inhale. He felt like a stranger in his own body, caught between the world outside and the turmoil inside.

"Keep your head down," Samuel's voice whispered, soft and almost soothing, weaving through the chaos. "Be invisible. It's safer that way."

Arthur's heart pounded, racing to the rhythm of their conflicting commands. Edmund pushed him toward the middle of the sidewalk, urging him into the open where eyes could see him, where mouths might speak. Samuel pulled him back, urging him to the edges, where shadows wrapped around him like an old, comforting friend.

"Show strength," Edmund urged, his voice ringing with the echo of defiance.

"Conserve energy," Samuel countered, his tone dripping with the knowledge of survival.

Arthur reached the crosswalk, his body stiff as the red hand held him back. Cars revved their engines impatiently, and when the light changed, the crowd surged forward, carrying Arthur with it like a leaf swept up in a river of steel and concrete. He moved past storefronts, their glass reflecting back a man who barely recognized himself—a face too plain, a figure too meek. But beneath the surface, a storm raged.

"Stand tall!" Edmund's voice boomed, his anger crashing like thunder in Arthur's mind.

"Disappear," Samuel murmured, his words like a soft caress, a plea to fade away.

Tourists, office workers, mothers with strollers—none of them knew what war raged beneath Arthur's skin. To them, he was just another man walking down the street, blending into the blur of city life. But each step was a battle, each breath a fight to keep himself from breaking under the pressure.

"Fight them!" Edmund shouted, his voice a roar demanding action, demanding that Arthur be something more than a shadow.

"Hide," Samuel whispered, his words full of quiet comfort. "Hide, and you'll be safe."

Arthur reached the towering office building that loomed ahead of him, its revolving doors spinning like a gateway between two worlds. He hesitated for a moment, suspended in the churn of glass and metal. For that brief second, he wasn't sure if he was even real anymore—neither the man the world saw nor the one who lived inside. Then the door pushed him through, and the sterile light of the lobby washed over him. He exhaled, not realizing until then that he had been holding his breath.

"Enough," Arthur pleaded silently to the voices in his mind. "Please... enough."

For now, the voices pulled back, retreating to the dark corners of his mind where they always waited. They never left for good, though. Arthur knew that much. They would be back, creeping in like the night, as persistent as the daybreak that followed.

Arthur Hall wasn't just one man. He was a legion. A battleground of selves all fighting for control, all pulling him in different directions. On the polished floors of the lobby, his reflection showed one figure walking toward the elevator. But inside, Arthur was many—a fractured collection of minds held together by sheer will.

At his desk, Arthur stared at his computer screen, fingers hovering over the keyboard. The office buzzed around him, phones ringing, keyboards clacking, and coworkers chatting. But Arthur might as well have been on a different planet. The report due by the end of the day blurred before his eyes. Words and numbers twisted into shapes he couldn't quite grasp.

His mind wandered, dragged back into memories he wished he could bury. His father's belt, the sting of his mother's hand. He learned early how to become invisible, to fade into the background when things got rough.

"Join them," Edmund urged, pushing Arthur toward a version of himself he'd never been able to become. "Be like them."

"Observe," Samuel whispered, his voice a cold echo. "Stay in the shadows where it's safe."

Arthur's gaze flickered to the family photos scattered on his coworkers' desks. Bright, smiling faces looked back at him—happy moments frozen in time. He didn't have anything like that. No pictures to show. No warm memories to keep. He didn't know what it was like to have those connections.

Lunchtime came, and the office emptied out as people went to eat. Arthur stayed behind. He never went out for lunch. He wasn't hungry, not anymore. Food had long since lost its appeal. He preferred the quiet, the stillness that came when everyone else was gone. The absence of others felt like a balm, a brief relief from the noise of the world.

Time dragged on, the ticking clock a slow reminder that every second brought him closer to the end of another day. He could hear the faint laughter from the break room, but it sounded distant, foreign, like something he couldn't quite understand.

When the day finally ended, Arthur slipped on his coat, its weight heavier than usual. The office lights flickered overhead as he made his way through the maze of cubicles, a shadow slipping through unnoticed. He stepped out onto the street, the city roaring back to life around him. People rushed past, wrapped up in their own worlds, oblivious to the war raging inside him.

As he walked home, the sky darkened, and Arthur wondered if the night ever truly ended for him.

In his tiny apartment, Arthur sat in the dark, the faint glow of a streetlamp filtering through the window. He closed his eyes, summoning an image of himself as a child—small, fragile, hiding in the corner of that old, broken house. The boy's eyes were wide, full of fear, his body trembling.

"Help me," the boy seemed to say, reaching out across time, his voice a distant echo.

Arthur opened his eyes, the image fading like a dream. But the plea stayed with him. It always did. Because the broken boy still lived inside him, shaping everything he was, everything he did.

And Arthur knew, deep down, that the pieces of his shattered mind might never fit together again.

Chapter 6

D ays blurred into one another, each one bleeding into the next like a watercolor left out in the rain. Arthur moved through them on autopilot, floating through the motions without fully forming a single thought. His mornings were a fog of alarms and showers, coffee cups and newspapers, each blending seamlessly into the monotony of his workday. He lost himself in the rhythm, the dull hum of life carrying him from one moment to the next, his mind adrift while his body went through the motions.

But beneath that thin veneer of normalcy, something darker pulsed.

Arthur's heart raced as he trudged through the sterile white corridors of the office, the walls towering above him like sentinels to his unease. Each breath he drew felt shallow, his chest tight as if the air itself were too thick to inhale. His footsteps echoed, a steady, heavy beat that mirrored the pounding of his pulse in his ears. The hum of fluorescent lights buzzed faintly overhead, but it was drowned out by the roar of his thoughts—disjointed, frantic, and growing louder.

His fingers twitched in his pockets, brushing against the fabric nervously. It felt like static under his skin, an electric buzz that surged through his veins. Every inch of him felt like a live wire, on the verge of snapping. The walls around him, painted in that bland, corporate gray, felt cold and sterile—an eerie reflection of the mask he wore to work each day. The mask was starting to slip. No matter how much he tried to force himself into routine, to blend into the background of office life, the cracks were showing.

He could feel it.

The facade that had once held him together—calm, composed, indifferent—was fracturing. A single misstep, a fleeting glance, and someone would see. They'd know what was festering beneath the surface, the guilt and the fear he tried to bury. His thoughts spiraled as he moved toward his desk, days of routine and normalcy giving way to flashes of memories, nightmares that clung to the edges of his mind.

The more he tried to push them down, the more they clawed their way to the surface. That decaying house. The splintered table. The feeling of being hunted.

And now, in the cold, neutral light of his office, those memories felt more real than ever.

His eyes flicked toward the glass reflection as he passed, catching the fleeting image of a man who wasn't really there. A shadow of himself, hollow and tense. What if someone saw through it? What if it was noticed, the storm barely contained beneath the surface?

Lisa stood by the photocopier, her chestnut hair swaying slightly as she moved. Calm and collected, she was the complete opposite of Arthur. Her hands worked smoothly, methodically feeding paper through the machine as if nothing could disrupt her quiet efficiency. The hum of the copier filled the office, a mechanical drone that only made Arthur's anxiety more palpable.

He stopped a few feet away, his breath shaky and uneven. This was the moment. Could he really do this? Could he break the barrier he'd spent years building, the one that kept everyone at a distance? He felt the pressure of isolation—years of keeping everything buried—pushing down on him like a crushing weight.

"Lisa..." His voice cracked, barely louder than the hum of the copier. He swallowed hard; his throat dry as sandpaper. "I know you've talked about.... Could I... have a moment of your time?"

Lisa turned, her brow furrowing in surprise, her brown eyes locking onto his. The copier continued its rhythmic churning, oblivious to the tension thickening the air. Arthur's heart pounded faster, each beat an urgent warning, but he forced himself to keep his hands buried in his pockets, trying to suppress the trembling that betrayed his calm exterior.

Her expression shifted from confusion to concern, her gaze softening as she tilted her head, studying him. It was as though she could sense the storm roiling inside him, see the cracks forming in the mask he had held onto for so long.

"Sure, Arthur," she said gently, her voice low and soothing. "What's up?"

Arthur felt the knot in his chest tighten, his instincts screaming at him to retreat, to say it was nothing, to walk away and forget this ever happened. But he couldn't. Not this time. The fractured pieces of himself were clawing their way to the surface, demanding to be acknowledged, to be heard.

He shifted on his feet, trying to muster some semblance of composure, but his hands shook violently in his pockets. He needed to speak, needed to connect with her, if only for a moment. Lisa was his only shot at grounding himself before he lost it completely.

"It's just..." The words stuck in his throat, heavy and jagged. He could feel the chaos in his mind building, swirling faster and louder, threatening to drown him if he didn't get something—anything—out. "I don't know how to say this, but something's wrong. Really wrong."

The look on Lisa's face changed. She wasn't just concerned anymore; she was worried. Arthur could see it in the way her brows drew together, her lips parting slightly as if to ask a question, but she didn't. She waited.

His heart thundered in his chest as he forced himself to stand taller, even though it felt like his entire body was about to give out. He had to say it, had to let her in, because if he didn't, the walls he'd built might come crashing down anyway—this time with no one around to help him pick up the pieces.

"I don't think I'm in control anymore," he whispered, the truth finally cutting through the silence, raw and jagged. His voice trembled, but there it was—out in the open.

Lisa took a step closer, her concern deepening, but she stayed calm, composed. Exactly what he needed.

"Arthur," she said softly, carefully, as if one wrong move might shatter him completely. "What do you mean? What's going on?"

Arthur's breath hitched, his mind racing. Could he really tell her everything? Could he risk it all, let her in to see the mess inside his head, the fear and guilt and confusion that had been choking him for so long?

He took a deep breath, his hands trembling as he pulled them from his pockets, finally exposing the raw fear he could no longer hide.

"I think I've done something terrible," he said, his voice barely a whisper.

"Arthur?" Lisa's voice broke through the haze, gentle but laced with concern. "Why? What do you mean? Is everything okay?"

Arthur's head jerked in a quick nod, though the movement felt like a lie. "It's...kind of personal. Can we talk during lunch? Somewhere private?"

He could see the shift in her expression—curiosity flickering, then uncertainty, and finally empathy. Her eyes darted to the clock, and for a moment, Arthur felt a flicker of doubt. Was this too much to ask? But then her gaze returned to him, and he sensed the balance tipping in his favor.

"Of course," she said softly. There was warmth in her voice, a kindness that chipped away at the suffocating tension wrapped around his chest. "The cafeteria has a quiet spot. We can meet there."

"Thank you." The words slipped out, shaky and unsure. Relief hit him like a wave, but it was premature. Inside, shadows shifted restlessly, the whispers in his mind growing louder. Arthur retreated, his feet moving him away from the photocopier, away from Lisa's concerned gaze, but not far enough from the storm brewing within.

As he walked back to his desk, the air in the office felt heavier than usual. The clatter of keyboards and faint murmur of voices faded into the background. All he could focus on was the looming lunch break, the private corner in the cafeteria, and the truth that he was about to reveal.

When noon arrived, Arthur's heart pounded, each beat echoing in his chest as he wound his way through the crowded cafeteria. His eyes scanned the sea of tables, but all he could hear was the roaring inside his head—Edmund urging him forward, Samuel pulling him back.

He finally spotted Lisa at the agreed-upon corner, tucked away from the throng of coworkers. She glanced up as he approached, a soft smile on her face, but her eyes held a deeper worry. Arthur's stomach twisted. He wasn't ready for this, but there was no turning back.

"Thanks for coming," he mumbled as he slid into the seat across from her. His hands immediately found each other, fingers knotting together as though clinging for dear life.

Lisa leaned forward slightly, her eyes scanning his face. "You sounded... urgent," she said. Concern tugged at her voice, her brow creasing. "What's going on, Arthur, how can I help?"

He took a breath—deep, shaky—and leaned closer, his voice dropping to a whisper. "I've been... dealing with something. Something I can't control." The words felt foreign in his mouth, like pieces of himself splintering off with each admission.

Lisa blinked, confusion flashing across her face, but she didn't speak. She waited, her silence urging him to continue.

Arthur stood frozen in front of Lisa, the weight of his confession crushing him as the words left his lips. "It's... Dissociative Identity Disorder," he blurted out before he could pull them back. His voice shook, the fear clawing at his throat. "There are... others. Parts of me. They have names. Lives. Fears."

He stopped, his heart thudding violently in his chest as he studied Lisa's face, waiting for her reaction. For a second, her expression flickered with shock. Her wide eyes betrayed a brief moment of disbelief—but then, as if something clicked, her face softened. It wasn't shock anymore; it was understanding.

"Arthur..." she breathed, leaning in just slightly, her voice trembling with a mix of surprise and compassion. "I... I had no idea."

Her hand twitched as though she wanted to reach out to him but hesitated, unsure of what to do. Arthur's chest tightened, but he could see it in her eyes—the recognition, the empathy.

"You know, my brother struggled with mental illness too," she continued, her words hitting him like a wave he hadn't expected. "I've seen... how hard it can be."

"I—I know, that's why I..." Arthur's voice trailed off.

The knot of dread lodged in Arthur's chest loosened just a fraction, but the weight of what he had just revealed still hung thick in the air between them. He had chosen Lisa for this moment for a reason. He knew about her brother—how she'd been there through his struggles, how she understood what it meant to live with someone whose mind could betray them. It wasn't just that she might understand; it was that she'd seen it firsthand. She wouldn't judge him, wouldn't write him off as broken or dangerous.

But even with that knowledge, the enormity of what he'd just said sat heavy in his gut. He didn't know what to say next, his mind buzzing with the fear that he'd made a mistake, that even her compassion wouldn't be enough to save him from the truth of what was happening inside his head.

Arthur dropped his eyes to the floor, his thoughts a storm he could barely contain. His hands twitched, trembling, as the reality of his admission sank in. The voices, the fragments of himself, had all been bottled up for so long, and now they were out. Exposed.

The silence stretched, but Lisa didn't pull away. She didn't retreat into discomfort like he feared she would. Instead, she stayed there with him, her presence steady, solid.

"You don't have to go through this alone," Lisa finally said, her voice low, firm. "I've seen how hard this can be. I know it's terrifying, but there are ways to get help, Arthur. You're not... you're not the only one going through something like this."

Her words were like a lifeline tossed to him in the middle of a raging sea. His pulse still thundered in his ears, but for the first time in what felt like forever, there was something to grab onto.

Arthur let out a breath he didn't realize he was holding, his hands finally unclenching. It wasn't much, but it was a start. A crack in the walls he'd built so carefully around himself.

"I don't know how to make it stop," he whispered, his voice thick with the weight of his struggle. "I don't know how to control it anymore."

Lisa nodded slowly, her eyes never leaving his. "You don't have to do it alone. We'll figure this out."

Her words wrapped around him like a shield, and for the first time in years, Arthur felt like maybe—just maybe—there was a way out of the nightmare.

The air between them thickens, heavy with the weight of words unsaid. Arthur watches Lisa closely, her calm expression contrasting with the storm raging inside him. His secret hangs between them, fragile, like glass, waiting to shatter.

"Thank you for trusting me, for telling me," Lisa whispers, her voice low and soothing. She reaches across the table, her hand finding his. The contact is gentle but steady, anchoring him to the moment. It feels like a lifeline, pulling him from the isolation he's been drowning in for so long.

The cafeteria hums with background noise—the clatter of trays, the low buzz of conversation—but in this corner, it's as if the world has paused. Arthur feels a shift, like the walls he's built around himself are starting to crumble, if only slightly. The darkness inside him seems to shrink, and for the first time in forever, he feels a flicker of something else. Maybe hope.

His fingers, still drumming nervously on the table, slow to a stop. His breath catches in his throat, every inhale strained, as if his lungs are fighting to work. The words he's kept locked up for so long press against him, demanding to be spoken.

"Lisa..." Arthur says, her name slipping out like a plea. He meets her eyes, trying to hold himself together. "I can't tell you how much this means—having you listen. Every day, it feels like I'm stumbling through a maze, blindfolded. There are parts of me... parts I can't control, parts I don't understand." His voice wavers, the cracks in his façade deepening with every word.

He stops, the weight of his confession settling in the space between them like a storm cloud. For so long, he's faced this battle alone. The different versions of himself have pulled him in every direction, dragging him further from who he once was.

Lisa doesn't flinch. Her gaze is steady, eyes filled with empathy and something else—something stronger, like determination. She leans in just a little, her fingers still resting on his hand, giving him the support he didn't know he needed.

"Arthur," Lisa says softly, her words cutting through the thick fog in his mind. "You don't have to go through this alone anymore. If you need to talk, or if you need help... I'm here. We can figure this out."

Her words settle over him, warm but dangerous. For so long, Arthur has kept everything locked away, hidden behind layers of control and distance. He's protected himself from the truth, even from the people closest to him. But now, with Lisa sitting here, looking at him like she actually *sees* him, those walls begin to fracture.

"Thank you," Arthur whispers, his voice barely more than a rasp. Relief sweeps through him like a wave, but beneath it, fear surges—sharp, biting. This was only the beginning, and he knows it. The chaos inside him isn't something that can be easily fixed. He's stood on the edge for so long that the idea of stepping back, of trying to confront everything, feels impossible.

His heart pounds in his chest, and before he can stop himself, the words spill out, heavier than he meant them to be.

"Claire... she doesn't understand." The sentence hangs between them, his voice breaking at the edges. He swallows hard, forcing himself to continue. "She tries. But she can't... She looks at me like I'm a stranger. Like I'm something broken." His hands clench into fists in his pockets as the bitterness rushes up. "I know she loves me, but it's not enough. Not for this."

The confession burns on its way out, the raw truth of it twisting in his gut. Admitting it feels like betrayal, but also like a release.

Lisa's eyes soften, and she leans forward slightly, her voice steady. "Arthur, it doesn't mean she doesn't care. This... it's hard for anyone to understand. But you're not alone in this. I know it feels that way, especially when someone you love doesn't get what you're going through. But it doesn't mean you have to carry it all by yourself."

Arthur's pulse pounds in his ears, his hands trembling now, exposed in a way he's never let himself be. The reality of what he's just shared, of laying his darkest truths bare, is suffocating. But there's something about Lisa's presence—her calm, unwavering attention—that anchors him. The air in the office feels thinner, like it's closing in, but Lisa is steady, her gaze holding him there, tethering him to something real.

"I don't know if I can keep doing this," Arthur finally admits, his voice raw, broken. "Pretending everything's fine. Trying to keep it all together."

"You don't have to pretend with me," she says quietly. "And you don't have to do it all alone. I know it's terrifying to let someone in, but I've seen this before. With my brother. I've seen what it's like to fight those battles in your head."

Arthur lets her words sink in, but they sit uneasily in his chest. He wants to believe her, to trust that she can help him through this, but the doubt gnaws at him, deep and relentless. Claire's distance, her confusion—it's all tangled in his mind, adding to the weight he's carried for so long.

And yet, in this moment, with Lisa sitting across from him, the burden feels just a little lighter. Maybe, just maybe, he won't have to face the nightmare alone.

Arthur draws in a sharp breath, his heart racing as the noise of the cafeteria fades into the background. His eyes dart nervously around the room, but they always come back to Lisa. She's sitting across from him, her gaze steady, patient, and unwavering. Her hands are clasped on the table between them, a silent offer of support that feels both comforting and terrifying.

The air between them feels charged, almost electric. Every second stretches out, heavy with the weight of his earlier confession. He told her things no one else knows—things he's kept locked away for years. Now, the question hangs in the air: What happens next?

"Arthur," Lisa says, her voice low and calming, cutting through the buzz of distant conversations and clattering trays. It's as if everything else falls away, and it's just the two of them in this moment. "I think we need to take this conversation somewhere more private. These parts of you... your alter egos... they deserve to be understood, by you and by someone who can truly help."

Her words hit him hard, stirring up a fear deep inside. Maybe he's made a mistake, maybe this is too much to share with her. But at the same time, there's a pull—something inside him wants to trust her, wants to believe that maybe she can help him unravel the mess he's been living with for so long.

"Would you be open to that?" Lisa asks gently, her eyes full of compassion but also a determination that's impossible to ignore.

Arthur hesitates, his throat dry. His hands twitch nervously on the table as he tries to find his voice. "Yes," he finally says, his words barely a whisper. "I would... appreciate that." The relief in his voice feels foreign, like hope, something he hasn't allowed himself to feel in a long time.

Lisa smiles, a small but genuine smile that softens her features. "Good. There's a coffee shop nearby—quiet, secluded. We could meet there after work. It might be easier to talk in a more relaxed setting."

Arthur nods again, this time a little more confidently. The idea of meeting somewhere outside the suffocating walls of the office, away from the constant pressure and the noise in his head, sounds like a lifeline.

"Thank you, Lisa," he says, his voice steadying. The names of his other personalities—Edmund, Samuel, Victor—swirl in his mind. Each of them is a part of him, each fighting for space in his crowded thoughts, but with Lisa's help, maybe he can start to make sense of it all.

"Let's plan on it then," Lisa says, standing from the table. The chair scrapes loudly across the floor, but the sound feels insignificant compared to what they've just shared. "I'll text you the address."

As she walks away, Arthur watches her go, feeling something shift inside him. The darkness that usually surrounds him feels a little less suffocating. It's still there, lurking, but now there's something else—a flicker of light, of possibility. For the first time in a long time, he dares to think that maybe, just maybe, he won't have to face this alone.

THE BELL ABOVE THE door rang out, its sound sharp and jarring as Arthur pushed into the coffee shop. The place was dimly lit, hushed, with shadows clinging to the corners like they belonged there. Arthur's eyes darted around, scanning the small space, but it was Lisa he sought out. She waved from a secluded corner by the window, her silhouette barely illuminated by the last slivers of daylight filtering through the streaked glass.

Each step he took toward her felt heavier, as if the weight of his secrets dragged him down. His feet hesitated, as if he expected—feared—that his other selves might follow him through the door. Finally, he slid into the seat across from her, feeling the distance between them close but somehow vast. The flickering candle on the table threw uneven shadows across their faces, hiding parts of him in the dark, just as he hid from himself.

"Thanks for coming," Lisa said softly, her voice cutting through the chaotic storm in his mind. The sound soothed him, but not enough to erase the gnawing fear inside.

Arthur nodded, wrapping his hands around the mug in front of him. Its warmth seeped into his cold fingers, grounding him, if only for a moment. He stared into the rising steam, watching it curl and vanish, much like the pieces of himself he was slowly losing.

"It's... good to be here," he muttered, but his voice wavered, betraying the lie behind his words.

He took a deep breath, steeling himself for what he had to say next. "Edmund," he began quietly, feeling the name stir in his mind like an unwelcome guest. "He's the oldest one. He's been with me the longest." Arthur paused, struggling to find the words. "He has this white hair... like he's seen things I never will. He talks to me like I'm a child, always giving advice, always calm. He's... wise, I guess. He tells me what to do when everything feels like it's falling apart."

Lisa stayed silent, her gaze never leaving him, allowing him to continue without interruption. He appreciated that.

"And then there's Samuel," Arthur added, his fingers trembling around the mug. "He's... he's scared of everything. He's small, frail. He hides in oversized clothes, like he's trying to disappear." Arthur's voice cracked, and he stared down into his coffee, the darkness in the cup reflecting the fear that constantly lurked in the back of his mind. "Samuel comes out when I'm terrified—when I feel like the world's too big, too dangerous."

The noise of the coffee shop—the clinking dishes, low murmurs of conversation—faded into a distant hum, leaving just the sound of his breathing and Lisa's steady presence.

"Victor," Arthur continued, his tone changing, the name sounding harsher. His body tensed, and he straightened up slightly in his chair. "Victor doesn't say much. He just watches, waits. He's... critical, always judging. I feel him when decisions need to be made, when I'm trapped between two terrible choices. He watches through my eyes, deciding what I do, if I should even move."

Arthur's grip on the mug tightened until his knuckles went white. Victor was always there, lurking in the background, measuring every risk, calculating every step.

The room outside the window was growing darker, the sun disappearing behind the horizon. Inside the café, they were sealed off from the rest of the world, hidden from the chaos outside. But in this small corner, Arthur knew he was far from safe. He wasn't even safe from himself.

Lisa shifted in her seat, leaning forward, her voice gentle but focused. "Arthur, when do Edmund, Samuel, and Victor come out? Are there certain situations that trigger them?"

Her question felt like a key turning in a lock, a small opening into the truth he'd been avoiding. He swallowed hard, his throat dry. "Stress," he said, the word barely audible.

"When things get bad, when I can't handle it anymore. Edmund steps up when I feel powerless... when anger is the only thing that makes sense."

"Anger is a way to take control when you feel like you've lost it," Lisa replied calmly, nodding as if understanding the chaos inside him. "What about Samuel?"

"Samuel... he shows up when I'm terrified. When I can't breathe, when the fear is so strong it crushes me." Arthur's voice cracked, raw with emotion. He felt like he was exposing his deepest wounds, laying them bare for her to see.

Lisa leaned even closer, her hand resting on the table, close to his but not touching, offering silent support. "And Victor?" she asked gently.

Arthur clenched his jaw, the name leaving a bitter taste in his mouth.

"Victor's the worst. He waits. He watches. When I'm stuck, when I don't know what to do, he's there, judging, pushing me to make decisions that feel impossible. He never says a word, but I can feel him in the back of my mind, always there."

Lisa's expression didn't waver. She didn't flinch or show fear—just empathy and understanding. "Arthur, these parts of you—they're trying to protect you in their own way. We need to understand them, but more importantly, you need to know that you don't have to go through this alone."

The café felt smaller, quieter, like they were the only two people in the world. Arthur's heart pounded in his chest, and for the first time in a long while, he felt a flicker of something he thought he'd lost—hope.

"Yes, that's what Dr. Thompson told me several days ago." Arthur said softly.

Arthur sank deeper into his chair, feeling the weight of Lisa's words hit like a hammer to his chest.

"Decision-making can be paralyzing," she'd said, and it felt like she'd peeled back another layer of his mind. He let out a shaky breath, shoulders drooping, as if her insight had given voice to the thoughts constantly swirling inside him.

For a moment, they sat in silence, the only sounds the occasional clink of spoons against ceramic and the low hum of distant conversations. But the quiet wasn't awkward—it was heavy with understanding. Each shared glance, each lingering second, was another step into the maze of Arthur's mind.

"Have you noticed any patterns? Something that could warn you when they're about to take over?" Lisa's voice was soft but insistent, like a gentle push toward a door Arthur wasn't sure he wanted to open.

He frowned, staring into his coffee as if the answers might be swirling somewhere in the dark liquid.

"Patterns..." he repeated, his voice barely audible. His eyes glazed over, sifting through memories, trying to piece together the fractured timelines of his other selves. "Edmund usually shows up after a fight... when I've kept things bottled up too long, and I can still feel the adrenaline running through me."

He took a deep breath, almost regretting what he was about to say next. "Samuel... he comes when it's too quiet. When I'm alone.

The silence... it feeds him." He clenched his jaw, trying to ignore the crawling feeling in his skin whenever Samuel appeared, small and afraid.

Lisa leaned forward, her brow furrowed in thought. "Isolation can magnify fear," she said, her voice quiet, almost as if speaking to herself.

Arthur nodded slowly. "And Victor... he's there when I'm facing a choice. A big one. It's like he's always watching me, waiting for me to mess up, ready to tear me apart if I choose wrong." His voice wavered, the realization sinking in deeper than ever. He'd always thought Victor was just judgmental, but now he saw it—Victor only showed up when everything was on the line.

Lisa's eyes locked onto his, her gaze steady. "Choices can be terrifying," she said, her words like a lifeline thrown into the storm. "But you're not facing them alone."

Their conversation carried on, unraveling more and more of Arthur's fragmented mind. Each piece they uncovered was another step toward understanding—toward making sense of the chaos that had haunted him for so long. The dim light of the coffee shop faded, the shadows growing longer as dusk settled outside, but inside, it felt like they were building something. Slowly, brick by brick, they were constructing a map of Arthur's mind, trying to find a way out of the labyrinth.

Arthur's hand tightened around the warm mug, the heat grounding him as the storm of thoughts raged on. He stared into the steam rising from his cup, a swirl of confusion and possibility. His fingers tapped nervously against the ceramic, the rhythmic sound echoing the pounding of his heart.

"Distraction," he said suddenly, the word cutting through the thick air between them. "When Edmund shows up, I need something to focus on. Something real." He blinked, feeling the weight of his thoughts ease just a little with the admission.

Lisa leaned in closer, her face illuminated by the soft glow of the candle.

"Something to ground you," she said, nodding. "A breathing technique might help, or a tactile object. Like a worry stone, something you can hold onto when things start slipping."

Arthur's eyes flickered with interest. "Something I can feel," he agreed, the idea starting to take root in his mind. The thought that he might have some control over Edmund, some way to keep him in check, was both foreign and strangely hopeful.

"And for Samuel," Lisa continued, her voice unwavering. "If silence makes him appear, then maybe filling that space with sound could help. Music, or an audio book—something to drown out the quiet."

Arthur nodded again, his mind racing. "And Victor..." His voice trailed off as he thought about the critical, judgmental figure lurking in the background of every major decision he'd ever made. "Maybe if I take smaller risks, he won't feel the need to step in. Like easing into it, so he doesn't feel like everything's on the line."

Lisa smiled softly, her confidence in him like a steady anchor. "Exactly. Small steps, Arthur. One at a time."

The coffee shop was nearly empty now, the once-busy space quiet except for the low hum of conversation from a distant table. Outside, the sun had completely disappeared, leaving the world draped in twilight. But for the first time in a long while, Arthur didn't feel swallowed by the darkness. The ideas they'd shared, the strategies they'd discussed, were like a flicker of light—a way forward.

Arthur exhaled, his breath shaky but relieved. "Thank you, Lisa. For listening. For not turning away."

Her hand brushed his arm gently, just for a second. "You don't have to face this alone, Arthur."

They stood up, the scrape of their chairs loud in the quiet room. As they stepped outside, the cool evening air hit them, crisp and fresh. Arthur stared up at the sky, the night vast and endless, but somehow... less overwhelming than before. The world was still big, still full of uncertainties, but now he wasn't facing it completely on his own. Somewhere inside him, a fragile sense of hope was beginning to bloom, nurtured by the understanding that maybe, just maybe, he didn't have to be afraid forever.

Arthur lingered at the doorway of the coffee shop, hesitating as the city buzzed around him—horns blaring, people moving, lights flashing. The night air was cold and sharp, biting into his skin. It was nothing like the warmth inside, where he and Lisa had just shared one of the most intense conversations of his life. Out here, it felt like he'd been ripped away from that safety, thrown back into the chaos of the real world.

"Arthur," Lisa's voice cut through the noise, pulling him back from the edge of panic. Her eyes found his, steady and sure. In the middle of the bustling street, she was his anchor. "You're not alone," she said, her words clear and firm.

Arthur tried to nod, but his body felt stiff, weighed down by the fear that had gripped him for so long. Still, he forced himself to meet her gaze. She stepped closer, her presence radiating warmth in the cold night. There was something about her—maybe the way she never flinched, never turned away—that made him feel like he could breathe again, even if just for a moment.

"We'll get you through this," she continued, her voice low but fierce, like she was promising him something more than just words. "Every step, every hard moment—you don't have to face it by yourself."

Her words hit like a jolt of electricity. They weren't just comforting—they were a lifeline. For so long, Arthur had felt trapped, buried under the weight of his own mind, the multiple versions of himself clawing for control. But here was someone, right in front of him, telling him that he didn't have to fight this battle alone.

"Thank you," he whispered, his throat tight, the words almost sticking on the way out. It was all he could manage, but he meant it more than he'd ever meant anything. He didn't know how they were going to get through this, or what would happen next, but he knew that having someone by his side made the future seem a little less terrifying.

Lisa's expression softened, but there was still a fierceness there. "It's not just about confronting your alters, Arthur. It's about healing, and it's a process. But I'm here, every step of the way."

Arthur felt a strange warmth bloom inside him—small, fragile, but real. It was a flicker of hope, something he hadn't felt in a long time. Lisa wasn't giving him empty promises; she wasn't pretending everything would be okay right away. But she was saying they would face it together. And that... that was enough for now.

They began walking down the street, side by side, the noise of the city fading into the background. Arthur still felt the weight of his fractured mind, the confusion, the fear, but there was something different now. A spark inside him, dim but growing.

As they moved forward into the unknown, with the night pressing in around them, Arthur felt like he could actually picture a future—one where the pieces of him weren't broken but might one day be whole. With Lisa in his corner, the long, dark road didn't seem so impossible. Together, they were stepping into something new—something that might just lead to dawn after all.

Chapter 7

The door to Dr. Turner's office creaked open, the sound slicing through the stillness like a warning. Arthur stood in the doorway, frozen, as a sliver of light stretched across the floor, barely touching his shoes. The familiar scent of antiseptic hung in the air, but beneath it, there was a hint of something softer—lavender, maybe—meant to calm. It didn't work. His heart raced wildly, slamming against his chest like a trapped animal.

"Arthur, come in," a voice called out, firm but gentle, slicing through the thick tension. Dr. Elaine Turner stood in the center of the room, her eyes on him, calm and inviting.

He swallowed hard, his throat tight, and stepped forward, crossing the threshold into the sterile office. The door clicked shut behind him, sealing him inside. The soft glow of a desk lamp illuminated Dr. Turner's kind face, but the room's silence was oppressive. He hesitated before sinking into the leather chair across from her, the cool material pressing against his back like an unwelcoming embrace.

Dr. Turner smiled slightly; the gesture warm but not enough to melt the icy fear gripping him. "Arthur," she said, her voice steady, "let's start with something simple. Close your eyes. Take a deep breath. In through your nose, hold it... and then let it out."

Arthur closed his eyes, forcing himself to follow her instructions. His chest rose and fell with each breath, but it felt like he was barely skimming the surface, afraid that if he breathed too deeply, he'd drown in the darkness inside.

"Good," Dr. Turner murmured, her voice low and soothing. "Now, tell me what's going on. Right here, right now."

His throat tightened again, words choking him. How could he possibly explain what he was feeling? How could he put into words the chaos inside him—the voices, the personalities, the constant battle for control? They were always there, lurking just beneath the surface, waiting for the right moment to take over.

"I..." Arthur's voice faltered, the confession clinging to the back of his throat. He forced the words out, even though they felt wrong, dangerous. "I'm not alone in here."

The moment the words left his mouth, the room seemed to grow colder, the silence heavier. The air felt charged, like something was waiting to happen.

Dr. Turner didn't flinch. She leaned forward slightly, her eyes never leaving his.

"Tell me more," she said, her voice steady, like she was talking about something simple, something normal.

But nothing about this was normal. Arthur's gaze drifted to the corner of the room, his breath quickening. He couldn't shake the feeling that if he said too much, if he opened the floodgates, the storm inside would swallow him whole. The alters—Edmund, Samuel, Victor—they weren't just parts of him; they were real, living forces inside his head, and any one of them could take over at any moment.

"They talk," he finally whispered, his voice barely audible. "They're always talking."

Dr. Turner stayed quiet, letting him continue. He could feel her watching him, waiting, but he couldn't bring himself to look at her.

"They... they tell me what to do. They tell me what to think. Sometimes, I'm not even sure I'm me anymore."

The room felt suffocating, the lavender scent now too sweet, too cloying. Dr. Turner was still calm, her face unreadable, but Arthur could feel the shift in the room, the tension building.

"You're not alone, Arthur," she said softly, but her words felt distant, like they couldn't reach him. The battle was raging inside him now, the voices louder, pushing, shoving, trying to take control.

He gripped the armrests of the chair, knuckles white, as if holding on to reality by a thread. Dr. Turner was still there, a lifeline in the storm, but he didn't know how long he could hold on.

"They want out," he whispered, his voice cracking with fear. "They want control."

Arthur's fingers dug into the leather chair, gripping it like a lifeline, as if the cool material could keep him tethered to reality. But he felt it—something was shifting inside him, unraveling his fragile sense of calm. His heartbeat, once steady, now pounded erratically in his chest, echoing the chaos in his mind.

"Arthur?" Dr. Turner's voice pierced the haze in his head, pulling him back just enough to hear her concern. "You've gone quiet. What's happening?"

He opened his mouth, trying to respond, but the words tangled on his tongue, refusing to come out. He couldn't describe it—the presence he felt inside, lurking in the corners of his mind like a shadow with no form. It was there, teasing at his thoughts, twisting them into something unrecognizable.

"Something's here," he finally forced out, his voice barely above a whisper. "Not in the room—inside me, I can feel it—them watching."

Dr. Turner leaned in, her eyes narrowing slightly as she tried to understand.

"Inside your mind?"

He nodded, swallowing the knot of fear that threatened to choke him. "It's like shadows, but there's no one casting them. Echoes of voices, voices I know but — they aren't mine."

Her pen hovered over her notepad, waiting to capture his words, but Arthur's gaze darted around the room, searching for something solid, something real to hold onto. But all he could see were shadows creeping along the walls, growing darker, thicker, like they were alive, watching him.

"Can you describe these shadows?" Dr. Turner's voice remained calm, but Arthur could feel the tension building between them. "What are they telling you? Are they asking you to do something Arthur?"

He tried to focus, tried to shape the chaos into words, but the feeling was too strong, too overwhelming. "It's... like a pressure," he said, his voice shaking now. "It's pushing against my thoughts, bending them, twisting them into things I don't recognize."

"Keep going," she urged gently, her voice soft but firm, like a lifeline thrown into the storm. "What are they saying to you?"

The moment she asked, it was as if the presence grew stronger, more real. Arthur flinched, his entire body tensing, as if the question itself had invited the darkness closer. He could feel it now, wrapping around his mind like tendrils of smoke, tightening its grip on him. His vision blurred, the room tilting as the pressure inside his head grew unbearable.

"They want control," he muttered, barely able to get the words out. "They want to take over."

Arthur felt like he was being dragged under, pulled into the depths of his own mind, where the shadows whispered things he didn't want to hear. His grip on the chair tightened, his knuckles white as he fought to stay present, but the voices grew louder, the whispers turning into demands, each one pulling him further away from himself.

Dr. Turner's voice was distant now, almost drowned out by the roar in his head. "Arthur, stay with me. You're in control. You can fight this."

But could he? Arthur wasn't so sure anymore. The shadows were closing in, and he wasn't sure how much longer he could hold them back.

Arthur's breath catches, barely a whisper in the thick air of Dr. Turner's office. A cold shiver runs up his spine as Victor—his darker, more dangerous side—starts to creep into his mind. It's subtle at first, like a shadow stretching across his thoughts, but soon it feels like it's everywhere, pulling him under. The room feels darker, like the shadows are reaching out to him, feeding off Victor's growing control.

"Arthur?" Dr. Turner's voice breaks through the heavy fog, clear but concerned. "You're awfully still. What's going on?"

He wants to answer, to tell her everything, but it's like his words are stuck, trapped behind clenched teeth. His hands grip the fabric of his pants tightly, his knuckles white, trying to hold onto something real, something solid. But Victor's presence is suffocating, filling every corner of his mind, silencing every scream before it even has a chance to escape.

Dr. Turner leans in, watching him carefully. She notices how tense he's become, how his eyes are darting around the room, searching for something that's not there. Despite the tension, she remains calm, her steady gaze unwavering as she assesses the growing storm inside him.

"Arthur," she says again, softer this time, her voice filled with empathy. "Stay with me. Focus on my voice."

She begins to guide him through breathing exercises. "Breathe in slowly... now breathe out." Her own breaths are calm, deliberate, trying to ground him. "Can you feel the chair beneath you? The floor under your feet?"

FRACTURED REFLECTIONS 101

Arthur manages a jerky nod, clinging to her words like they're the only thing keeping him afloat. But even as he tries to focus on her voice, Victor is there, wrapping around his thoughts like smoke, clouding his reason and feeding his fear. His chest tightens, each breath harder to take as panic grips him like a vice.

"Good," Dr. Turner continues, unfazed by the fear on Arthur's face. "Stay here, in the moment. You're in this room, with me. You're safe."

Her words are like a light in the darkness, but Victor's presence refuses to let go, pulling Arthur deeper into the abyss. His control is slipping, his grip on reality starting to fray as Victor's whispers grow louder, drowning out everything else.

"Arthur, I need you to tell me what's happening. It's important that you try to describe it."

Arthur struggles, his thoughts splintering under the pressure. Finally, he forces out one word: "Pressure." His voice is hoarse, shaky. "He's... everywhere."

"Who, Arthur?" Dr. Turner asks, her voice steady but urging him on. "Who's 'he'?"

"Victor." The name comes out in a strained breath, like admitting it gives Victor more power. It's like surrendering to the dark part of himself, the one that's always waiting, ready to take over.

"Remember, Victor is just one part of you," Dr. Turner says firmly. "But he doesn't define who you are. You can confront him. You can take control."

Arthur wants to believe her, but Victor's presence feels too strong, too consuming. Still, he holds onto Dr. Turner's words, her steady confidence the only thing keeping him from falling apart completely. As the session dives deeper into the chaos inside his mind, Arthur clings to her voice, desperate for something—anything—that can help him fight the darkness closing in around him.

Arthur's heart pounds in his chest, the walls of Dr. Turner's office seeming to close in around him. The air feels thick, heavy, like a weight pressing down on his lungs. Shadows crawl along the floor, creeping toward him, as if alive. Victor's voice—a dark, twisted presence in his mind—slithers through his thoughts like a snake.

"You think you can shut me out?" Victor hisses, his voice cold and sharp. "I am the truth you're too weak to face."

Arthur's hands grip the arms of the chair, his knuckles turning white as he fights to keep control. The leather beneath his fingers feels real, solid, but it's not enough to anchor him. Victor's words coil around his mind, tightening, squeezing the life out of his resolve.

"Go away," Arthur whispers, his voice barely audible, drowned out by the pounding in his ears.

Victor's laugh echoes inside his head, cruel and mocking. "Go away? You'd be nothing without me. I'm the only thing keeping you from falling apart."

Arthur clenches his teeth, his muscles tensing as a surge of fear grips him. His gaze darts to Dr. Turner, her calm eyes watching him closely. He can see the concern in her face, but there's something else—hope. A tiny flicker of it. It gives him just enough strength to push back.

"Why?" Arthur croaks, his voice shaking. "Why won't you leave me alone?"

Victor's voice darkens, a sinister growl. "I'm not here to torment you, Arthur. I'm here to show you who you really are. Weak. Fragile."

"Enough!" Arthur's shout bursts from him, breaking the silence like a crack of thunder. His entire body trembles with the force of it, his chest heaving as he struggles to hold onto the last shred of control he has left. "You don't get to control me!"

The room goes still, the only sound the rapid thudding of his heart. Victor is quiet for a moment, and Arthur feels the air shift. But the darkness lingers, hovering on the edges of his mind, waiting for him to falter.

"Arthur, stay with me," Dr. Turner's voice cuts through the haze. She leans forward, her tone gentle but firm. "Listen to my voice. Focus on your breathing. Slow, deep breaths."

Arthur fights to focus, his breaths coming fast and shallow. He forces himself to follow her lead. Inhale... exhale. The room feels less oppressive, the shadows less menacing.

"You're here, in this room," Dr. Turner continues, her voice steady and calm. "Feel the chair beneath you, the floor under your feet. Victor is only in your mind. He has no power outside of it."

Arthur nods slightly, his fingers gripping the chair as if it's the only thing keeping him from being swept away. He can still feel Victor lurking, but the oppressive weight begins to lift, just a little.

"Now tell me," Dr. Turner says, her eyes locking onto his. "What is Victor saying to you?"

Arthur's throat tightens, fear threatening to choke him. But he forces himself to speak.

"He says I'm weak," Arthur whispers. "That I'm nothing without him."

"And do you believe him?" she asks, her tone even.

Arthur swallows hard, his mind racing. He wants to say yes, to give in to the terror that Victor feeds on. But something inside him—something small, but strong—pushes back.

"No," Arthur says, his voice barely more than a breath. "I don't believe him."

Dr. Turner smiles, a soft, encouraging smile. "Good. Victor's words are just that—words. They don't define you. You define you."

Arthur's heart slows, the frantic pounding in his chest easing. The shadows in the room seem less alive, less threatening. Victor's voice, though still present, is quieter now, more distant.

"You can fight him, Arthur," Dr. Turner says, her voice unwavering. "You have the power to push him away."

Arthur nods, feeling a flicker of strength return. It's not much, but it's enough. Enough to keep Victor at bay, enough to keep himself grounded.

"I'm in control," Arthur whispers to himself, his hands relaxing their death grip on the chair. "Not him."

Dr. Turner nods in approval, her eyes full of reassurance. Arthur knows the battle isn't over, that Victor will come back, stronger and more relentless. But for now, in this moment, he's won. And that's enough.

Arthur's chest tightens, his breaths ragged as if the very air in the office is suffocating him. The room seems to close in, the walls pressing down like invisible hands squeezing his lungs. Sweat trickles down his forehead, stinging his eyes, as Victor's cold, mocking voice coils around his mind.

"You think you can escape me?" Victor sneers, his tone slithering like a snake. "You're nothing without me, not even with the help of your doctor, you will never be free of me Arthur, you weak pathetic shit."

"Victor doesn't own you," she insists, her words ringing clear and true.

He clings to her mantra, letting it fuel a fire inside him. With clenched fists, Arthur pushes back against the suffocating darkness that Victor casts over his thoughts.

"You will not control me!" he shouts, the defiance in his voice growing louder, reverberating off the walls like an echo of strength.

Victor's laugh echoes inside his skull, but there's something different this time—an edge of uncertainty, a crack in the facade. Victor's voice snakes out from the shadows, cold and mocking. "Weak, pathetic fool." it hisses. but Arthur senses the shift. He knows Victor is afraid of losing control.

"Edmund," Arthur calls out silently, searching for the wisdom of his mentor. In the midst of the chaos, Edmund's familiar figure appears, a beacon of experience amidst the storm. His eyes, bright with understanding, lock onto Arthur's.

"Remember your anchors, Arthur," Edmund advises, his voice a calm presence amidst the chaos. "Your history, your truth—let them guide you."

Arthur grasps at Edmund's words, picturing the sturdy oaks from his childhood, their roots deep and unyielding. He can almost feel their strength wrapping around him, anchoring him firmly to the here and now, grounding him in reality.

"Samuel," Arthur whispers next, summoning the timid soul within who knows all too well the taste of dread. Samuel's presence, while small, exudes a surprising resilience, forged through countless nights spent weathering storms of anxiety and fear.

"Y-you're not alone," Samuel stammers, his voice shaking but determined.

"Together, we are stronger than he is."

With their combined strength, a protective shield begins to form around Arthur, a barrier that Victor's taunts cannot penetrate. The malevolent figure flinches, his influence starting to wane as Arthur's defiance swells.

"Your time is over," Arthur declares, his voice cutting through the oppressive gloom like a sword. It's a proclamation filled with newfound power, each word a step toward reclaiming his identity from the depths of despair.

Victor's laughter, once chilling and confident, begins to dissolve in the air. "You think you can win?" he scoffs, but his sneer falters as Arthur stands his ground. The more Arthur asserts himself, the more Victor shrinks back, reduced to a mere echo of his former self.

Dr. Turner watches intently, her gaze unwavering, a sentinel guarding the fragile gates of Arthur's sanity. She nods slightly, a silent sign of approval for the man fighting to reclaim himself piece by piece.

Arthur stands tall, an inner legion gathered behind him, a united front against the usurper of his mind. As Edmund's wisdom intertwines with Samuel's quiet support, Arthur creates a fortress of self, a bastion against the darkness that has haunted him for so long.

The oppressive weight in the room begins to lift. The shadows recede, their grip loosening as a profound silence settles in the aftermath of the battle. Arthur's breath comes easier now, each inhale a step away from the edge, each exhale a release of Victor's lingering influence.

As the tumult within subsides, a fragile peace envelops Arthur Hall, his consciousness his own once again, if only for this moment—a hard-won reprieve in the ongoing war for his soul. He knows Victor will return, but for now, he has emerged victorious, stronger than before, ready to face whatever darkness may lie ahead.

Arthur's fingers slowly unclench, the tightness in his knuckles melting away as he takes in his surroundings with new clarity. The shadows in Dr. Turner's office, once ominous, now appear as nothing more than ordinary patterns cast by the fading afternoon light. He draws in a deep breath, feeling the remnants of Victor's icy grip dissolve with each inhalation.

"Thank you," he whispers, a blend of gratitude and awe in his voice. "I couldn't have faced him without you." His gaze locks onto Dr. Turner's, finding reassurance in her steady presence.

Dr. Turner nods, acknowledging the weight of his struggle. "Arthur, your courage today speaks volumes about your resolve. Remember, this is a journey, and I'm here with you every step of the way."

Arthur's heart swells at her words, a warmth igniting inside him. The resolve within him hardens like steel forged in fire; he knows the battle with Victor is far from over, but the will to endure and reclaim his life from The Shadow's clutches burns brighter than ever.

"Victor won't give up easily, he'll be back with a vengeance, I'm afraid." Arthur admits, the reality of his internal war settling deep within him. Yet, there's a newfound defiance in his voice, a spark that wasn't there before.

"He may not," Dr. Turner agrees, her tone a blend of warmth and authority. "But neither will we. Your progress today is a testament to your strength, Arthur. Through therapy and self-awareness, you'll learn to navigate these turbulent waters."

Rising from the chair, Arthur feels more grounded than he has in months. The fragmented pieces of his psyche still swirl around, but he senses the potential for wholeness, an intricate puzzle waiting to be solved. He glances back at Dr. Turner one last time before the session ends, her silhouette framed by shelves laden with books, a guardian of minds.

"Until next time," he says, hope threading through his simple farewell, a promise of continued resistance against the darkness within.

"Until next time, Arthur," she replies, her eyes sparkling with the understanding that their fight could lead to either triumph or tragedy. For now, they stand on the precipice of possibility, poised between the abyss of the mind and the ascent toward recovery.

As Arthur steps into the chill of the late afternoon, the door to Dr. Turner's office closes softly behind him. The pulse of the city beats a rhythm that feels foreign to his own elevated heart rate. His breath mists in front of him, each exhalation a ghost of the turmoil that still lingers inside his mind.

The air bites at his skin, a stark contrast to the sweat still clinging to his palms. He can feel Victor's icy grip trailing him like a dark shadow, an unwelcome presence that haunts his every step. But with each stride along the concrete path, Arthur's resolve hardens. The confrontation with Victor has not crushed him; it has forged him anew.

The buildings loom overhead, their windows reflecting the waning light like eyes hiding secrets within their depths. Arthur's own secrets churn inside him, a storm of identities battling for control. Yet as he walks, the cacophony of voices dulls, the clamor becoming whispers he can choose to ignore. He's learning the delicate art of selective listening, distinguishing Victor's taunts from his own true thoughts.

Passersby blur past him, their faces distorted by the speed of his march. They remain oblivious to the man fighting demons in plain sight, their indifference a shield that allows Arthur to move unseen through the crowd. It's a skill he's perfected—the art of invisibility.

As he approaches the corner, the city's hum swells into a deafening roar. Cars zip by, headlights cutting through the encroaching dusk. The crosswalk signal blinks—red to green—and Arthur takes it as a sign. He crosses the threshold, leaving behind the sanctuary of Dr. Turner's office and stepping into the battlefield of the real world.

A fierce gust of wind rips through the street, ruffling his coat and tousling his slightly graying hair. It carries the scent of rain, of change. Arthur tilts his head to the sky, where dark clouds gather ominously, promising a storm. There's a strange comfort in the brewing tempest, a reflection of his own inner chaos.

He understands now, more than ever, that the struggle for control is far from over. Victor, The Shadow within, will not retreat quietly into the dark corners of his mind. But Arthur is no longer a passive victim. He's an active participant in this war, armed with the tools Dr. Turner has provided and the knowledge of his own inner strength.

As he turns the corner, disappearing into the vibrant throng of city life, Arthur embraces the complex mosaic of his identity.

Each step he takes is a declaration—a commitment to confront the fractured parts of himself and piece them together into something whole. Despite the uncertainty that lies ahead, one thing is clear: Arthur Hall strides forward into the night, not as a victim but as a man resolutely determined to reclaim his life from the shadows.

And as the first drops of rain begin to fall, they mix with the sweat on his brow, a baptism of resilience, washing away the remnants of fear and doubt. The storm is coming, but Arthur is ready.

Chapter 8

Arthur snaps his eyes open, jolted from the void of sleep by the blinding, sterile whiteness above him. The sharp light pierces his skull, confusion crashing through his veins like ice. His breath quickens, ragged gasps tearing through the oppressive silence as his mind struggles to orient itself.

Where am I? What the hell happened?

The cold, hard surface beneath him feels alien—he's on the floor, sprawled in a position that sends panic flaring in his chest. The sickly, metallic scent of blood fills the air, twisting his stomach into knots. It's everywhere, overwhelming, suffocating. His throat tightens as nausea claws at him, threatening to take over. He forces himself to take shallow, desperate breaths to calm his racing heart.

Arthur pushes himself up, hands trembling, and recoils in horror. His palms are slick with blood, warm and fresh, glistening under the harsh light. The sight slams into him like a freight train. His pulse hammers in his ears, drowning out everything but the visceral, gnawing panic coursing through him. He scrambles to his feet, his legs unsteady, his body screaming at him to flee even as his mind fights to comprehend the horror.

Whose blood is this?

The question spirals through his head, frantic and unrelenting.

His eyes dart around the room, wild and desperate, searching for anything—*anyone*—that can explain the nightmare he's just woken up to. The sterile walls loom around him, cold and indifferent, offering no answers, no relief. It's a void—empty except for the creeping realization that something has gone horribly wrong.

His chest tightens, breaths coming in shallow, sharp bursts as the walls seem to close in on him. His mind races, but there's nothing to hold onto, no memory, no thread to pull.

How did I get here? What did I do?

The pounding of his heartbeat is the only rhythm, the only answer in the silence. Arthur stumbles backward, his back hitting the wall as his legs threaten to give out. His hands shake violently, the blood on his skin feeling like it belongs to someone else—*someone else's life, someone else's nightmare.* He wipes his hands on his pants, but the blood smears, and the terror only grows.

The thought crashes into him like a tidal wave—*What if this blood isn't mine?*

His eyes widen, the weight of that possibility suffocating him. He frantically checks his own body, patting down his arms, his torso, his legs—no pain, no wounds. He feels unharmed, physically intact, but that only deepens the dread. If it's not his blood, then... *Whose is it?*

A scream builds in his throat, but he swallows it, choking on the terror that has lodged itself deep inside. His mind claws at the void, desperate for answers, for memories that refuse to surface.

What happened here?

The blankness of his memory is more terrifying than anything else, a gaping hole that could swallow him whole.

He presses his back harder against the wall, trying to steady himself, his body trembling as the questions pile on top of each other, smothering him.

What if I did something?

The thought gnashes at him, relentless, echoing through his skull like a violent whisper.

There's nothing but the weight of his uncertainty, a suffocating darkness that refuses to let him go. Arthur's mind spirals further, his breath coming in panicked gasps.

I have to remember... I have to know...

But the room remains silent, a bleak witness to whatever horror has just unfolded. And Arthur stands alone, blood on his hands, the truth slipping further from his grasp.

Desperation claws at him as he stumbles backward, bracing himself against the cold wall. His mind races, each thought colliding with the next, swirling in a maelstrom of confusion and fear. He can't remember.

What is happening?

There must be something in this room that can help him piece together the puzzle. But all he finds is the overwhelming weight of his own uncertainty.

Arthur takes a deep breath, steeling himself. He must focus. He can't let the panic consume him. With trembling hands, he pushes off the wall and takes a step forward, ready to confront the reality of his situation. Each step feels like a leap into the unknown, the floor beneath him unsteady, as if he's walking on the edge of a precipice. The darkness of his mind battles against the stark, cold reality surrounding him.

He needs to find answers. He needs to remember. But as he takes another step, the questions grow louder, echoing in the corners of his mind like the sound of distant sirens, drawing closer with every passing second. Arthur knows he must uncover the truth—before whatever is lurking in the shadows can reach out and claim him.

DETECTIVE JAMES LAWSON sits behind his desk, the glow of the desk lamp casting long, flickering shadows over the scattered photographs and reports that tell stories of lives interrupted. The precinct is quiet, a stark contrast to the chaos of the world outside. Just as he begins to lose himself in the details of his latest case, the shrill ring of the phone shatters the stillness, cutting through his focus like a knife. He answers it with the practiced precision of a seasoned detective, his voice steady despite the late hour.

"Lawson here."

"James, we've got another one," the voice on the other end says, sending a chill racing down his spine. Another murder. Another life violently snuffed out; a candle extinguished in the darkness.

"Details," he commands, his pen already in hand, hovering above a blank page, ready to capture every word, every nuance. He leans in, the room around him fading away as he listens intently. The scratch of his pen on paper is the only sound in the otherwise silent precinct, a rhythmic reminder of the weight of the news being relayed to him. Each detail is a thread, and James Lawson is a master weaver, turning them into a tapestry that slowly reveals the haunting face of a killer.

The voice continues, detailing the crime scene—where it happened, how the victim was found, the chilling evidence that suggests a pattern. As the information pours in, a grim determination ignites within him. This is more than just another case; it's a chance to bring closure to the grieving and justice to the dead.

"Understood. I'm on my way," he says, ending the call with a decisive click. His heart races with purpose, but the case files stacked high on his desk beckon him. Yet, he resists the pull. There will be time for that later, after he's stood on the scene, after he's absorbed every silent scream and whisper of violence that lingers in the air like a ghost.

He rises, shrugging into his coat with the ease of someone who has done this countless times before. His movements are deliberate, methodical. This isn't just a job for Lawson; it's a calling, an obsession fueled by the desire to understand the darkness that lurks in the human heart. As he steps out into the night, the cold air wraps around him like an old friend, familiar yet foreboding, and he heads toward the latest point on a map that's becoming far too crowded with death.

The streets are eerily quiet as he drives, the neon lights of the city casting a haunting glow on the pavement. In the back of his mind, a profile begins to form, piecing together the fragments of information into a picture that's still frustratingly incomplete. The faces of the victims flash through his mind, each one a reminder of the life snuffed out too soon, the laughter silenced forever.

Yet James knows that patience is key. Every killer slips: every murderer leaves a trace. He grips the steering wheel tighter, his knuckles whitening, and vows to himself that when they do, he'll be there, ready to bring the monster lurking in the shadows to justice.

As he approaches the scene, he feels the familiar thrill of the hunt pulse through him—a dark adrenaline that fuels his determination to unveil the truth hidden beneath the layers of grief and horror. Tonight, he will face the darkness head-on, and he won't back down until the killer is brought to light.

Detective James Lawson steps through the door and is immediately hit by the overwhelming scene before him. The room, once ordinary, has been transformed into a horrific slaughterhouse, drenched in chaos and horror. The sharp, metallic scent of fresh blood fills the air, suffocating him like a thick fog. It clings to his skin, making him acutely aware of the violence that unfolded here.

He squints against the dim light, his flashlight beam cutting through the shadows like a knife. The walls are smeared with dark streaks, grotesque splatters that tell a story of brutality. Furniture lies overturned, and the floor is slick with a grim mix of blood and broken glass, making every step feel treacherous.

Lawson's heart pounds in his chest, adrenaline surging through his veins. He forces himself to breathe, to focus. His training kicks in. This is what he signed up for—this is the darkness he must confront.

He scans the room with a steely gaze, taking in every detail, each element a crucial part of the puzzle he needs to solve.

In the center of the chaos lies a body, lifeless and still. The sight stops him in his tracks. A woman, her features twisted in a final grimace of terror, stares unseeing at the ceiling. Her eyes, wide open, seem to plead for justice that has come too late. A shiver runs down his spine as he kneels beside her, struggling to sort through the whirlwind of emotions swirling inside him.

He pulls out his notebook, hands shaking only slightly as he writes down observations. A single drop of blood glistens on the floor, catching the light, as if beckoning him closer. The room is silent, except for the sound of his pen scratching against the paper, a sharp contrast to the horror that surrounds him.

He sets to work, placing evidence markers with precision. A hairpin glints in the corner, a potential clue to the victim's identity. A broken chair lies nearby, its splintered wood suggesting a violent struggle. Each piece of evidence tells a story, and Lawson is determined to hear it.

The cold grip of fear clings to him, but he shoves it deep down, refusing to let it take control. He knows he must be strong—not just for himself, but for the victim. He has to find out what happened, to bring her killer to justice.

As he continues to examine the scene, the weight of the room settles over him. Every corner holds secrets, every shadow could hide a witness. He feels the pressure of time ticking away, the killer potentially still lurking nearby. The darkness of the night outside seems to mirror the chaos within the room, each moment amplifying the tension.

He stands and surveys the area, adrenaline coursing through him. This isn't just a job; it's a battle—a battle against the evils that walk among them, against the monsters that lurk in the shadows.

Lawson knows he will stop at nothing to piece together the fragments of this crime, to weave them into a narrative that will lead him to the truth. With determination in his eyes, he sets to work, ready to face whatever darkness lies ahead, prepared to dive deep into the nightmare that has unfolded in this once-innocent room.

The air is thick with the heavy, metallic scent of blood and the stench of death, each breath he takes feels like swallowing iron, a visceral reminder of the violence that unfolded here. Shadows cling to the walls, their dark shapes twisting and contorting in the weak light of his flashlight, a feeble attempt to push back against the consuming darkness that has seeped into every corner of the room.

He crouches beside the body—a woman, lifeless and cold, her life brutally snuffed out. Her eyes, wide open, stare up at him in a haunting expression of silent accusation, as if they demand answers that he knows he must find. The horror of the scene presses down on him, yet Lawson doesn't flinch. Years on the force have hardened him to such gruesome sights, but they have never extinguished the flame of determination burning within him.

Methodically, he pulls out small evidence markers, placing them with precision near potential clues. He pauses over a single strand of hair, its color contrasting sharply against the pale floorboards. A partial shoe print by the door catches his eye, and he notices a fiber caught on the splinter of a broken chair. Each piece is cataloged with a quiet reverence, each item a fragment of a larger story begging to be uncovered. They are whispers of the victim's final moments, secrets that must be heard if justice is to be served.

Lawson's hands are steady, each movement deliberate as he sets the markers in place, but his mind races with possibilities. He dissects angles and examines the layout of the room, reconstructing the scene in his mind. Every detail matters—every drop of blood, every scuff on the floor. He envisions how the struggle unfolded, the chaos of the last moments of the woman's life replaying in his mind like a disturbing film.

The sound of sirens wailing in the distance becomes a reminder of the urgency that drives him. Time is of the essence. He knows that the killer is still out there, lurking in the shadows, perhaps even watching him now. Lawson's resolve hardens. This isn't just another case; it's a race against time to bring a murderer to justice before they strike again.

As he studies the blood spatter fanning out across the floorboards, he notes the grotesque ballet of crimson against the wood, each arc telling a story of desperation and pain. He breathes deeply, forcing the weight of the scene to settle into his chest, fueling his determination. With every piece of evidence he uncovers, he feels the fire within him grow stronger. He is a hunter in pursuit of a shadow, and he won't rest until the killer is found.

With each passing moment, Lawson's theories take shape, the puzzle coming together bit by bit, yet he knows he'll have to dismantle and rebuild them countless times before he finds the truth. But that's the nature of his work—a relentless pursuit of justice in a world that can be so dark.

With one last glance at the victim, Lawson stands, determination etched into his features. This room, this scene, will not be the end. It will be the catalyst for his relentless quest to uncover the truth. He steps back into the darkness, ready to face whatever horrors lie ahead, knowing that he will do whatever it takes to ensure that this woman's story does not fade away into silence.

ARTHUR HALL SITS ALONE in the stifling silence of his apartment, where the shadows seem to laugh at his desperate attempts to maintain his sanity. His heart races, pounding a frantic rhythm against his ribs, each beat a reminder of the dread creeping through him. Beads of sweat collect on his forehead, mixing with the grime and blood he can't remember smearing on his skin.

The fear hits him in waves, crashing over him like a tidal wave, forcing the air from his lungs. It feels alive, a writhing thing inside his chest, gnawing at his insides with sharp, unyielding teeth. He squeezes his eyes shut, desperately trying to push away the horrific images that flash behind his eyes—splashes of crimson and echoes of screams that aren't his.

His senses are on high alert, every creak of the building settling and every distant siren igniting a sense of impending doom. He feels hunted, the prickling sensation of unseen eyes tracing every curve of his body. Paranoia whispers that everyone he encounters knows what he's done, that they can see the guilt etched on his face as clearly as he feels it within his very soul.

His hands tremble as he fumbles with the faucet, scrubbing them raw beneath the water. No matter how much he washes, it's never enough to erase the stains that seep beyond his skin, tainting the very marrow of his being. He glances into the mirror, searching for a hint of recognition, but the stranger staring back offers nothing but silent questions:

Who are you?

Tears blur his vision, cascading down his cheeks and carving clean tracks through the grime. They are tears of frustration, confusion, and sheer terror. Arthur is adrift in the chaotic sea of his own mind, clinging desperately to the fragments of who he was, who he is, and who he fears he might become.

Chapter 9

Detective James Lawson strides through the bustling precinct, a folder tucked firmly under his arm, the purposeful echo of his footfalls cutting through the noise of the late-night chaos. He steps into a dimly lit interrogation room where a woman sits, her fingers nervously twisting the hem of her shirt. The flickering fluorescent light casts erratic shadows, mirroring the tension in the air. Lawson flips open the folder, revealing pages filled with notes and photographs, each marked with meticulous annotations.

"Mrs. Henderson," he begins, his voice calm yet authoritative, "I need you to think back to last night. Tell me everything you remember."

The woman's eyes dart around the room, never resting in one place for too long. Lawson observes her carefully, patient as a spider weaving its web. He senses the tension in her body as she speaks, her words skimming the surface of the truth like leaves drifting on a pond.

"Did you see anyone near Mrs. Edwards' apartment?" he asks, his tone gentle yet probing. Mrs. Henderson hesitates, a subtle shift in her posture telling Lawson that she's hiding something important.

"Well, there was this man..." she trails off, her gaze finally locking onto Lawson's, a flicker of recognition dawning in her eyes.

"Can you describe him?" he presses, leaning forward slightly, eager for the details that could unlock this case.

She describes an unremarkable figure, a shadow among many in the city's grey landscape. But it's not the description that hooks Lawson; it's the pause before she speaks, the flicker of uncertainty that tells him she has seen more than she realizes.

"Thank you," Lawson says, closing the folder with a soft thud. Every interview, every fragment of overheard conversation is another piece of the puzzle — and Lawson knows how to wait for the picture to emerge from the chaos.

ARTHUR STANDS IN THE cramped confines of his bathroom, his eyes locked onto the man staring back at him in the mirror. The blood on his hands is a vivid red against the white porcelain sink, a glaring contrast to his pale skin that seems almost translucent under the harsh light. His heart pounds against his ribs, each thud echoing like a drum, drowning out the silence that envelops him.

With shaky hands, he turns on the faucet, watching as the water spirals down the drain, tainted pink as it washes away the remnants of his guilt. He scrubs at his skin with a frenzy, the soap slipping through his fingers like the truth he desperately tries to cling to.

"Get it off," he whispers, a mantra that battles the rising panic threatening to consume him.

He can hardly bear to meet his own gaze, haunted eyes staring back at him, the lines of fear etched deeper on his forehead as the weight of his secrets bears down on him.

In the sterile, tiled walls of the bathroom, he fights to wash away the evidence. Yet the coppery scent of blood lingers in the air, a ghost that clings stubbornly to his senses. It's not just the physical traces he yearns to erase; it's the memories that claw at the edges of his consciousness—the darkness lurking within him, waiting to strike.

He dries his hands with a towel, the fabric snagging against the rawness of his skin. With every thread of evidence he conceals, the overwhelming guilt sinks its claws deeper into him, a cruel reminder of the horror that dwells beneath the surface of Arthur Hall—the quiet office worker with tired eyes and a mind fractured by dread.

DETECTIVE JAMES LAWSON stands over a cluttered desk, fingers sifting through a mountain of photographs and notes scattered across the surface. The dim light from his desk lamp casts long shadows in the room, echoing the dark puzzle sprawled before him. Something glints beneath a pile of witness statements, a sliver of metal catching the weak glow. He reaches for it, and his breath catches in his throat—a key chain, plain but for a small, enameled emblem. It's a logo he recognizes from an office building downtown, the very place where Arthur Hall spends his days, lost in anonymity.

A surge of adrenaline courses through Lawson's veins, igniting his senses. This is the lead he's been waiting for, a tangible thread woven into a web of shadows. The detective's mind races, piecing together timelines and movements, constructing a mosaic that centers around Arthur.

"Could it really be this simple?" he mutters, though deep down, he knows there's nothing straightforward about the chase. The hunt for truth in a sea of deceit is never easy, and the stakes have never felt higher.

Detective Lawson feels a quiet excitement building inside him, a small flame flickering in the darkness of the unknown. He carefully tucks the key chain into an evidence bag, his eyes bright with determination. This clue could be the breakthrough he desperately needs, the first real step toward exposing the killer who has been stalking the city during its restless nights.

Meanwhile, Arthur navigates the twisted streets of the city, feeling like he's being swallowed whole by the shadows. His frantic footsteps echo off the cold concrete, each sound amplifying his rising panic. He darts into a narrow alleyway, the stench of rotting garbage wrapping around him like a suffocating blanket.

The police presence looms in his mind like a predator circling its prey, a threat to the fragile balance of Arthur's crumbling world. Paranoia clings to him, much like the blood still staining his hands. It whispers that every shadow is watching, that every stranger's glance carries an unspoken judgment.

Arthur takes a different path, making careful turns designed to throw anyone off his trail. His heart races like a trapped animal, pounding against his ribs as he slips through darkened backstreets. He avoids the main roads, those open spaces where prying eyes might linger too long, where recognition could seal his fate.

At each corner, he hesitates, his senses on high alert as he scans for any sign of the police or anyone following him. His thoughts are a chaotic jumble, threads of logic fraying under the weight of his fear. With each close call, he feels the noose of inevitability tightening around his neck. He knows it's only a matter of time before the hunter becomes the hunted, before the truth he dreads emerges like a body rising from still water.

Arthur retreats deeper into the city's maze, becoming a ghost among the living, haunted by the knowledge that the police's net is slowly tightening around him.

Victor prowls through the night, a shadow slipping between darker shadows, his steps silent on the damp pavement. The city's heartbeat pulses through him—a predator attuned to the rhythm of unsuspecting prey. He pauses for a moment, inhaling deeply, savoring the intoxicating scent of vulnerability that hangs in the air, almost tangible in its allure.

A soft click, the sound of metal against metal, barely pierces the urban noise, but it's there. Victor is patient as he picks the lock, the door giving way under his skilled touch. With a soft thud, it swings open, revealing a darkened interior that invites him in.

The room is steeped in silence, the stillness broken only by the soft, rhythmic breathing of a sleeping figure within. Victor moves with deliberate grace, excitement swelling in his chest as he approaches. A dim light from the street filters through the curtains, casting eerie shadows that flicker on the walls, as if celebrating the sinister events about to unfold.

Victor stands over the bed, his eyes fixed on the steady rise and fall of the chest beneath the sheets. A cruel smile spreads across his face; this moment—this perfect, chilling moment—is his and his alone.

With a calm that belies the chaos he's about to unleash, Victor grips the blade tightly. It glints in the dim light, a flash of silver that reflects his dark intent. In one swift motion, he plunges the knife down. Blood bursts forth, blooming like dark roses against the stark white sheets, creating a horrific masterpiece that only he can appreciate.

The body jerks once, a weak protest against the inevitable, then falls still. The room is silent, save for the soft rustle of the sheets and the steady thrum of Victor's heartbeat, a rhythmic reminder of the life he has just extinguished.

Satisfied, Victor steps back, admiring his handiwork for just a moment longer. The thrill of power courses through him as he turns to leave, knowing that chaos now reigns in his wake. With each drop of blood seeping into the fabric of the bed, the danger to Arthur intensifies, a ticking clock that inches closer to detonation. Victor's heart races with anticipation—he's set a dark plan in motion, and nothing will stop him now.

DETECTIVE LAWSON SITS across from the witness, the room suffused with tension thick enough to smother. His blue eyes, sharp as ever, never waver from the figure before him. The man fidgets, seems to shrink under the weight of the detective's gaze.

"Take your time," James says, his voice tempered steel wrapped in velvet. "Every detail matters."

The witness nods, moistens dry lips, and then it comes—a hesitancy in speech, a faltering that signals the crux of it all. Words stutter out, fragmented pieces of a puzzle that James has been meticulously assembling in his mind.

"Seen 'im around... always thought he was just some quiet office guy... But that night, I saw Arthur—"

"Arthur Hall?" Lawson interjects, urgency creeping into his tone. The mention of the name feels like a spark igniting a powder keg.

"Yeah, that's the one." The witness's eyes dart nervously, shifting away then back to meet James's gaze. Conflict plays out in his expression, a battle between fear and the need to tell the truth.

"He was carrying a bag—looked heavy—down the alley. It was late, too late for someone like him to be out there."

"Go on," James encourages, his instincts firing up like a hunter catching a whiff of prey.

The witness swallows hard, his voice dropping to a whisper. "His hands... they were bloody. At first, I thought it was paint or something, but now..." His words hang in the air, the weight of their meaning crashing down like thunder.

Lawson leans back, a surge of adrenaline rushing through him. This could be the breakthrough he's been waiting for—the thread that, when pulled, unravels the tangled web of murders plaguing the city. And at its center, maybe, just maybe, is Arthur Hall.

A chill runs down his spine, and he knows they're onto something big. The room seems to close in around them as he takes a deep breath, focusing on the path ahead. Time to chase down the truth, no matter where it leads.

ARTHUR PACES BACK AND forth in his cramped apartment, the walls closing in around him. The air is still thick with the metallic scent of blood, a grim reminder that no matter how much he scrubs, it won't wash away. His breaths come in shallow gasps, each one escaping his lips like a puff of steam in the frigid room. Every creak of the aging floorboards beneath his feet sounds like a siren calling to his paranoia, and the shadows cast by the flickering streetlight outside seem to point fingers at him, accusing him of unthinkable acts.

He frantically grabs newspapers and piles of clothing—the tangible remnants of his chaotic life—and shoves them into trash bags with shaking hands. The pulse of the city vibrates through the walls, a relentless beat that syncs with the frantic thump of his heart.

"Control," he whispers to himself, trying to anchor his spiraling thoughts. But control is a ship that has long since sailed, now adrift on a stormy sea stirred by fear and guilt. With trembling fingers, he lights a match and drops it into the sink, watching as flames engulf the papers, devouring secrets too dangerous to keep. The flames dance and flicker, a brief moment of chaos mirroring the turmoil inside him.

Tick. Tick. Tick. The clock on the wall mocks him, its steady rhythm counting down the moments until someone discovers his terrible secret. Desperate, he grabs a bottle of bleach, scrubbing the counter top, erasing fingerprints that scream of his presence. Deep down, he knows it's pointless; the truth is like a relentless hound on a scent, closing in on him. Yet, desperation breeds a warped sense of logic.

Peering through the window, the outside world becomes a blur of unfamiliar faces. He scans each one, his eyes darting with suspicion, searching for the slightest hint of pursuit. Paranoia clings to him like a second skin, whispering dreadful thoughts into his ear with every passing glance. He can feel the noose tightening around his neck, woven from strands of Detective Lawson's determination and his own unraveling mind.

IN A DIMLY LIT ROOM, Detective James Lawson stands surrounded by whiteboards covered in timelines and photographs pinned like moths trapped in a web. His blue eyes narrow as they land on a new piece of evidence—an overlooked photograph that has resurfaced: a ticket stub from the night of the third murder.

This ticket is a direct link, a silent witness to the killer's secret journey through the darkest corners of the city. Lawson runs a hand through his graying hair, feeling the weight of the revelation settle heavily on his shoulders.

"Arthur Hall," he murmurs to himself, piecing together the chilling puzzle laid out before him. A grim pattern begins to emerge, undeniable and horrifying. This quiet man, this unremarkable office worker with his soft-spoken demeanor and careful steps, might just be the mastermind behind the horrors they've been chasing.

As he studies the grainy security camera footage, his heart races with recognition. There, in the flickering light, is Arthur—a figure shrouded in shadows, but unmistakably familiar. The pieces fit together all too well to be mere coincidence.

"Gotcha," James whispers into the heavy silence, the thrill of the chase igniting a fire within him. The hunt has become a game of cat and mouse, and now, for the first time, the prey is finally within reach.

Chapter 10

The flickering light of the television bathes the living room in an eerie glow, casting long shadows that seem to stretch and curl like tendrils of darkness reaching for Arthur. He sits rigidly in his chair, a statue of dread, his mind a storm of turmoil. The anchor's voice cuts through the heavy silence, detailing the latest murder with a chilling detachment that only deepens the chill running down his spine. To Arthur, the report feels like a funeral dirge, each word a haunting reminder of the chaos churning within him.

"City officials are urging everyone to stay vigilant," the reporter states, her expression impeccably calm, as if she were discussing the weather rather than a brutal killing.

Arthur's fingers curl tightly around the arms of his chair, knuckles white with tension. The tremor in his hands betrays a terror that claws its way up his throat, threatening to suffocate him. His heart pounds violently against his chest, each beat a cruel echo of the guilt gnawing at his insides. Another life snuffed out, another victim added to the grim tally, and his mind spins in a sickening dance of fragmented thoughts and memories he wishes he could forget.

Just then, a voice cuts through the haze of his thoughts—soft yet edged with an unsettling undercurrent that makes his skin prickle.

"Arthur?"

He looks up, startled. Claire stands in the doorway, her silhouette framed by the flickering light, her presence a stark contrast to the darkness closing in around him. Her eyes, deep pools of concern mixed with something more—something that feels alarmingly like fear—lock onto his. As she takes a tentative step closer, the floorboards creak softly beneath her feet, the sound amplifying the tension in the room.

"Are you okay?" she asks, her voice barely above a whisper, as if afraid the shadows themselves might overhear.

Arthur can't find the words; his throat feels tight, as though the truth he's been holding at bay is choking him from the inside. He nods stiffly, but the lie hangs heavy in the air between them.

Claire steps forward, her expression morphing from worry to something more resolute. "You've been watching the news again, haven't you? It's eating you alive."

Her words strike a nerve, and the room seems to close in on him, the walls pressing against his chest. Every heartbeat feels like a drum roll heralding his impending doom. Arthur can feel his breath quickening, panic bubbling just beneath the surface.

"I... I just need to know what's happening," he stammers, the words tumbling out like marbles rolling down a hill.

But Claire isn't buying it. "It's more than that. You're not just scared, Arthur. You're hiding something."

The accusation hangs in the air, thick and suffocating. Arthur's heart races, a frantic rhythm that drowns out the television's droning voice. He glances at the screen, where a grainy image of a crime scene flickers, the blurred outlines of police tape and flashing lights a grim reminder of the world outside.

As Claire steps further into the room, the shadows seem to close in around her, making her look fragile against the backdrop of chaos. "You can't keep running from this," she says, her voice firm yet laced with fear. "You need to talk to someone. You can't carry this alone."

Arthur's breath hitches, his mind racing. She's right—he can't escape the truth forever. But what if talking about it drags her into the darkness with him? The weight of his secret presses down, a heavy shroud that threatens to suffocate him.

"Claire, I—" he begins, but the words die in his throat, choked by the fear of what he might reveal.

Suddenly, the television blares a siren, jolting them both. Arthur's heart skips a beat as he watches the reporter's face twist into a mask of urgency.

"Stay indoors and lock your doors," she warns, her voice cutting through the tension like a knife. "Authorities are advising caution as the investigation continues."

The air around them grows electric with fear, the shadows deepening as the night stretches on. Arthur's eyes dart to Claire's, the unspoken dread pooling between them like poison. In that moment, he knows they're both standing on the precipice, teetering between the past and an uncertain future, with danger lurking just beyond the door.

"Arthur, I need you to talk to me about this."

The words barely register in his foggy mind. His gaze is locked onto the television screen, where images of a city caught in a nightmare flash before him—a montage of chaos, fear, and destruction. The news anchor's voice drones on, detailing the latest horrors, but all Arthur can think about is how he's entwined in that darkness. He feels like a puppet, his strings pulled by unseen forces that lurk deep within the fractured corners of his psyche.

As he sits there, Claire moves closer, her hand reaching for him, hovering just above his arm. When she finally makes contact, it's like a jolt of electricity surging through him, igniting the raw, frayed edges of his mind. He flinches instinctively, an involuntary reaction that sends hurt flashing across Claire's face. She quickly masks it with a practiced calm, but he sees the tremor in her expression, the flicker of fear.

"Please, Arthur," she urges, her voice steady yet tinged with something frantic. "You're scaring me."

"I can't..." His voice is a hoarse whisper, the words slipping from his lips like smoke, dissipating into the still, oppressive air. Can't what? Can't stop the chaos? Can't remember how he ended up here? Can't hold the splintered pieces of himself together any longer?

"Arthur— Arthur look at me." Her command slices through the thick fog clouding his thoughts. He turns slowly, his weary eyes meeting hers. In that moment, he sees a flicker of desperation in Claire's gaze—a frantic search for the man she once knew, the man buried beneath layers of fear and guilt.

"Whatever this is, whatever you think is happening," she continues, her tone carefully balanced between firm and gentle, "we'll figure it out. You're not the only one in this marriage, that means we are a team, we will figure it all out together, I promise."

But her reassurance feels like a fragile lifeline, and he's terrified of what might happen if he reaches for it. The weight of his secrets presses down on him, suffocating.

"I'm a danger to you, Claire," he admits, the truth spilling out like venom. "I don't even know who I am anymore."

Her expression shifts, shifting from fear to resolve.

"That's exactly why we need to talk. You're not just running from yourself, Arthur. You're running from the truth. And hiding won't make it go away."

His heart pounds in response, each beat resonating with the chaos swirling in his mind. The noise from the television blares louder, drowning out the haunting echoes of his thoughts. The world outside is a cacophony of sirens and screams, a reflection of the chaos that has taken root inside him.

"Look at this city," he says, desperation bleeding into his voice. "Look what's happening out there. I feel like I'm at the center of it all, and I can't escape. Every time I close my eyes, I see... things."

Claire's eyes widen, a mix of concern and determination flickering within them. "Things? What kind of things?"

He hesitates, wrestling with the words that threaten to spill out—the dark memories, the nagging doubts, the horror that lurks just out of sight.

"I can't explain it. It's like a nightmare I can't wake up from. And I'm terrified that if I let you in, you'll become a part of it too."

"But you don't have to face this by yourself," Claire insists, her voice rising with urgency. "You have to trust me. Let me in, I can help you. We can figure this out together."

In her plea, Arthur can see the flicker of hope—a glimmer that feels impossibly distant, yet achingly close. It's there in the way her brow furrows, in the way she holds his gaze, as if anchoring him to the present moment. The fear swirling inside him begins to ebb, just a fraction, as he grapples with the choice laid before him.

He swallows hard, the weight of his decision pressing down. "I don't want to lose you," he finally admits, his voice barely more than a whisper, but it feels like a confession, a vow.

"You won't," Claire promises, her hand tightening around his arm. "We'll face whatever comes our way united, you and me, just like we are supposed to be. Just take a breath, okay?"

As the cacophony of the outside world blends with the quiet rhythm of their shared moment, Arthur feels the first stirrings of resolve within him. The darkness is still there, clawing at the edges of his mind, but for the first time, the prospect of confronting it doesn't feel quite as terrifying.

"Okay," he breathes, allowing a flicker of hope to ignite amidst the shadows. "I'll try."

But as they stand there, the emptiness between them widens, gaping like a dark abyss filled with the ghosts of their shared past—the moments they've tried to forget, the pain that lingers like an unwelcome shadow. Each memory weighs heavily in the air, a silent specter haunting their fragile connection.

Their conversation becomes a rickety bridge over turbulent waters, swaying precariously beneath the weight of unspoken fears and the oppressive silence that stretches between them like a taut wire. The air is thick with tension, a palpable force that seems to pulse with every shallow breath they take.

Arthur can feel the dread swirling in his gut, a serpent of anxiety tightening its grip as Claire's gaze searches his face for answers. Her eyes, usually filled with warmth, now flicker with uncertainty, the reflection of a heart torn between love and fear. The truth hangs there, suspended in the space between them—something chilling, something neither of them is ready to name.

"Arthur," Claire finally breaks the silence, her voice trembling just slightly. "We can't keep pretending that everything is okay. This... whatever is happening to you, it's tearing us apart."

Each word hits him like a hammer, reverberating in his chest. He knows she's right, but admitting it feels like standing on the edge of a cliff, looking down into a bottomless pit.

"But Claire, I— I told you, I don't want to lose you," he whispers, the confession falling like a stone into the abyss, sinking deep into the chaos swirling around them.

Claire steps closer, her expression softening, but the distance remains, a rift filled with doubts and unspoken words.

"Then let me in," she pleads, desperation creeping into her voice. "I can't help you if you won't let me see what's going on. We can face this together, but you have to trust me and trust that I am not going anywhere."

The silence stretches, heavy and suffocating, as Arthur grapples with his own turmoil. He wants to reach out, to bridge the gap, but fear claws at him, whispering that revealing the truth will only shatter what little they have left.

"You don't know what you're asking," he warns, the tremor in his voice betraying his resolve.

"Maybe I don't," she replies, her eyes locking onto his with a fierce intensity. "But I do know that living in this limbo is killing us both. You're not alone in this, Arthur. You don't have to be. I think 25 years of marriage has proven that I am here to stay, here for you in good times and bad. I am not going anywhere Arthur, I swear it."

With every heartbeat, the gulf seems to expand, threatening to swallow them whole. The weight of their shared history hangs like a storm cloud, dark and foreboding. The truth, unspoken but ever-present, lingers in the air, heavy with the promise of chaos.

As the shadows close in around them, Arthur feels the tremors of fear and uncertainty shift into something else—a flicker of defiance igniting within him.

"Maybe it's time to face the ghosts," he mutters, his voice steadying as determination washes over him. "If I fall, at least I won't be falling alone."

Chapter 11

The door swings open with a sudden rush, flooding the dim living room with a sharp burst of light that cuts through the shadows like a knife. Gary stands in the doorway, his tall silhouette a stark contrast against the evening gloom, looming like an unwelcome reminder of what once was.

"Hey there!" he calls out, his voice a bright chime that clashes with the heavy atmosphere thickening around Arthur and Claire. Arthur's lips twitch, trying to form a smile, but it feels more like a grimace—a mask for the turmoil brewing beneath his surface.

"Hey Gary," Arthur managed, the name foreign on his lips, as if it belonged to someone else. Speaking felt like dragging stones, each word an anchor pulling him deeper into his own mind. His chest tightened, making every breath feel like a struggle for air.

"Claire? You okay, love?" Gary's voice, casual and concerned, sliced through the fog, his focus shifting to her.

Claire nodded, but her eyes betrayed her. A storm raged behind them, her gaze flickering between Arthur and Gary. She could feel something was wrong—something deeper than she could grasp—but Arthur couldn't bring himself to look at her. His head was a battlefield, his thoughts spiraling out of control, drowning him in the weight of his own guilt.

Gary, oblivious, clapped Arthur on the back with a force that reverberated like thunder in the silence. It was a gesture meant to be friendly, but Arthur felt it as a painful reminder of how far he'd drifted from the camaraderie they once shared. It rattled through his body, amplifying the tension that had already settled into his bones.

"Rough day?" Gary asked, trying to lighten the mood. He hugged Claire and kissed her cheek, the picture of comfort, as if everything were normal.

"Something like that," Arthur mumbled, his voice barely rising above a whisper. Hollow. He couldn't look Gary in the eye. Beneath the surface, too many unspoken horrors stirred. Victor's actions—*his* actions—coiled like serpents at the edge of his mind, waiting to strike.

Gary didn't push, not right away. Instead, he launched into stories about the office, ridiculous antics and harmless pranks, his laughter filling the air. Arthur nodded, but the sound felt distant, like it belonged to another world—one he no longer lived in. Gary's voice was a lifeline, pulling him back, but Arthur's grip on reality was slipping, his thoughts sinking further into the darkness that had taken root inside him.

"Arthur?" Claire's voice broke through the haze, her tone a quiet plea. She could see him unraveling. "Are you alright?"

Arthur blinked, jolted back to the moment. "Sorry, what?" His voice wavered, shaky, betraying the storm within.

"You seem... distant," Claire said, her eyes locking onto his, searching for something—*anything*—that would explain the man standing in front of her. "Is there something you need to talk about?"

Arthur opened his mouth, but the words wouldn't come. His mind was a hurricane, and he couldn't find a way to explain it. "Nothing important," he lied, the words tasting bitter, hollow. But even Gary wasn't fooled.

Gary's gaze lingered, suspicion creeping into his voice. "Okay, mate. If you say so." His tone was light, but the tension beneath it was unmistakable. He could feel Arthur slipping away, thread by thread, unraveling before them both.

Arthur tried to respond, but the knot in his chest tightened, suffocating him. Silence stretched, the weight of it crushing. His guilt clung to him, choking his words, leaving only his shallow breaths to fill the room.

Claire moved closer, her hand hovering just above his arm, uncertain. She wanted to reach him, to help, but there was something fragile in Arthur, something that might break if pushed too hard. She hesitated, sensing the danger in his silence.

Arthur's breathing quickened, each inhale sharp and painful, like shards of glass. He wanted to tell them, to scream that he was spiraling out of control, that everything was slipping through his fingers. But the words stayed trapped in his throat. All he could do was stand there, suffocated by his own fears, praying they couldn't see just how close he was to breaking.

Somewhere in the house, a clock ticks steadily, each tick echoing in his mind, marking the time until everything comes crashing down. Arthur knows he can't maintain this act for much longer; the truth—whatever horrific shape it takes—claws at him from within, desperate for release.

"Arthur?" Claire's voice is soft yet urgent, threading through the dim light like a lifeline. "Please, talk to me." Her concern is palpable, filling the air with an electric tension, urging him to confront the chaos within before it consumes them both.

As her gaze holds his, Arthur feels the walls closing in, the shadows growing darker, and he knows the time has come to face what he's been running from.

A pounding pressure builds behind Arthur's eyes, his pulse quickening, echoing against the stillness of the room. Flickering flashes of the evening news invade his mind—gruesome images of crime scenes, police tape cordoning off chaos, and a city gripped by fear. They blend with the familiar walls of his home, turning his sanctuary into a haunting reminder of darkness.

"Something's wrong," he finally admits, the words clawing their way up his throat like a desperate plea for release. His voice is barely above a whisper, a ghostly echo that hangs heavy in the air between him and Claire. "I think... I might be responsible for... for the murders."

His confession looms like a specter in the room, palpable and undeniable, casting a chilling shadow over their fragile moment.

Gary's easy smile shatters, his face draining of color as if Arthur's words possess the power to drain the life from him. He blinks rapidly, the jovial facade crumbling away to reveal a raw astonishment that strips him of words.

"Responsible?" Gary echoes, disbelief lacing every syllable as if saying it aloud might somehow unravel the nightmare. "But you're—you're not capable of—" His sentence breaks apart, the pieces falling away amidst the rubble of his understanding. "We're here for you, mate. Whatever it is, we'll figure it out."

Claire's eyes lock onto Arthur's, searching for a spark of the man she once knew, desperately begging him to emerge from the shadows of this horrifying confession. But all Arthur can see is the reflection of his own fractured soul staring back at him, a mosaic of identities shattered and hidden beneath layers of fear and guilt.

"Please, Arthur," she urges, her voice trembling slightly, as if the very air is charged with the weight of her worry. "What do you mean? How could this happen?"

Arthur feels the walls closing in, the truth clawing at him, desperate to be acknowledged. His heart races, each beat pounding louder in his ears, drowning out the doubt and confusion swirling around them. He takes a deep breath, trying to steady himself, but the very act feels futile.

"I don't know how it happened," he admits, the words spilling out in a rush. "But I remember things... flashes of a night I can't fully recall. The blood, the panic... it's all jumbled in my head, and I can't tell what's real anymore."

His voice cracks, the raw vulnerability escaping him like a dam bursting. Gary and Claire exchange glances, their expressions a mixture of concern and fear. Arthur can see the way their trust wavers, like a tightrope straining underfoot.

"Arthur, you're scaring me," Claire breathes, her voice trembling. "You need to explain this to us, tell us everything. Please."

The silence that follows is deafening, a thick wall of unspoken fears and uncertainties that isolates Arthur in a sea of dread. He's trapped, ensnared by his own mind, and the revelation feels like a noose tightening around his throat.

"I can't lose you both," he whispers, the confession punctuated by the weight of his desperation. "I can't bear the thought of either of you thinking I could ever hurt anyone, not on purpose."

As the truth settles like a heavy fog, Arthur feels the reality of his situation crashing down around him. He's standing on the edge of his own unraveling, and he knows that the moment he steps forward, there will be no going back.

The air is thick with tension, charged with the electricity of his admission, and Arthur realizes that the only way out of this nightmare is to confront the darkness within himself, no matter how terrifying it may be.

Arthur's chest tightens, each breath feeling like a struggle against invisible hands closing in around him. The walls of the room seem to inch closer, pressing in on his mind, while shadows cling to the corners like lurking specters, whispering secrets only he can hear. He sits motionless, a ghostly figure lost in the dim light of the living room, his gaze unfocused, fixated on something beyond their understanding—something dark and menacing.

Gary shifts uneasily beside him, throwing a worried glance toward Claire, whose brows knit together in a silent conversation filled with unspoken concern. The air is thick with tension, heavy with the weight of things left unsaid, punctuated by the relentless ticking of the clock—a sound that mirrors the frantic thud of Arthur's heart.

"Arthur?" Claire's voice slices through the thick silence, tentative yet insistent. "You're not by yourself in this." Her hand hovers near his arm, trembling as if afraid that touching him might shatter whatever fragile barrier holds him together.

But Arthur feels like a statue, frozen in place as his thoughts spiral down into a dark abyss. In his mind, whispers twist and turn, morphing into screams of accusation, while faces from his past contort into monstrous figures that loom large with blame. Reason battles against paranoia in a relentless war, and every breath he draws is laced with the poison of doubt and fear.

"Please," Claire urges, her voice growing stronger, filled with desperation. "If you won't talk to us, you need to talk to Dr. Turner. She can help make sense of all this."

The mention of the doctor sends a jolt through Arthur's numbed senses, igniting a flicker of something deep within him. The possibility of help—real help—hangs before him like a lifeline tossed into a stormy sea. His eyes, usually vacant and clouded, flicker with the faintest spark of hope, fighting against the dread that threatens to extinguish it.

"Dr. Turner..." Arthur murmurs, the name stirring a flood of memories—images of sterile rooms, the soft scratch of pen on paper, and the calm reassurance of a professional who might untangle the chaos within. Beneath his fear lies a fragile desire for salvation, clinging desperately to the prospect of healing like a lifeboat amidst the wreckage of his mind.

"Think about it, Arthur," Claire says, her voice a mix of steely resolve and deep compassion. "She can help you untangle these thoughts, these fears. But you have to be brave enough to face them."

In the grip of his internal chaos, Arthur's eyes finally meet Claire's. For a brief moment, the world around them fades into silence, the shadows retreating just enough for him to catch a glimpse of a path forward—a path filled with uncertainty and darkness, but still a path, nonetheless.

The weight of his emotions swirls within him, each pulse a reminder of his struggles, yet in that fleeting moment of clarity, he feels the slightest thread of determination weave through his fear. With the softest whisper of resolve, he nods, the movement a tiny spark igniting against the suffocating gloom.

"Okay," he breathes, his voice trembling yet resolute. "I'll think about it."

As the words leave his lips, a rush of adrenaline courses through him, breaking the paralysis that has held him captive. For the first time in what feels like an eternity, the darkness doesn't seem quite so all-consuming, and the journey toward healing feels possible—a daunting task, but a necessary one.

Arthur's chest heaves, the fabric of his shirt clinging to his skin as if it senses the gravity of Claire's words. His fingers twitch, an involuntary spasm that betrays the turmoil roiling within him. Hope, a fragile thread, begins to weave its way through the fog in his mind, urging him to break free from the dark prison he's built around himself. The air in the room feels electric, thick with the promise of change and the possibility of redemption.

"Okay," he rasps, the word barely more than a whisper, yet it reverberates through the heavy silence like a bell tolling in the distance. "If you insist, I-I'll see Dr. Turner again."

As he speaks, the tension in the room shifts. The weight of his silent promise anchors him to reality, a grounding force in the chaos swirling inside him. He knows he must confront the turmoil, the chaotic cluster of voices that have long turned his mind into a battleground. Regaining control over his fractured psyche feels like a monumental task, but Claire's plea ignites a flicker of determination—a small flame that refuses to be extinguished.

Claire exhales, a soft sob of relief escaping her lips, her eyes shimmering with unshed tears. She steps closer, bridging the gap that once felt insurmountable. Her hand finds his, gripping it tightly, a warm anchor against the storm that rages within him. In this moment, she is his lighthouse, unwavering and constant amid the darkness.

"We're here for you, Arthur," she whispers, her voice steady, a soothing balm against the rawness of his fears. "No matter what."

Gary, who has been standing awkwardly to one side, finally shifts forward, his broad shoulders relaxing as the initial shock dissipates. His blue eyes, usually bright with laughter, are now deep pools of genuine concern, reflecting the gravity of the moment.

"Absolutely, mate," Gary adds, his voice warm and reassuring. "We've got your back, no matter what it takes."

The moment hangs in the air, fragile like the surface of a pond just before a leaf falls. Arthur looks up, leaving the safety of his solitude behind. Tears brim in his tired eyes, threatening to betray the stoicism that has shielded him for so long. Gratitude wells up inside him, an overwhelming tide that washes over the jagged edges of his guilt and fear.

"Thank you," he manages to say, his voice thick with emotion. It's a whisper of vulnerability, an acknowledgment of his need for their support, their steadfastness in the face of his internal storm.

Their presence is a life raft in the turbulent sea of his mind. Though the journey ahead looms daunting and treacherous, Arthur clings to it with newfound resolve. This decision, born from desperation and shaped by love, marks the first step toward navigating the labyrinth of his own thoughts—a journey not just toward healing, but toward reclaiming the identity that has been slipping through his fingers like grains of sand.

As they stand together, the shadows seem less oppressive, the room less confining. Together, they are united in purpose, ready to face whatever darkness lies ahead, fortified by the bonds that tether their lives in this moment of shared resolve. The path may be fraught with challenges, but for the first time, Arthur feels a glimmer of hope—a flicker that promises a brighter dawn beyond the storm.

The silence in the room feels heavy, like a thick fog that wraps around the trio, muffling even the steady tick of the wall clock. Arthur sits frozen on the couch, his eyes glued to the worn fabric beneath him. His hands clasp tightly together in his lap, desperately trying to still their trembling. The air is charged with unspoken thoughts, each breath echoing the chaos that churns within him.

Claire occupies the armchair next to him, her fingers knotted in her lap. She looks like a statue carved from worry and determination. Every glance she casts toward Arthur is a lifeline, a silent plea for connection, trying to bridge the widening chasm between them with empathy and understanding.

Gary slouches on the other end of the sofa, his expression a mix of concern and disbelief. His usually bright eyes, filled with humor, are now dimmed by the weight of Arthur's confession—a haunting shadow that lingers in the air, suffocating in its intensity.

The room feels smaller, the walls pressing in as if they want to hear the cacophony of their inner thoughts. Arthur's mind is a battlefield, each thought a skirmish between guilt and hope. Fragments of his identity clash within him, waging a silent war for control.

Time stretches, a taut rubber band pulled to its limit, ready to snap.

Then, as if summoned by the collective tension, a single word breaks the stillness.

"Tomorrow," Arthur whispers, his voice low but resonant in the quiet room. Claire's head snaps up, her eyes searching his face for strength behind his quiet determination. Gary leans forward, eyebrows raised, silently asking for more.

"Dr. Turner," Arthur continues, his voice gaining strength as he speaks the name of the psychiatrist who embodies both his greatest fear and his only glimmer of hope. "I'll try to see her tomorrow."

The words hang in the air like a lifeline, a beacon cutting through the fog of uncertainty. It's a commitment etched into the darkness, a promise that binds them together on the path ahead.

Chapter 12

Claire's hand reaches out, hovering just shy of touching Arthur's arm, respecting the fragile space he occupies. The gesture speaks volumes—support without pressure, presence without intrusion.

Gary nods, determination solidifying his features. "We'll be right there with you, mate." he says, his voice steady and full of camaraderie, a reassuring anchor amidst the storm.

Arthur allows himself a nod, a simple dip of his head that acknowledges their solidarity and shared determination to face the brewing storm together. He draws in a deep breath, the air heavy with apprehension but also tinged with a faint hint of relief.

The air around them buzzes with a charged stillness, each of them trapped in their own thoughts, yet irrevocably linked by the weight of the moment. Arthur sits at the edge of the couch, his shoulders hunched, fingers clenched into tight fists. The ticking of the clock on the wall becomes a metronome for his racing heart, each tick echoing the uncertainty that looms over him. He feels like a ship caught in a storm, surrounded by uncharted waters, unable to see where the waves might lead.

Claire, still in the armchair, can sense the disturbance swirling in the room. Her brow furrows as she struggles to find the right words, the ones that will penetrate Arthur's fog of despair.

"I know this is hard, Arthur," she begins softly, her voice breaking the silence like a fragile glass against stone. "But you don't have to face this alone. We're in this together." Her words hang in the air, both a promise and a plea, a reminder of the bond they once shared, now tested by shadows of doubt.

Across from them, Gary shifts in his seat, his earlier levity replaced by a solemnity that weighs heavily on his broad shoulders.

"We've always got your back, man," he adds, his voice steady but tinged with concern. "No matter what it takes." There's an uncharacteristic seriousness in his tone, a shared understanding that this is more than just a fleeting moment of vulnerability. It's a turning point, a potential pivot from despair to healing.

As Arthur looks up, meeting their gazes, a flicker of something stirs within him. It's a spark of hope, fragile but persistent, fighting against the overwhelming darkness that has consumed him for so long.

"I'll see Dr. Turner tomorrow," he finally manages to say, the words tumbling out like a fragile lifeline thrown into the chaos.

Claire's expression brightens with relief, her eyes shimmering with unshed tears.

"That's a brave step, Arthur," she responds, her voice steadying with a renewed sense of purpose. "You're stronger than you think."

The tension in the room shifts, the oppressive silence giving way to a tentative optimism. The unspoken fears begin to lose their power as Arthur acknowledges the support of his friends. He feels the walls of his own mind beginning to crack, the tightly woven threads of his life starting to unravel, but in that unraveling, he senses the potential for something new to emerge.

With a deep breath, he leans back slightly, his body relaxing just enough to allow a moment of clarity.

"I know it won't be easy," he admits, his voice barely above a whisper, "but I have to try. I can't keep living like this." The admission feels like a weight lifted, each word shedding the burden of secrecy he has carried for far too long.

Gary nods, the warmth of camaraderie washing over them like a comforting blanket.

"We're right here with you, every step of the way. You don't have to face this alone," he reassures, offering a supportive smile that ignites a flicker of strength within Arthur.

As they sit together, the silence transforms again—not as a weight, but as a shared moment of understanding. They are poised at the edge of something profound, a journey into the depths of Arthur's troubled psyche, where darkness and light will clash, revealing truths long hidden in the shadows.

The clock continues its relentless ticking, each second marking the passage of time that will lead them to tomorrow. Arthur glances at Claire and Gary, feeling the warmth of their presence seep into him, like sunlight breaking through dark clouds. They are ready to face the unknown together, and as he contemplates the road ahead, he realizes that this journey will not only test their resolve but will also redefine their bonds, carving out new paths in their hearts.

In this moment, the story of Arthur's struggle transforms from one of isolation into a tapestry of connection and resilience. He feels the first stirrings of hope within him, a small flame ignited by the support of those he loves. With the promise of tomorrow looming, he prepares to dive headfirst into the depths of healing and self-discovery, ready to confront the reality of his condition under the skilled gaze of Dr. Elaine Turner.

And as the evening draws to a close, he understands that he is not alone in this fight. The road ahead may be treacherous, but he is surrounded by allies—friends who will walk beside him into the unknown

Chapter 13

Fingers poised above the keyboard, Dr. Elaine Turner hesitates, the cursor on her screen a steady and rhythmic pulse in the dim light of her office. The soft hum of the computer fans blends with the distant sounds of the city at dusk as shadows claw at the edges of her vision. With each passing moment, the weight of suspicion grows heavier, a tangible pressure against the walls of her resolve.

She exhales slowly, a calculated breath to steady her nerves, and begins to sift through the case files once more. Her eyes, sharp behind the lenses of her glasses, scan for elusive threads that might weave Arthur's fragmented existence into this tapestry of tragedy. She searches for patterns and signatures in the chaos that could link him to the horrors that have unfolded on her watch.

The digital folders open one by one, revealing their contents like secrets whispered in hushed tones. Images of crime scenes, autopsy reports, witness statements—they all blend into an intricate, grisly mosaic. It's within this morbid collection that she seeks the truth about Arthur Hall, the unassuming man whose psyche splinters into shadowy alcoves she has yet to illuminate entirely.

Elaine clicks on a folder labeled "Surveillance" and leans closer, squinting at the grainy footage that flickers onto her screen. Time stamps crawl across the bottom, moments captured in monochrome. She scans through the videos, pausing intermittently when a familiar silhouette enters the frame.

There he is—Arthur, or so it seems, casts in the stuttering glow of a streetlight near the first crime scene. His movements are indistinct, shrouded by the poor quality of the footage and the cover of night. She rewinds and plays it again, her heartbeat keeping time with the flickering images.

"Could it really be you, Arthur?" she whispers to herself, not expecting an answer from the silent room. The figure on the screen lingers at the periphery of the recorded area, his presence both incriminating and inconclusive. Enough to fuel doubt, but not enough to convict.

Elaine's fingers tremble over the mouse, the chill of possibility seeping into her bones. As the last glimmers of daylight succumb to the encroaching darkness outside her window, the office feels colder, more isolated. She watches the figure disappear from the frame, a ghost retreating into the night's embrace.

The surge of adrenaline fades, leaving behind a residue of dread. Logic battles intuition; professionalism wars with gut instinct. In her heart, she wants to believe in Arthur's innocence, to attribute his proximity to coincidence or some benign explanation. But the seed of doubt had already taken root, spreading through the fertile ground of her uncertainty, twisting between what she knew and what she feared.

Dr. Elaine Turner saves the footage, locks her computer, and rubs her temples. The night is far from over, the darkness both within and without just beginning to unfold its narrative—one she must navigate with care, lest she become ensnared in its deceptive web.

Elaine rummages through the paper file, her hands guided by an instinctual sense that there is more to unearth. Her fingers stumble upon an anomaly—a subtle unevenness in the folder's bottom. With deft movements, she teases open a cleverly disguised compartment. The breath catches in her throat as clippings and articles cascade onto her desk like macabre confetti.

The dim office light casts long shadows as Elaine sifts through the paper trail of death with meticulous care. Each clipping is a silent scream, headlines blaring the gruesome details of each murder. The arrangement is unnervingly precise, a chronological testament to a sinister fascination. Arthur's handwriting, unmistakable in its neatness, annotates margins with chilling notes and dates.

Her pulse throbs in her ears, a relentless drumbeat echoing the gravity of her discovery. Elaine can't shake the image of Arthur's soft-spoken manner, the gentle tilt of his head when lost in thought—could this be the same man who cataloged atrocities with such cold dedication?

She shakes off the horror, focusing on the task at hand. She retrieves Arthur's alibis from another section of the file and begins the painstaking process of cross-referencing. Dates, times, locations—each element scrutinized under Elaine's vigilant gaze. Page after page, the alibis crumble beneath the weight of inconsistency. Meetings that never took place; errands that left hours unaccounted for.

With each discrepancy, the walls of Arthur's fabricated world seem to close in, the air growing thinner. Elaine feels the unease crawling up her spine, a serpentine doubt constricting around her resolve. It's not just the gaps that unsettle her, but the way they align with the timeline of terror so neatly laid out in his hidden archive.

"Arthur, what have you done?" She murmurs, though the question is rhetorical. The evidence sprawled before her paints a damning portrait, yet she knows it is not complete. Arthur's mind is a twisted web, and she has only just stepped over the threshold.

The weight of responsibility presses down on Elaine; she is both arbiter and confidant, caught in the crossfire of her own empathy and the stark reality of potential guilt. The shadows in the room grow longer, reaching out like spectral fingers to remind her that daylight offers no sanctuary from the darkness of the human psyche.

Elaine stared at the plain envelope in her hand, unsure of how it had found its way to her. It had been slipped under her office door just moments before—no return address, no markings to indicate its origin.

Her fingers hesitated at the edge of the manila folder, her pulse quickening. Something about it felt wrong, heavy with an unspoken threat.

Her breath shuddered as she pulled back the cardboard flap, and the folder fell open with an unsettling rustle. The contents tumbled out in slow motion, scattering across her desk like a series of unspoken confessions.

Her gaze locked onto the crimson-stained fabric nestled among the documents. She blinked once, twice, unable to fully comprehend what she was seeing. The dark red stain was unmistakable.

Her throat tightened. Whoever sent this knew exactly what they were doing.

A shirt—ordinary in make but grotesque in its adornment of dried blood—lies folded with sinister precision. It resembles the one that covered the figure that crept away into the night after each heinous act, as described in hushed tones by terrified witnesses. Elaine's hands tremble, not merely from fear but from the cataclysmic implications of the garment lying before her. Her heart throbs in her ears, a drumbeat growing louder with every realization.

"Victor," she murmurs, the name tasting like bile on her tongue. Arthur's other half, his darkness incarnate, now seems all too real, a specter haunting the edges of this investigation.

Elaine knew there was no time to waste. The weight of the discovery pressed down on her, and she couldn't afford to second-guess herself. With trembling fingers, she grabbed her phone and dialed James' number. Each beep in the suffocating silence of her office stretched the moment, making her pulse race.

James responded with a gruff "Lawson," his voice a recognizable anchor in the confusion and one that had become hardened over time from years of chasing shadows.

"James, it's Elaine." She didn't pause, the urgency in her voice evident. "I received an envelope this morning—no return address. It was shoved under my office door. Inside, there's a blood-stained shirt. It matches the description of what the killer was wearing at the scene."

There was a brief silence, the weight of her words hanging between them. She could feel the tension mounting, the shift in the atmosphere as James processed the gravity of her revelation.

"I think... it belongs to Arthur Hall," she added, the name heavy on her tongue. "He's been making some disturbing confessions in our sessions. He's losing control, James. I think Victor, his alter ego, might be more than a psychological threat."

Another pause, but this time it wasn't hesitation. It was understanding - Lawson knew exactly what this meant.

Elaine's pulse quickened, her professional calm beginning to fray at the edges. "James, please, be careful." The concern in her voice slipped through, raw and real. "Arthur's alter ego, Victor—it's not just a figment or some convenient excuse. He's dangerous. More dangerous than we thought."

"I hear you. We'll catch him," Lawson replied, his tone unwavering, a rock in the chaos. "I give you my word."

As the call ended, Elaine stood still, the cool metal of her phone now a distant sensation. The envelope remained on her desk, its dark secret revealed, but the storm it had unleashed was only beginning.

But Elaine knew words could only go so far. The path ahead was dark, riddled with unknowns, and every step felt like it could trigger another nightmare. She hung up, the silence of the room pressing in on her as she stared at the blood-stained shirt laid before her—evidence of horrors still lurking in the shadows.

She couldn't afford to falter now. Victor's darkness loomed closer with every second, and Arthur's soul hung in the balance, as did the lives of the innocents Victor might already be hunting. Elaine pushed down the rising fear, steeling herself. The fight wasn't over—it was just beginning.

Elaine's gaze flits over the dense text, the psychological assessments of Arthur Hall scattered across her desk like pieces of a jigsaw puzzle. In the dim light of her office, shadows cling to the corners, as if mirroring the dark recesses of Arthur's mind she's attempting to navigate. Her fingers trail along the timelines, the recorded instances of dissociation, each episode a potential gateway to the alter who calls himself Victor.

The clock ticks a rhythmic warning, and Elaine leans back in her chair, rubbing her temples. She sifts through the fragmented evidence with forensic precision, constructing a narrative from the chaos. There's an elusive pattern here, whispers of a deeper malaise beneath Arthur's placid surface—a quiet man, a ghost in his own life, overshadowed by an entity born from trauma.

A tremor courses through her hands as she aligns dates and events, noting the vacillations in Arthur's demeanor, the days unaccounted for, the nights that match the timeline of terror painted in police reports. The man who hides in plain sight, could he truly harbor a killer within?

She pulls up a video file, a therapy session where Arthur's voice slips, contorts, becomes something else—Victor's cruel sneer etched in pixels and sound waves. Elaine watches, breath tight in her chest, as Arthur's eyes darken on screen, the transformation subtle yet unmistakable.

The phone pierces the silence, its shrill ring startling her from the depths of analysis. Elaine's heart lurches, and she snatches the receiver to her ear. "Elaine Turner."

"Elaine, it's Lawson." His voice is granite, etched with resolve. "I spoke with my superiors. We're moving forward—full investigation. We'll turn over every stone, chase down every lead. We *will* find him."

Relief washes over her, mingling with a gnawing anxiety that coils in her stomach. The truth is close now, a specter rising from the fog.

"Thank you, James," she says, her voice steady despite the storm of emotions. "We need to understand what drives him, what feeds Victor's compulsion."

"Leaving no stone unturned," he affirms, the line crackling with his intensity.

"None," she promises, the weight of the responsibility grounding her. She replaces the receiver, her resolve hardening. For Arthur, for the victims, she will unravel the mystery of this fractured mind. And in the gathering darkness, she knows the battle for Arthur's soul is only just beginning.

Elaine's fingers dance across her keyboard, summoning a network of professionals with a flurry of emails. Her office, once a haven of order, now mirrors the chaos of Arthur's mind—papers strewn about, books on psychological disorders stacked precariously high. The dim light from her desk lamp throws long shadows across the room, giving the illusion of figures lurking just out of sight.

She composes her messages to several Specialists with clinical precision, requesting insights into Dissociative Identity Disorder, specifically its correlation to violent behavior. Each sent email is a beacon in the dark expanse of uncertainty, seeking guidance from those who have tread similar paths in their own practices. Elaine knows she must sharpen her understanding of Arthur—and Victor—before she can intervene.

As the night deepens, her inbox pings with incoming responses. Experts share case studies, theories, and anecdotal experiences. They speak of the rare instances where alternate personalities carry out acts unimaginable to their hosts. The words on the screen blur together, painting a harrowing picture of what could lie within Arthur. She pores over each detail, cross-referencing them with notes from her sessions, searching for any sliver of insight that might illuminate the path forward.

Elaine then stumbles upon an article discussing a pioneering therapy technique—Integration Therapy—a method designed to unify fragmented identities within the mind. Her pulse quickens. Could this be the key to reining in Victor's influence over Arthur? Her hand hovers over the mouse, the cursor blinking expectantly on the link.

Click.

The article details the delicate process, a mental labyrinth navigated through trust, patience, and the precarious balance of power among the personalities. The risks loom large in her mind; triggering trauma could shatter Arthur's psyche beyond repair. But the alternative—leaving Victor unchecked—is unthinkable. Sweat beads at her temples as she leans into the screen, absorbing every word, every warning sign, every glimmer of hope.

Time ticks away mercilessly. Elaine weighs the potential harmony against the cacophony of destruction. If successful, Arthur could be whole again, saved from the clutches of his darker half. But if it fails...

She reaches for a blank notepad, scribbling fervently, charting out the myriad possibilities. With each stroke of the pen, Elaine feels the immensity of the decision she must make. There's no margin for error—not with lives hanging in the balance.

"Arthur, what have you done?" she whispers into the silence, the question lingering like a specter in the room. Her gaze returns to the computer screen, where the profiles of Arthur and Victor stare back at her, two halves of a divided soul. In the depths of those digital eyes, she searches for the answer that will either restore or condemn.

Tonight, Elaine is both the keeper of secrets and the seeker of truths, wrestling with the perilous choice that lies before her. The clock on the wall ticks on, indifferent to the psychological precipice upon which they all now stand.

Elaine's fingers hover above the keyboard, each tap a deliberate echo in the quiet of her office. The screen in front of her is filled with a grim collection of evidence—a disturbing puzzle that's impossible to ignore. She compiles the report methodically, her mind a whir of clinical precision and human concern.

"Subject exhibits traits consistent with," she types, pausing as she considers the gravity of her next words, "a potential for extreme violence." The cursor blinks, an accusatory flash in the dim light. Elaine sifts through the digital folders, aligning surveillance stills alongside Arthur's timetables, noting every discrepancy with a surgeon's care.

The report grows, a living document that breathes unease into the room. It outlines the dual existence of Arthur, the subdued office worker, and Victor, The Shadow within him—both entities bound to a single, tormented soul. She includes the blood-stained shirt, the clippings, the chilling footage, each piece another knot in the noose of suspicion tightening around Arthur's life.

Elaine leans back, her eyes tracing the lines of text that seal a man's fate. She knows the psychiatric board will scrutinize every claim, every inference. Her reputation affords her words weight, but with it comes the burden of proof. The clock on the wall ticks away, indifferent to the urgency pressing down upon her like a heavy shroud.

Taking a deep breath, Elaine steels herself for the confrontation that looms. Her hand reaches for the phone, its cold plastic an unwelcome reminder of the reality she must face. She dials, arranging a meeting with Arthur, her voice steady despite the tremors that threaten her composure.

Taking a deep breath, Elaine braces herself for the confrontation ahead. Her fingers hover over the phone, the cold plastic a stark reminder of the reality she's about to face. With steady resolve, she dials Arthur's number, each ring dragging out the tension that clings to the air around her.

"Thursday, 10 AM—no, it has to be sooner." Her voice wavers with impatience, a rare crack in her professional demeanor. She reschedules the meeting for the following morning, urgency spilling into her tone as she realizes the seriousness of what she's uncovered. There's no time to waste.

She turns off the computer, the screen's glow fading into obscurity. In the silence, Elaine practices the words she will say, rehearsing the offer of therapy, the promise of integration. She imagines Arthur's tired eyes, searching for a sign of the man she believes still exists beneath the fractured exterior.

"Choose the light, Arthur," she whispers, more prayer than plea. Shadows play across the walls, dancing specters that mock her efforts to dispel them. Elaine's heart beats a rhythm of both dread and determination; tomorrow, she will face Arthur—and Victor—and the battle for one man's soul will reach its crescendo.

Chapter 14

Thursday, 10am

Elaine's hand hovers over the door handle, the metal cool and unyielding beneath her touch. She presses down, feeling the mechanism give way, and steps into the meeting room where a slant of morning light cuts through the blinds, casting long shadows across the floor. Her heart drums a staccato beat in her chest as she closes the door behind her with a soft click that seems to echo too loudly in the confined space.

Arthur sits at the far end of the room, his hands folded neatly in front of him. His eyes, dark pools of uncertainty, fix on her as she approaches. In them, Elaine sees the flicker of the quiet, reserved man who has become an enigma wrapped in the mundane. The air between them is fraught with unspoken words, a tense anticipation for the revelations to come.

"Arthur," she begins, her voice steady despite the storm of emotions swirling within her. "Thank you for coming."

"Dr. Turner, what is it? You sounded like it was an emergency." he replies, his tone level but infused with a wariness that wasn't there before. His measured response is a testament to the internal struggle that must be raging behind his calm facade.

Elaine takes her seat opposite him, placing her folder on the table. The sound of paper against wood feels like a verdict waiting to be delivered. She reaches out, bridging the distance with a gesture meant to convey solidarity rather than confrontation.

"Arthur, I've been reviewing your case, and there are things we need to discuss," she says, her eyes locked onto his, searching for a sign of recognition or denial. "It's about the murders."

He blinks slowly, a shutter closing momentarily over the window to his soul. Elaine wonders which personality is peering out from behind those tired eyes. Is it Arthur who listens with bated breath, or Victor, lurking in the depths, ready to spring forth?

"Victor is a part of you, but he doesn't have to define you," Elaine continues, her voice a lifeline thrown into the turbulent sea of his mind. "There's a path to recovery, a chance for integration."

Arthur's Adam's apple bobs as he swallows, his hands clenching then unclenching under the table. He remains silent, but the subtle shift in his posture speaks volumes. It is as if he stands at a crossroads within himself, teetering on the brink of decision.

"Your life, the lives of others... they hang in the balance," Elaine urges, leaning forward. "You can choose to fight this, to seek the help you want and need it."

The room is steeped in suspense, each second elongating as if time itself is holding its breath. Elaine can feel the weight of the moment pressing down upon them both, the gravity of the situation pulling at the very fabric of reality.

Finally, Arthur nods, just once and barely perceptible, but it is enough. Enough for Elaine to know that the battle for Arthur's soul is not completely lost, that the first step toward reclaiming the fragmented pieces of his life has been taken.

As they sit across from each other, shadows pool in the corners, as if hiding secrets waiting to be exposed. Arthur senses their presence, a suffocating weight that mirrors the turmoil swirling inside him. The air feels electric, alive with anticipation.

"Arthur, is there something else that you'd like to talk about today?" Dr. Turner's voice slices through the tension, but it resonates differently now, as though she senses the growing danger in the room.

Before Arthur can respond, a laugh—not his own—suddenly echoes in the sterile office. It's a chilling sound that reverberates with unnerving familiarity, a dark ripple across the waters of his troubled mind. Victor's presence creeps in, unsettling the delicate balance within him. He knows something is coming, something he cannot control.

"Ah, Elaine," says the voice, smooth as glass, yet edged with venom. "Always so direct, even when you don't understand the gravity of what's unfolding before you."

Dr. Turner's eyes narrow slightly, her pen poised above the notepad, but she doesn't flinch. "Victor," she acknowledges, her voice steady despite the chill that has crept into the room.

Arthur's chest tightens, his heart thudding with a dread that threatens to choke him. Victor, The Shadow within, emerges without warning, seizing the reins with a confidence that terrifies him. He is at once a spectator in his own body, watching helplessly as the darkness speaks with his lips, smiles with his mouth.

"Your little sessions," Victor continues, the malice practically dripping from each syllable, "they're quite touching, really. But they're meaningless. You see, I've planned far ahead of these quaint attempts at 'healing.'"

Dr. Turner leans forward, her gaze unyielding. "What is it you want, Victor?"

"Want?" The word rolls off Arthur's tongue with a sardonic twist. "I want what has always been mine—control, dominance, freedom from the pathetic constraints of morality."

Arthur feels the presence of Victor coming through him like a cold hand gripping his mind, squeezing until spots dance before his eyes. Yet, even as fear washes over him, a part of him marvels at the terrifying elegance of Victor's control, the sheer force of will with which he holds court.

"Freedom," Victor whispers, and the room seems to darken with the promise of his intentions.

Victor leans in, his cold breath a sinister whisper sending shivers down her spine.

"But it's not just about Arthur and me. Others must be cut free from our little dance. Dr. Turner," he pauses, a cruel smile playing on Arthur's lips, "and dear Claire."

Arthur's eyes snap wide open, his gaze locking with Dr. Turner's. The horror in them is naked and raw, a silent scream for help that he cannot voice. Claire—his anchor, his light—how could Victor? His voice, no longer his own, coming from his mouth, but it is Victor in control, yet Arthur is watching from within himself.

"Eliminate?" Dr. Turner's voice cuts through the thickening air, her eyes sharp as flint despite the tremor Arthur senses in the depths of his own consciousness. She sits back, her posture straight as a blade, refusing to let the shadow before her see any flicker of fear.

"Yes." The word slithers out, devoid of warmth. "A necessary pruning, Elaine. You've become... inconvenient. And Claire, she hinders Arthur's true potential."

Dr. Turner's fingers lace together on the desk, knuckles whitening for just a moment before she regains control.

"Is that your plan, Victor? To rule over a wasteland of Arthur's mind?"

"Better a wasteland under my reign than a kingdom shared with weakness," Victor retorts. His confidence is unshakable, a fortress built on malice and meticulous strategy.

"Your threats don't scare me, Victor," Dr. Turner says, each word a measured drop of defiance into the pooling darkness. "And they won't work. We can fight this together, Arthur and I."

Victor laughs, a sound like ice cracking on a winter lake, full of dark amusement. "Together? There is no together. There's only Arthur's illusion of sanity and my inevitability."

Dr. Turner rises smoothly, her movements betraying none of the shock that must surely course through her veins. "We'll see about that," she declares, her tone a beacon in the encroaching gloom that Victor casts over the room.

Arthur wants to reach out, to warn her, to protect—but he is trapped in the audience of his own life, watching the battle unfold with a growing sense of dread knotting in his stomach.

Arthur's fingers clasp and unclasp, the fabric of the chair coarse beneath his touch. Sweat beads on his brow, a silent testament to the terror threading through his veins. He fixates on Dr. Turner, her image a lighthouse in the tempest that Victor conjures within him. She is calm, a still point in the chaos, but Arthur knows the ferocity of the storm she faces.

"Protect them," he whispers to himself, a mantra that beats in time with his racing heart. How? The question ricochets around the confines of his skull, each rebound a jarring reminder of his helplessness.

Victor leans forward, his movements a serpentine slithering from the shadows that have become his domain.

"Oh, Arthur," he croons, his voice laced with venomous honey. "Can you hear the shatter of your little world? It's music to my ears."

Dr. Turner's eyes flicker toward Arthur, a silent plea for him to find strength. But Victor is relentless, weaving a narrative designed to unravel the very fibers of Arthur's being.

"Your precious Claire, so innocent and pure," Victor continues, the words dripping with malice. "But oh, how fragile innocence is. A single touch could spoil it all."

Arthur feels the walls closing in, the air thinning. His chest constricts, each breath a battle against the weight of impending doom. Victor's presence looms larger, an eclipse casting a shadow over Arthur's soul.

"Stop," Arthur chokes out, but his voice is a mere wisp, lost amid the cacophony of his own fractured thoughts.

"Stop?" Victor echoes with mock incredulity. "Why, we're just getting started. You've kept me at bay, Arthur, but no longer. I am inevitability. I am your truth."

The room spins, the edges darkening as if night itself seeps through the walls, drawn to Victor's chilling embrace. Arthur grapples with the encroaching darkness, his psyche splintered between his fervent desire to protect and the dread that Victor may already be too powerful to overcome.

"Think, Arthur, think!" he urges himself. But thoughts scatter like leaves in a gale, each one caught up in Victor's whirlwind of terror and manipulation.

Dr. Turner leans forward, her eyes locking onto Arthur's, a silent message of urgency passing between them. She slides a notepad across the polished surface of her desk, the motion discreet yet deliberate. Her voice is soft but carries a steel edge as she addresses both the man before her and the shadow within him.

"Arthur, I want you to listen to me very carefully. We're going to take some steps to keep everyone safe. Claire is my priority, as are you."

Arthur nods, the action jerky, as if he wrestles with invisible restraints. His gaze flickers to the notepad, where Dr. Turner has scribbled a few words—a phone number, an address, a time. Instructions form a lifeline in the swirling darkness.

"Victor can't win," Dr. Turner says, her tone imbued with conviction. "You have more strength than you realize. Together, we can secure safety for Claire, for you... for all of us."

Arthur's breath hitches, a spark igniting within the hollows of his fear. He clings to the plan laid out on the paper before him, each word an anchor against the tide of Victor's malice.

"Enough," he rasps, his voice gaining volume, pushing through the layers of trepidation that Victor has woven around him. His hands clench into fists, knuckles whitening. "I won't let you hurt them."

Victor's laugh, a sinister echo in the corners of the room, fails to smother the flame of Arthur's resolve. "Brave words, Arthur. But what can you do? You are nothing but my shell."

"I am more than you'll ever be," Arthur counters, standing with a newfound steadiness. The room tilts, yet he remains erect, facing the void where Victor lurks. "I care. I love. And I will fight."

Dr. Turner watches, her expression a mixture of concern and admiration. The battle lines are drawn within Arthur, the schism between his fractured selves now a battlefield upon which the fate of their intertwined lives hangs precariously.

"Then fight, Arthur," she murmurs. "Fight for control, for your life. For Claire. I'm with you."

With those words as his shield, Arthur steps into the fray, his declaration a war cry against the darkness threatening to consume him.

Victor's voice slithers through the silence, a cold whisper that claws at the edges of Arthur's consciousness. "You're weak, Arthur. You've always been weak."

Arthur's pulse hammers in his ears, sweat beads on his brow, but he stands his ground, his gaze locked on Dr. Turner for grounding. Her nod is subtle, almost imperceptible, but it's enough.

"Strength isn't about instilling fear," Arthur fires back, the words tumbling out with more conviction than he feels. "It's about facing it."

Dr. Turner's voice slices through the tension, calm and clear. "Focus on your values, Arthur. Victor feeds on doubt. Starve him."

The room seems to shrink, the walls closing in as Victor's presence looms larger, a dark cloud ready to burst. But Arthur plants his feet, an oak amidst the storm, his resolve hardening like stone.

"Values..." he whispers, clinging to the lifeline Dr. Turner has thrown. The word is a beacon, guiding him away from the tempest that is Victor. "I value life. I value Claire. And you, Victor, are nothing but death."

A chuckle, dry and hollow, echoes from the void where Victor resides. "And what is life without death, Arthur? A meaningless cycle."

"Life is connection. It's hope," Arthur insists, each word a brick in the fortress he builds around his mind. He feels Dr. Turner's supportive gaze, her silent encouragement empowering him.

"Hope can be shattered," Victor taunts, his tone dripping with malice.

"Then we build it again," Dr. Turner interjects firmly, her eyes never leaving Arthur's. "You have the power to rebuild, Arthur. Remember who you are beyond the fragments."

Arthur nods, a small yet significant gesture. His chest rises and falls with each steadying breath, the air charged with the electricity of his determination. He reaches inward, toward the core of his being, where light flickers defiantly against the encroaching darkness.

"Victor is just a shadow," he asserts, his voice gaining strength. "And shadows only exist because of light."

"Poetic nonsense," Victor sneers, but there's a tremor in his voice now, a crack in the armor of his confidence.

"Truth," Arthur corrects, stepping forward mentally, pushing against the boundaries Victor has set. "And truth is my light."

Dr. Turner's hand rests gently on his arm, a physical reminder of her presence, of reality. "Use that light, Arthur. Illuminate the path back to yourself."

Arthur closes his eyes, focusing on the warmth of her touch, letting it guide him through the labyrinth of his mind. Victor's influence recedes with each breath, like shadows retreating before the dawn.

"Your time is over, Victor," Arthur declares, a sentinel standing watch over his own psyche. "I am in control."

Victor's laughter fades into silence, a specter vanishing in the face of Arthur's will. The room suddenly feels brighter, the air lighter, as if a great weight has lifted.

Arthur opens his eyes, meeting Dr. Turner's gaze. There's a battle ahead, but for now, he basks in the victory of this moment, the triumph of self over shadow.

The office flickers with shadows as dusk settles outside the window, encroaching upon the last vestiges of daylight. Arthur's heartbeat is a staccato rhythm in his chest, echoing the ticking of the clock on Dr. Turner's desk. He sits rigid, every muscle taut with anticipation and dread.

"Arthur," Victor whispers, his voice a silk thread wrapping around Arthur's thoughts. "Do you really think she can protect you from me?"

Dr. Turner watches him, her eyes sharp and calculating, yet brimming with an unwavering empathy. She knows the stakes are high, higher than any session that has come before. The room holds its breath, the air thick with the silent battle waging within Arthur.

"Victor won't win," Arthur murmurs, though it's unclear if he's trying to convince himself or assert his defiance to the darkness that gnaws at the edges of his mind.

"Confidence," Victor taunts, "but is it enough, Arthur? Will it shield you, or all of them when I strike?"

The threat slithers through the room, a tangible presence that makes Arthur's skin crawl. Dr. Turner remains still, her composure a fortress against Victor's psychological siege.

"Focus, Arthur," she urges softly. "Remember why you're here."

He nods, his hands clenched into fists as he grapples with the specter of Victor's malice. Claire's face flashes before him—her gentle eyes filled with concern, her smile a beacon in his darkest moments. The thought of her in danger because of him, because of Victor, ignites a fire within.

"Enough!" Arthur's voice shatters the silence, his declaration a challenge to the malevolence that seeks to consume him. "You will not touch them. I won't allow it."

A chuckle, dark and menacing, reverberates off the walls. Victor's amusement is a cold wind that chills the soul.

"Bold words for someone so broken," Victor sneers. But beneath the bravado, there's an edge, a hint of uncertainty.

"Broken can be mended," Arthur counters, locking onto Dr. Turner's steady gaze.

"Time is up for today," she says quietly, but her tone carries an unspoken message—they are on the brink of something pivotal.

Arthur rises, his movements deliberate. He knows this is not the end; it's merely the calm before the storm. As he steps toward the door, he feels Victor receding into the dark corners of his mind, biding his time.

"Be careful," Dr. Turner calls after him, her voice a lifeline thrown across turbulent seas.

Arthur pauses at the threshold, a silhouette framed by the dying light. His next move is a mystery, even to himself. How will he confront Victor? Can he save Dr. Turner and Claire without losing himself in the process?

"Always," he replies, then slips out into the evening, leaving the question hanging in the air like a specter, haunting the silence of the room.

The door clicks shut behind him, the sound of the latch hinting at the dangers ahead.

Chapter 15

Arthur paced restlessly, his apartment walls seeming to close in tighter with every frantic step. The dim light flickered, casting jittery shadows that mirrored the tremors running through his hands. He was unraveling, a puppet on fraying strings, each movement dictated by the relentless pull of Victor lurking in the dark recesses of his mind. The air was suffocating, heavy with the sour tang of cold sweat and fear.

"Help," he whispered, his voice barely more than a breath, lost in the oppressive quiet.

A sharp knock sliced through the silence. Arthur froze, his breath catching in his throat. He stared at the door, dread pooling in his chest. It was Lisa and Detective Lawson, standing just outside, ready to step into the chaos he could barely contain.

They entered, eyes immediately scanning the room, taking in the clutter—the visible reflection of the storm raging inside him.

"Arthur?" Lisa's voice was gentle, but steady, like a tether pulling him from the edge. "I brought Detective Lawson with me. He's here to ask a few questions, to help you with your concerns. I hope that's alright."

Arthur swallowed hard, his pulse thudding in his ears. "It's fine," he murmured, though his words felt hollow.

"Something's not right," Lawson said, his gaze cutting through the haze of tension. "Talk to us, let us help you."

Arthur's heart raced, the confession clawing its way up, desperate to be heard yet choked by the fear tightening around him. He opened his mouth, but the words stuck, trapped by the enormity of what he was about to reveal.

"It's... I have..." His voice trembled, each word a step onto a narrow ledge.

"Victor's not just a name I made up," he finally confessed, the truth slipping out like venom from a wound.

Lisa's eyes widened, the shock clear, though she held steady, her presence a beacon of reassurance. Detective Lawson's expression remained controlled, but his eyes sharpened with interest.

"Dissociative Identity Disorder," Arthur forced out, the diagnosis feeling foreign, bitter.

The room hung in stunned silence, but beneath the shock was a growing resolve—a determination to face what was coming next.

Arthur's breath catches, a tremor in each word as if his voice is shattering along with his composure. "There are... others," he confesses, the admission spiraling from his lips like leaves caught in a whirlwind. "Edmund is... kind, elderly; he helps me remember to breathe." His fingers twitch, mimicking the turning of pages that Edmund, no doubt, would find solace in. "Samuel, he's a child but also the protector, always bracing for impact." He clenches his fist, embodying Samuel's readiness to shield.

"Then there's Victor." The name comes out as a hiss, a serpent coiled in the depths of Arthur's psyche. "He's the storm, chaos incarnate, and he's trying to... to overthrow everything I am."

Lisa moves closer, her presence a stark contrast to the tempest within him. She reaches out, her touch light on his arm, grounding—like an anchor in his tumultuous sea.

"Arthur, it's okay," she whispers, her voice a melody amidst dissonance. "I—We're here to understand, to help you through this storm. I told you I would help you; I won't betray your trust."

Her gaze holds a depth of empathy, eyes reflecting a soul that has seen sorrow but still knows how to find the dawn. In her look, there's no judgment, only the silent promise of being a confidante, a safe harbor for his fragmented truths as she had promised.

"Victor is strong," Arthur murmurs, afraid yet finding solace in her unwavering support. "But I'm still here, fighting to keep the light on in the lighthouse, hoping not to crash against the rocks."

Lisa nods, her assurance not needing words, her belief in him as clear as the resolve shining in her eyes. "You are the lighthouse keeper, Arthur. And we'll make sure that light never goes out."

Detective Lawson leans in, the table between them groaning under the weight of his forearms. His eyes, sharp and blue, dissect Arthur's haunted expression with clinical precision. He squints, as if to peel back the layers of Arthur's soul and pulls out a small notepad from his inner jacket pocket. The scratch of his pen against the paper is a staccato rhythm in the charged silence.

"Arthur," he begins, voice steady, "you mentioned Victor. Can you describe what triggers his emergence?"

Arthur feels the question like a jolt, a direct current probing the fissures of his fragile psyche. Lisa's hand on his arm is a lifeline, her warmth a counterpoint to the detective's cold inquiry. He swallows, searching for the words that skitter like shadows just beyond his grasp.

"Stress," he manages to say. "Conflict... It's when I feel cornered, threatened. That's when he... appears."

"Good, good. And how often does this occur?" Lawson's gaze never wavers, capturing every nuance of Arthur's response, cataloging it, analyzing it.

"Too often," Arthur whispers, his voice barely above a sigh. "Sometimes I don't even know when he has been and gone. Times like..."

Lisa's hand brushes soothing circles on Arthur's back, her presence a soft beacon in the encroaching darkness. She speaks up, her tone laced with conviction.

"We are going to help you, Arthur. We are here, and we won't leave until you are ready."

Arthur lifts his head, eyes meeting hers. In those brown depths, he finds an echo of his own struggle—a shared understanding of pain—and it cradles his heart. A sense of relief washes over him, diluting the poison of isolation that Victor has injected into his veins for so long.

"Thank you," he breathes out, the words carrying the weight of countless unspoken fears. "Thank you both."

Lawson nods, closing his notepad with a snap that punctuates the moment.

"We'll do everything we can to keep you safe and stop Victor. This isn't just your battle anymore, Arthur. We're in this together."

The words settle around Arthur, forming a shield against the chaos Victor thrives on. For the first time in a long while, hope flickers in the dark recesses of his mind, its light fragile but fierce. With Lisa's gentle support and Detective Lawson's unwavering resolve, Arthur dares to believe that victory over the tempest within might just be within reach.

Arthur's gaze flickers to the window, a silent sentinel guarding against the shadows that threaten to seep through the cracks. With each breath, he steels himself, the air in his lungs a testament to newfound resolve.

"Dr. Turner," he starts, voice uncharacteristically firm, "I need to see her again. It's time I face this head-on." His hands, once trembling, now rest steady on the tabletop, anchoring him to the here and now.

Lisa nods, her eyes reflecting the gravity of his decision. "She could be our key to understanding Victor better."

Detective Lawson's pen pauses mid-scratch. "Risky, but necessary," he concedes, the words rolling off his tongue like marbles. "Victor is a wildcard, unpredictable. Dr. Turner's help could give us insight into his patterns, maybe even predict his next move."

Their voices, once scattered by the weight of uncertainty, begin to weave together, forming a tapestry of shared purpose. The risks are clear—delving deeper into Arthur's psyche might provoke Victor, yet the benefits of gaining an advantage beckon them forward.

"Tracking him..." Arthur leans in, his mind churning with strategy. "We could keep a log. Document everything—the triggers, the switches. Patterns will emerge. They have to."

"Patterns," Lawson echoes, his blue eyes sharpening like blades as they dissect each word. "Yes, evidence. We'll need solid proof if we're going to contain him."

"Contain...yes, and protect," Arthur adds, the latter word wrapping around him like a shield. "My friends, my colleagues. I can't let Victor hurt them."

Lisa reaches across the table, her touch grounding. "You won't be alone, Arthur. We'll set up a system, checks and balances. You're not just fighting for control; you're safeguarding lives."

Their plan takes shape, murky and malleable, but gaining definition with every spoken thought. Arthur's input weaves through their conversation, no longer a passive victim but an active participant in his own rescue.

"Dr. Turner will help us make sense of it all," Arthur insists, his heart thrumming with the potential of reclaiming the life that had been splintered by Victor's chaos. "I trust her."

"Then it's settled," Lawson declares, his voice a bastion of authority. "A meeting with Dr. Turner. Surveillance on Victor. We'll build a case so tight he won't have room to breathe."

The room is charged with a sense of unity, the darkness held at bay by their collective determination. A plan is more than words;

it's a promise—a vow to chase away the night that has held Arthur captive for far too long.

Arthur's fingers trace the rim of his coffee mug, a small, grounding ritual against the storm brewing in his mind. The room is silent except for the scratch of Detective Lawson's pen and Lisa's steady breathing.

"Arthur," Lisa begins, her voice a beacon in the murkiness of his thoughts, "can you describe what it feels like when Victor... comes forward?"

He nods, his gaze fixed on the dark liquid that mirrors the swirling shadows within him. "It's like... being shoved into the backseat of my own body. I'm there, but not in control. He takes over, and I'm just... screaming behind soundproof glass."

Detective Lawson leans in, his blue eyes intent and searching. "What does Victor want?"

"Chaos," Arthur whispers, the word a serpent slithering through the room. "He thrives on fear, on power. It's a game to him—everyone else, mere pawns."

Lisa's hand is warm on his arm, a soothing contrast to the chill of his revelation. She turns to Lawson, determination etching her features. "We need to approach this holistically. Victor isn't just a personality; he's a threat that requires a multifaceted strategy."

"Agreed." Lawson's nod is resolute. "We're dealing with more than just criminal behavior; it's psychological a war from within your own mind."

"Then we should consider forming a team," Lisa suggests, her chestnut hair catching the light as she tilts her head. "Family, friends and some professionals who understand the nuances of mental illness and can profile someone like Victor. Someone to keep a constant eye on him."

Lawson's lips quirk into a semblance of a smile, the first glint of excitement in his eyes. "A team... Yes. With the right expertise, we could anticipate his moves, counteract them before they happen."

Arthur feels a spark ignite within him, hope fanning into flame. The idea of a collective force against the darkness is both terrifying and exhilarating.

"People who can help me hold him back," he says, strength threading through his voice.

"Exactly," Lisa replies, her eyes alight with the possibilities. "Together, we can all safeguard you and your environment against Victor's influence."

"Imagine that, Arthur," Lawson adds, standing now, the energy in the room rising with him. "A fortress of minds, each one a bulwark against the siege."

Their excitement is palpable, a current that sweeps away some of the heaviness that has long clung to Arthur's shoulders. For the first time in too long, he allows himself to believe in a future where he is the master of his own fate, a future where Victor's shadow is nothing but a distant, fading echo.

Arthur taps his phone against his palm, the digits of Detective Lawson's number now a lifeline etched into the screen. Lisa hovers close, her phone aglow with a new contact—Dr. Elaine Turner—her thumb hovering over the 'save' button.

"Friday, 10 AM," Lawson says, his voice a low rumble that seems to ground the moment, tethering their newfound alliance to reality. "That's when we meet with Dr. Turner."

"Friday," Arthur repeats, the word tasting like promise on his tongue. He keys in a reminder and feels the gentle pressure of Lisa's hand on his shoulder—a physical anchor amidst the tempest of his thoughts.

"Be sure to charge your phones, you two," she quips, a lighthearted note in her voice that belies the gravity of their situation. The corners of Arthur's mouth lift in an almost-smile; it's been ages since he felt part of something resembling a team.

"Will do," he murmurs, locking eyes with each of them in turn. There's a silent pact in that gaze—a shared commitment that tightens around his chest, both suffocating and exhilarating.

"Victor won't know what hit him," Lisa says with conviction, her earlier shock now replaced by steely resolve.

"Indeed," Lawson agrees, folding his notepad away. His nod is firm, a silent oath sealed between them. In this solemn moment, Arthur senses the tiniest fissure in Victor's armor, a hairline crack in the fortress that has imprisoned him for so long.

"Thank you," Arthur breathes out, feeling the words inadequate to express the magnitude of his gratitude. They stand together, three figures cast in the fading light of day, bound by a common cause.

As they disperse into the darkening city, Arthur's apartment door clicks shut behind him, sealing him away from the world. A shadow detaches itself from the corner of the room, formless yet heavy with intent. Victor's presence is palpable, a dark whisper against Arthur's consciousness.

"Plans and little helpers," Victor's voice slithers through the silence, a taunting caress. "How... quaint."

His eyes gleam in the gloom, twin orbs of malice that reflect no light but seem to consume it. Sinister delight twines around his words, anticipation curling at the edges of his tone. Arthur shivers, the glimmer of hope within him flickering like a candle in a storm.

"Enjoy your fleeting courage, Arthur," Victor purrs, the darkness coiling tighter around him. "I relish the challenge."

The finality in those whispered threats sends a shudder down Arthur's spine, and he knows that the real battle has yet to begin. Outside, the city stretches on, oblivious to the psychological maelstrom brewing within its midst. And as night falls, the stage is set for a confrontation that will test the very limits of Arthur's fragmented soul.

Chapter 16

Arthur leans over the shared desk, pointing to a line of text on Gary's screen.

"Right there, that's where we integrated the new algorithm," he murmurs, his voice barely rising above the hum of the office.

Arthur leans against the edge of his desk, papers fanned out before him like a deck of cards strewn in the aftermath of a game. The office buzzes around him, a hive of ceaseless activity, but his world narrows to the conversation at hand.

"Gary, this analysis you pulled off—it's meticulous," Arthur murmurs, thumbing through the sheets, each number a testament to their collective effort.

Gary stands across from him, hands tucked into his pockets, an easy smile playing on his lips. "Well, when you've got a human calculator like yourself checking the work, it's hard to go wrong."

The quip draws a small, fleeting smile from Arthur, a rare crack in his stoic facade. It's a momentary lapse, a glimpse of the camaraderie they once shared freely.

"Calculator, huh? Guess we'll see if the higher-ups agree when the presentation rolls around," Arthur replies, the lightness in his voice belying the gravity he feels pressing down on him.

"Ah, they will," Gary assures him, his tone light, almost dismissive of any other possibility. He leans in, lowering his voice conspiratorially. "And if they don't, we'll just blame it on the intern, right?"

Arthur's smile broadens ever so slightly, a quiet acknowledgment of the humor meant to be a balm for the stress of their looming deadline. It's a brief respite, Gary's levity a stark contrast to the shadows that seem to cling to the edges of Arthur's thoughts, veiling them with whispers of doubt and fear.

The light from the computer screen casts a pale glow across Arthur's hands as they hover over the keyboard, fingers trembling with a hesitation that belies his usual precision. His eyes, shadowed and distant, flicker away from the spreadsheet before him to Gary, who is oblivious to the undercurrent of tension threading through the room.

"Did you catch the game last night?" Gary asks, the words meant to be an anchor in the drift of casual office banter.

"Ah, no," Arthur starts, the response fractured by a pause too long, "I had... other engagements." The phrase feels hollow, even to his own ears.

"Too bad, it was a hell of a match," Gary continues, unaware of the turmoil knotting tighter within Arthur.

Arthur nods, but his gaze slips past Gary, fixating on something unseen. There's a taste of panic, sharp and metallic, at the back of his throat. It's the forewarning of a darkness that creeps along the fringes of his consciousness, threatening to engulf him whole.

"Gary..." Arthur's voice is a whisper, almost drowned out by the hum of fluorescent lights overhead. "There's—there's something I've been meaning to tell you."

Gary pivots toward him, his expression open, expectant. "What's up?"

"It's... complicated," Arthur manages, each word sounding more strained than the last. "I've been having these... lapses. Moments where time just... escapes me."

"Like you're forgetful?" Gary's brows knit together in confusion, his attempt at lightness falling flat between them.

"More than that," Arthur presses on, the confession clawing its way up his throat. "Full blackouts. There are hours, sometimes days, I can't account for."

"Blackouts?" Gary repeats, the joviality seeping out of him, replaced by a dawning concern that he tries to mask with a poorly timed chuckle. "You sure you're not just sneaking off for some secret life as a spy or something?"

Arthur's laugh is a brittle thing, shattering against the gravity of his revelation. "I wish it were that simple," he says, a bitter edge to his tone. "This is serious, Gary. I'm losing pieces of myself."

The air between them grows heavy, charged with a truth too weighty for mere words. Arthur's admission hangs suspended; a dark cloud ready to burst.

"Remember the other day when you came by the apartment, and I told you that I felt like I was responsible for the deaths?" Arthur prepares himself for this deep conversation with his friend. "Yeah, mate, I remember." Gary's brow furrows, a deep line etching itself between his eyes as he leans back in his chair, creating a small but noticeable distance between him and Arthur. The office seems to contract around them, the walls inching closer, trapping the tension in the confined space.

"Well, I have... problems. Blackouts." Arthur said in a hushed voice.

"Arthur, that sounds like... I don't know, man, something out of a movie," Gary says, his voice laced with incredulity. He runs a hand through his sandy blonde hair, a gesture of unease that belies his typically relaxed demeanor. "Oh mate, I mean, A—Are you seeing someone about this? A professional?"

Arthur's fingers grip the edge of the desk, knuckles white. "Yes, but it's more than just blackouts. It's... there are times when I'm not myself." His voice drops to a hushed tone, heavy with the weight of unspoken fears. "It's called Dissociative Identity Disorder."

"Dissociative what?" Gary leans away, his eyes squinted skeptically, searching Arthur's face for a hint of jest. "That's like, multiple personalities, right? You're saying you've got other people living in your head?"

The words hang in the air, stark and surreal. Arthur watches as Gary's amiable mask slips, replaced by a look of discomfort. There's a subtle shift in the room's atmosphere, a silent signal that their familiar dynamic has been irrevocably altered.

"Other... parts of me," Arthur corrects gently, trying to steady his voice. "It's not like I'm making it up. It's real, Gary. And it's terrifying."

"Right, mate." Gary's response is terse, clipped. He casts a glance over his shoulder, as if contemplating an escape route. For the first time since Arthur has known him, Gary avoids meeting his eye, his gaze darting to the papers scattered on his desk, the clock on the wall—anywhere but Arthur's pleading stare.

"Look, Arthur, this is... a lot," Gary stammers, standing up abruptly. His chair scrapes against the floor, the sound sharp in Arthur's ears. "I'm not sure what you want me to say."

"Nothing," Arthur responds, a hollow feeling spreading through his chest. "I just needed you to know."

"Sure, yeah." Gary clears his throat, his once-warm eyes now cold and guarded. "I need to get some air. We'll talk later, okay?"

He doesn't wait for an answer, leaving Arthur sitting alone, the echo of his footsteps a stark reminder of the widening chasm between them. Arthur's gaze settles on the empty chair across from him, a silent sentinel to his unveiling secret.

As the office buzzes around him, Arthur feels the creeping tendrils of isolation wrapping around him, cold and unforgiving. He remains motionless, fixated on the screen before him, yet seeing nothing but the reflection of his own fractured identity staring back at him from the darkened glass.

Arthur's fingers trace the edge of his desk, a slow and deliberate motion that mirrors the pacing of his heart. The office hums around him, indifferent to the storm brewing in silence—a tempest swirling through his mind. He lifts his gaze, finding Gary's retreating figure paused at the threshold of the room.

"Gary," Arthur calls out, his voice a strained whisper grappling for strength. "Please."

The word hangs in the air, a plea wrapped in vulnerability. Gary turns, the hesitance etched into the lines of his face a stark contrast to the easy smiles that usually reside there.

"Arthur, it's not that I don't want to understand," Gary begins, shifting from foot to foot. The fluorescent lights above cast a harsh glow, deepening the shadows beneath his eyes and throwing his inner turmoil into sharp relief.

"I need you to believe me," Arthur insists, rising from his chair with a purpose that belies his shaking hands. His words are a lifeline thrown into the chasm that's opened between them. "It's real, Gary. Every day is a struggle to remember who I am, to hold onto myself amidst the chaos."

Gary's Adam's apple bobs as he swallows, his discomfort palpable. "I... Arthur, this is beyond anything I've dealt with before. I can't even begin to imagine what it's like."

"Then just listen," Arthur implores, stepping closer. His shadow intersects with Gary's, a visual reminder of the connection he so desperately seeks. "I lose hours, days even. There are moments when I'm not... myself. And when I come back, it's like waking up in someone else's life."

A flicker of uncertainty crosses Gary's face. He takes a tentative step back, the distance between them growing once more. "I hear you, mate, but this—"

"Is terrifying, I know." Arthur's voice cracks under the weight of his own fears. "But think about how it feels for me. I'm living it. Every single day."

Gary's mouth opens, then closes, no words escaping. His eyes, once bright with camaraderie, now reflect a wariness that sends a chill down Arthur's spine. "I'm not sure what to do with this information, Arthur."

"Neither am I," Arthur admits, his breath faltering. "But I don't have the luxury of walking away from it."

There's a beat of silence, the kind that thrums with unspoken thoughts and unanswered questions. Gary looks at Arthur, really looks at him, and for a fleeting second, there's a glimmer of the old warmth. But it's quickly extinguished, snuffed out by the complexity of the revelation that looms over them, an opaque veil that neither knows how to lift.

"Let's just take this one step at a time, okay?" Gary suggests, though his voice lacks conviction. "We'll figure something out."

Arthur nods, more to himself than to Gary. He watches as Gary retreats once again, leaving him alone with the ghostly afterimage of their fractured rapport. The screen before him offers no solace, merely a blank canvas awaiting the keystrokes of a man whose greatest adversary lies within the confines of his own mind.

Arthur watches Gary from across the room, the once familiar territory of friendship now a foreign landscape. The exchanges of casual banter have dwindled to nothingness, replaced by a cold silence that spreads between their desks like frost on glass. When their eyes do meet, Gary's are quick to divert, evading the unspoken plea in Arthur's tired gaze.

A question lingers on Arthur's tongue, one he dare not voice—why? Yet the answer is etched in the stiff line of Gary's shoulders, the barrier he erects with every curt nod and mumbled greeting. The office air grows thick with the scent of betrayal, stinging Arthur's nostrils and tightening his chest.

He takes a deep breath, attempting to quell the tempest brewing within. Each heartbeat echoes the rhythm of rejection. The camaraderie they had built feels as if it were a figment of his imagination, an illusion shattered by the weight of his confession.

In the cavernous space of his mind, Arthur's thoughts spiral. What worth does he hold if the complexities of his condition are enough to sever ties? The fragmented pieces of himself claw for dominance, each identity pulling at the seams of his consciousness, threatening to unravel him completely.

"Get it together," he murmurs under his breath, a mantra meant to stitch the fraying edges of his sanity. But words are feeble threads against the onslaught of doubt and loneliness.

The clock ticks, slow and taunting. Time, once a reliable companion, now marks the growing distance between Arthur and the world around him. It's as if he speaks a language only he can understand, the words lost on those who once listened.

And as Gary laughs, a sound that once brought Arthur solace, he realizes it's directed elsewhere, a shared moment to which he is no longer privy. A pang of something sharp and bitter—a mix of envy and sorrow—cuts through him.

Arthur sits back, fingers pressed against the cool surface of his desk, grounding himself in the present. He is alone in a room full of people, a solitary figure adrift at sea while life continues on the shore, vibrant and oblivious to his plight.

Arthur's fingers hover above the keyboard, still, as if the chatter and clinking of coffee mugs around him have erected invisible walls, sealing him within his cubicle. His colleagues' voices blend into a distant hum—white noise to his solitary existence. He glances up from his perch, surveying the office landscape: clusters of people leaning into conversations, animated gestures painting stories he's no longer a part of.

The chair beside him, once warmed by Gary's presence, now holds nothing but absence. The emptiness feels tangible, an unspoken reminder of the chasm that has opened between them. Arthur swallows hard, the lump in his throat a silent testament to his growing solitude.

He tries to focus on the spreadsheet before him, numbers blurring into meaningless smudges of black on white. Each cell is a cage, trapping his thoughts, which dart like panicked birds against the confines of his mind. He presses a hand to the smooth surface of his desk, grounding himself in the solidity, yet it does little to anchor the drift of his spirit.

His eyes betray him, drawn again to the empty chair. It mocks him with its vacancy, a throne for ghosts of camaraderie lost. Arthur recoils inwardly, the sting of isolation sharper in this sea of indifference.

He forces his gaze back to the computer screen, the cursor blinking expectantly, waiting for input that doesn't come. The pixels seem to pulse with the rhythm of his racing heart, a silent echo of the turmoil swirling within him. On the monitor, a half-written email addressed to no one hangs suspended—the words a bridge to nowhere.

A shiver runs down Arthur's spine as he sits motionless, the weight of Gary's disbelief pressing down on him like a physical burden. The office buzzes with life, but none of it reaches him; he is an island amid a flowing stream of human connection.

The clock on his desktop ticks away seconds, indifferent to his plight. Time stretches, pulling at the edges of his reality. Arthur leans into the glow of the screen, allowing the artificial light to wash over him, a pale substitute for warmth. The project files sit untouched, icons on a desktop that hold no meaning anymore.

"Understand," he whispers to the vacant space, a plea lost in the void. But there's no response, only the relentless tapping of keys from the next cubicle—a Morse code of normalcy he can't decipher.

As the office dims with the approach of evening, shadows creep across the floor, reaching for him. They're companions, these shades, in their silent understanding of what it means to be unseen, unheard, unknown.

Arthur remains at his desk, long after the bustle has faded, the glow of the computer screen a beacon in the gathering darkness. He stares into the digital abyss, grappling with the echoes of Gary's retreat and the suffocating embrace of his own concealed agony.

It's just him—the fractured keeper of secrets—and the unblinking eye of the monitor, bearing witness to a man who wears invisibility like a second skin. Alone, Arthur sits adrift in the quiet aftermath, the fading resonance of rejection wrapping around him, as palpable as the encroaching night.

Chapter 17

The night is a shroud, but Victor does not hesitate. He moves with sinister grace, a shadow amongst shadows. The streetlight flickers, casting an eerie glow on Claire's unsuspecting form as she fumbles for her keys at the front door. She doesn't hear him approach; the silence is his accomplice.

Claire turns, and the keys jingle like a death knell in the chilly air. Victor's hand clamps over her mouth before the scream can claw its way out. His other arm encircles her waist with iron certainty. Her eyes widen, mirrors of moonlight reflecting raw terror. He feels the vibration of her muffled cries against his palm, the desperate plea for mercy that he will never grant.

"Shh," he whispers, his voice a serpent's hiss. "Struggle, and it ends badly."

Her body tenses, ready to fight, but Victor's cold gaze paralyzes. Those eyes, devoid of warmth, promise a darkness deeper than the one that envelops them. Claire's resistance fades: the realization dawns that this is not just a man—this is The Shadow, the one who thrives in the abyss of Arthur's fragmented mind.

He drags her back, away from any chance of safety the light offered. Each step he takes is measured; a predator confident in his hunt. Claire's thoughts race, tripping over themselves in panic. But even as her mind screams for escape, her limbs feel leaden under Victor's unyielding grip.

"Please," she manages, the word distorted against his skin.

Victor tilts his head, considering her plea with mock curiosity. "There's no 'please' with me, Claire. You know that." His tone is chillingly calm, a contrast to the chaos he orchestrates with each calculated move.

He opens the car door, still cloaked in darkness, and shoves her inside. The interior swallows her up, and the door slams with the finality of a coffin lid. Victor slides into the driver's seat, his silhouette outlined by the faint glow of the dashboard. The engine roars to life, a beast awakened, as they pull away from the curb, leaving behind the safety of the known world.

Claire is trapped, caught in the web of Victor's meticulous design. The road stretches before them, leading towards an uncertain fate where the only certainty is that Victor, The Shadow within, holds all the power.

Arthur's heart crashes against his rib cage. He watches helplessly from inside the eyes he shares with Victor. Guilt gnaws at him, a ravenous beast feasting on his insides. It's his fault. His presence, his condition, has painted a target on Claire's back.

"CLAIRE!" he bellows into the void, his voice shattering the silence of the deserted street. The name rips from his throat, a desperate incantation in the darkness.

"CLAIRE!" he screams again, but she can't hear him, swallowed by Victor's dark machinations. Arthur stands alone inside of his head, the echo of his cry hanging in the air like an accusation.

Arthur struggles to regain control, the weight of this reality crushing him. The Shadow of Victor has outmaneuvered him again, and the thought gnaws at his resolve like a worm through an apple. He wants to save Claire, to be the hero she deserves, but fear's icy tendrils coil around his heart. Victor is in control now, and where Victor leads, darkness follows.

His mind races, thoughts clashing in violent disarray. With every breath, Arthur fights for dominance over his own fragmented psyche, battling against the cold grip of Victor's influence. Save her, his conscience urges, yet the terror of confronting that part of himself that is The Shadow whispers caution, seducing him into inaction.

"Must save her," he mumbles, voice barely audible over the din of his internal tempest. His hands tremble, not just with adrenaline but with the seismic force of his warring selves. To defeat Victor would be to defeat the very demon within, and for a man fractured by his own mind, the prospect is as terrifying as the abyss itself.

A room devoid of warmth or comfort, walls stained with the residue of old fears—it's here that Claire is held captive. The air is thick with the musty scent of neglect, the only sound the slow drip of water from a rusted pipe somewhere in the shadows. The single bulb hanging from the ceiling flickers erratically, casting erratic shadows that dance across the room like macabre specters.

Claire, bound and motionless, lies on a bare mattress, the fabric stained and torn. Her breaths come in shallow gasps, each one a silent plea for salvation. The room feels alive with malice, as if it, too, is an extension of Victor's will—a physical manifestation of the terror he exudes.

Every corner seems to whisper threats, and the scant light does little to banish the gloom that clings to the place like a second skin. It is a chamber designed not just to hold a body, but to imprison a soul, to strip away hope until nothing remains but raw, unfiltered dread.

Arthur's mind was a battlefield, torn between the urge to break through and the force holding him back. He needed to get into the room, to tear down the walls and save Claire from the terror inside. But every time he caught sight of Victor's cold, taunting smile in the reflection of the windows, he froze. The darkness lurking within him—Victor—was capable of creating this nightmare, and Arthur knew it.

He stared at his trembling hands, caught between the need to save and the fear of destruction. He knew what had to be done, but the way forward was unclear, each step a plunge deeper into his own worst fears.

Victor's silhouette looms over her, a dark sentinel against the meager light that filters into the room. Claire's heart hammers in her chest, each beat echoing the terror that courses through her veins. She meets his gaze, eyes wide with fear, her lips parting to draw in a breath that feels too thick to swallow.

"Please," she whispers, her voice barely audible above the sound of her own frantic pulse. "Let me go, Victor. You don't have to do this. Let Arthur come back to me, please Victor, please."

He tilts his head, considering her with an indifference that chills her to the bone. His shadow stretches across the floor, as if reaching out to claim her very essence. The calmness in his eyes, the absence of empathy, it freezes the words in her throat.

"Reasoning with me?" Victor's tone is soft yet laced with a threat that sends shivers down her spine. "You should know better by now, Claire."

Tears brim at the edges of her eyes, but she fights them back, refuses to show the depth of her vulnerability. Instead, she scans the room, desperate for anything that might aid her escape.

Her gaze snags on a shard of metal, half-hidden beneath the mattress's frayed edge—a sliver of hope amidst the despair. Her mind races, calculating the distance between her restrained wrists and the jagged piece that promises a chance at freedom.

"Thinking of running?" Victor's voice betrays no emotion, as if he's reading her thoughts, but his attention shifts momentarily to the door, contemplating something only he understands.

Claire seizes the moment, fingers stretching, straining towards the shard. It digs into her skin, a pain that is welcome if it means liberation. Her breath catches in her chest, a silent triumph rising within her, even as the fear of discovery looms.

She must be swift, she must be silent—her life depends on it.

The shard betrays her. The metallic scrape against the concrete floor is a siren wail in the silence, dragging Victor's attention back. His head swivels, eyes locking on Claire's fingers now bloodied with effort and desperation.

"Did you really think..." His voice trails off as he steps closer, looming over her like an eclipse casting a shadow over any flicker of hope she harbors.

"Victor, please," she whispers, but the plea hangs in the air, unanswered. Her heart thunders against her ribs, each beat a drum of impending doom.

"Escape is not an option." Victor's tone is icy, his words solidifying into chains that constrict tighter around Claire's resolve.

Arthur watches helplessly from the corners of his mind, trapped in silence, his breath betraying his fear. Every step Victor takes toward Claire sends a jolt of rage and guilt through him. He wants to scream, to leap forward and protect her from the darkness he knows is part of himself. But he's frozen, paralyzed by regret, unable to move as the horror unfolds.

Moments stretch into eternity as Arthur's mind splinters, the fractured pieces battling for supremacy. He needs a plan—one that accounts for Victor's cunning and his own fragmented state. Resources are scant; his greatest weapon lies within the labyrinth of his psyche.

The desperation mounts, clawing at his throat, demanding action. He must out think Victor. If he fails, Claire pays the price. He can't allow that—his love for her is the anchor in his storm-tossed mind.

"Think, Arthur, think!" he admonishes himself silently for fear of Victor hearing his thoughts. There's no room for error, no second chances. It's a game of chess with lives in the balance, and he's been playing at a disadvantage all along.

Victor's mocking smile flickers, echoing in Arthur's mind. "You can't beat me, Arthur. I've won. I'm here, and you're stuck with me now."

Arthur, sharing the same body, feels the taunt as though it's his own thought, the divide between them razor-thin. He recalls the building's layout, the security routines, the guards—all memorized with precision. These details should guide him, but with Victor in control, each step could lead to salvation or a trap.

"Tonight," Arthur silently vows, his thoughts echoing within Victor's consciousness. He'll reclaim his body, rescue Claire, or lose himself completely.

As they move, Arthur's mind tracks every twist, every turn Victor makes. The derelict building looms closer. Arthur feels Victor's presence smothering him, a constant shadow within their shared thoughts. Claire is close, but Victor's grip tightens.

Anxiety presses in, a force that both Arthur and Victor feel, yet only Arthur fights against. Victor moves with an eerie confidence, his body blending into the night while Arthur fights to suppress panic. The tension thickens with every step they take toward Claire's prison.

Inside the building, Arthur's awareness sharpens. Victor is in control, but Arthur clings to the periphery of their shared mind, fighting to break through. As they pass through the hallways, the sterility and coldness only intensify the dread. Arthur knows Victor is playing a game, taunting him with each calculated move.

Then, at the door, Victor's hand hovers over the knob. Arthur pushes, trying to wrestle control, but the door opens under Victor's will. Inside, Claire is there, bound, her eyes filled with fear. Arthur's heart pounds, his body moving without his command. It's Victor, savoring the power.

"Arthur?" Claire's voice trembles, hope mixed with terror.

Victor steps forward, and Arthur screams inside their mind, desperate to stop him. But a flood of thoughts about Claire betray his thoughts. Victor's head snaps up, eyes narrowing with malicious amusement.

"Thought you could outsmart me, Arthur? You should've known better."

Arthur struggles, fighting for control, but Victor's grip is too strong. His mind races, colliding with Victor's, chaos clashing with Victor's cold, calculating nature. Claire's eyes lock with Arthur's—a silent plea—but Arthur can't act. He's trapped, watching through Victor's eyes.

Then the lights flicker and die, plunging them all into darkness. In the confusion, Arthur pushes, seizing the opportunity to strike. Their body lunges in the dark, a desperate grasp for freedom. They fight blindly, Arthur's will against Victor's in a brutal, unseen clash.

Blow after blow, they struggle in the void, Victor's presence a suffocating force inside their shared mind. Arthur's hand finds flesh—his triumph short-lived as Victor retaliates with searing pain. They are one, yet divided, battling for control of the same body.

"Arthur, please come back!" Claire's voice cuts through the darkness, a lifeline.

But returning isn't an option. Arthur refuses to let Victor win. He fights, not just for his body, but for Claire, for redemption. The battle rages in silence, a deadly dance of willpower until—

Silence.

Arthur gasps for breath, unsure who has won. His body aches, his mind frayed from the internal war.

"Arthur?" Claire's voice quivers.

"I'm here," he whispers, barely audible, unsure if it's him or Victor speaking.

His hand reaches out, finding hers. For a moment, Arthur feels in control, but Victor is still there, lurking, waiting.

They stand in the dark, both the victorious and victim, unsure which of them holds the future in their hands.

Chapter 18

Arthur sits alone, the dim apartment swallowed by the flickering light of a single lamp, casting jagged shadows across the walls. The room feels suffocating, but it's not the darkness that unsettles him—it's the silence, the unbearable quiet left in the wake of Claire's hurried departure. He had sent her away, forced her to flee from Victor and the storm of violence that was sure to follow.

His hands, pale and trembling, clutch a worn photograph of Claire. The edges are frayed, the colors faded, but her smile remains vivid, a ghost of happier times piercing through the gloom. The tremors running through his fingers seem to echo in the air, amplifying the tension that coils tight around his chest.

Arthur's eyes, bloodshot and heavy, trace the delicate lines of her face in the photograph, searching for some semblance of peace. But her smile offers no comfort—only a cruel reminder of what's at stake. His fractured mind claws at him, the weight of his own thoughts pressing down, suffocating. Each breath feels labored, as if even the air has turned against him, matching the crushing burden of his fading resolve.

He rises abruptly, the photograph nearly slipping from his grasp as he begins to pace. The carpet muffles his steps, a silent witness to the turmoil that propels him back and forth. With each stride, doubts gnaw at the edges of his consciousness, fears whispering like specters in the dark corners of the room.

"Can I stand against him?" Arthur's voice is a mere breath, a ghost of sound that lingers in the charged air. "Am I strong enough to resist Victor's pull?"

The questions hang unanswered, multiplying with the rhythm of his footsteps. Victor is relentless—a constant adversary whose dominance looms larger with every passing moment. Arthur feels it, the push and pull of an unseen tide, threatening to sweep away the remnants of his sanity.

With each turn across the floor, the boundary between himself and Victor blurs, like ink bleeding into water. The thought of succumbing sends shivers down his spine, ice spreading through his veins.

"No," he whispers fiercely, the word barely audible over the pounding of his heart. "I refuse to let him win."

But the declaration does little to steady the shaking of his hands or quiet the overwhelming doubt. Arthur knows that his next move could very well dictate the course of this shadowy chess game he's been ensnared in, a game where the stakes are his very soul.

Arthur halts his pacing and stands before the tarnished mirror that hangs askew on the wall; its silvering flawed with age. Flecks of darkness mar his reflection, but it's the look in his eyes that truly distorts the image staring back at him. Tired eyes, rimmed red and swimming with uncertainty, lock onto their own gaze. He watches himself, a man fractured by the very mind that should be his refuge.

The glass surface becomes a battleground, reflecting not just Arthur, but all the tumultuous possibilities that lie ahead. Each breath he takes fogs the mirror, as if his deepest fears are clouding the reality of what he might become. Losing control to Victor is not just a loss of self—it's the annihilation of every bond he's ever cherished, every semblance of normalcy he's struggled to maintain. The impact would ripple outwards, leaving Claire and anyone else who dares to get close caught in the wake of his destruction.

His hands, once trembling, now clench into fists so tight that his knuckles whiten with strain. There's an unsettling resonance in his chest, a primal drumbeat urging him on to fight, to protect, to survive. Yet beneath that rhythm lies a seductive whisper, a call from the shadows where Victor resides, promising power, promising relief from the ceaseless struggle within. It's enticing, this notion of surrender—to let go and allow the darkness to consume him, to relinquish the responsibility of the war he wages against himself.

But no, Arthur refuses. His heart pounds, thrumming against his rib cage like a caged bird desperate for release. A line of sweat trails down his temple, testimony to the battle raging inside him. Protect and preserve—these words echo in the hollows of his mind, a mantra against the encroaching night. Protect those he loves, preserve the essence of who he is, who he must believe he still is.

He releases his fists, fingers unfurling as if letting go of the dark promise they held. A tremor courses through him, a visible shiver of resolve that hardens his stance. Arthur will not succumb to Victor today. Not when there's still fight left in him, not when there's still light, however faint, guiding him through the turmoil. His reflection, once besieged by doubt, now bears a look of determination, even if marred by the weariness of eternal vigilance.

"Today," he murmurs to the man in the mirror, "I stand my ground."

Arthur paces the length of his cramped living room, each step a silent argument with himself. Confrontation is inevitable, an inescapable truth that gnaws at the edges of his resolve. The photograph of Claire lies abandoned on the coffee table, her smile a stark contrast to the storm brewing within him.

"Face him," one thought insists, a surge of adrenaline propelling it forward. "It's the only way to protect her." But another voice, quieter, laced with trepidation, whispers, "What if you lose? What if Victor is too strong?"

He halts mid-step, glancing around the dimly lit room as though expecting to see the dark figure of Victor materializing from the shadows. A confrontation could mean liberation, or it could mean giving Victor the reins, allowing the darkness to seep out and infect everything he holds dear.

"Can I risk it?" Arthur's question hangs heavy in the silence of the room. There are no easy answers; there never have been. Each move feels like a gambit in a chess game where Victor is always two steps ahead, and the stakes are soul-crushing.

"Enough!" His own voice startles him, a low growl of frustration breaking free. It's time to gather what's left of his frayed wits.

Arthur closes his eyes, inhales deeply. He imagines the breath as a wave, washing over him, clearing the debris of fear and doubt. Exhale, and with it, dispel the image of Victor's sneering face. Inhale, draw in strength and the memory of those fleeting moments of lucidity when he is wholly himself. Exhale, release the tendrils of Victor's influence that seek to choke his will.

"Find the light," he coaches himself, each breath a lifeline back to the surface. "Hold onto who you are."

The rhythm of his breathing steadies, a metronome to the chaos. With each breath, Arthur finds a sliver of hope, a flicker of determination that refuses to be extinguished. His eyes open slowly, and in them, the ember of resolve sparks to life.

"Victor doesn't define me," he whispers, the words a shield against the encroaching dark. "I'm more than this struggle. I am Arthur Hall, and I will fight."

His thoughts, once a storm of chaos, now focus sharply, like a blade being honed. Arthur's pulse races, pounding in his ears as he grips the photograph tighter. Every breath is shallow, quick, as if the air around him is thickening. Claire's face in the picture taunts him—a reminder of everything he's about to lose if he doesn't act.

His mind sharpens, the weight of his fractured psyche forgotten, replaced by a fierce, single-minded drive. There's no room for doubt. Only one thing matters now: defeating Victor before it's too late., now align with purpose. He stands still, letting the newfound calm anchor him. The battle for his mind rages on, but armed with clarity and a trace of optimism, Arthur knows he has what it takes to keep fighting Victor's influence.

Arthur lurches forward, his silhouette a stark outline against the faint glow of streetlights seeping through the blinds. His fingers claw at his scalp, nails scraping skin as he tries to anchor himself in the now, to not slip into the abyss where Victor waits with open arms. The pain is real, tangible—it's Arthur's pain, not Victor's.

"Stay," he grunts, a voice half-lost between identities. His own plea echoes off barren walls, a call for help from within. He grips tighter, as if holding the fragments of his mind together, binding them with sheer force of will.

The room spins and tilts, but Arthur forces himself to focus, pressing his fingers hard against his temples, fighting the vertigo. Each line, each groove under his touch feels like a map of his own mind—territory Victor has invaded but is still Arthur's to control.

A flicker of memory then, like the soft beam of a distant lighthouse piercing through fog: Dr. Turner's steady gaze, her words that weave through the darkness. "You are not alone, Arthur. We're here with you."

With this, his breathing evens out, the tightness in his chest loosening. Dr. Turner believes in him, not just in the broken man plagued by an inner demon, but in the strength that lies beneath, waiting to emerge victorious.

Lisa's smile radiates through another shard of recollection—her warmth, the unwavering friendship that doesn't falter, even when fear would dictate otherwise. She has never seen him as a lost cause;

she sees the man fighting back, reaching for light in a shadowed world.

Detective Lawson's firm nod materializes next, the unspoken promise of an ally in battle. The detective's belief isn't rooted in naivety, but in evidence, in actions taken and choices made—the very essence of Arthur's struggle against Victor.

These thoughts, these allies, they weave a tapestry of support around Arthur, each thread a testament to his resilience, a counterargument to the doubt that Victor sows. Their faith in him is armor, their conviction his sword.

"Stand up," he tells himself, the words resolute now, no longer a whisper but a command. There's power there, power in remembering who stands with him, in knowing that while Victor may be part of him, he does not have to walk this dark path alone.

"Fight." And Arthur knows he will.

Arthur's fingers stretch across the desk, brushing against the cool surface before they close around a notebook and pen. His movements are deliberate, a silent declaration of war against the entity that threatens to consume him. The photograph of Claire, captured in happier times, gazes back at him from the table, her eyes an anchor in the tempest of his mind.

He flips open the notebook, the pages crisp and unmarred—a blank canvas for the battle plans that will shape his destiny. The pen trembles slightly in his grasp as he steadies his hand, refusing to let Victor's shadow interfere with this moment of clarity. This is Arthur's stand, his line drawn firmly in the sand.

The first word spills onto the page, and then another, each one etched with the gravity of their intent. He scribbles furiously, thoughts racing faster than he can write, outlining scenarios where he confronts Victor head-on, strategies to outmaneuver the malevolent presence that has haunted his every step.

Lines and arrows crisscross the paper. Arthur's brow furrows as he charts pathways through the maze of his own fractured psyche, seeking leverage points, weaknesses to exploit. Each plan is a trap laid for The Shadow, each decision a potential pivot point toward victory or ruin.

He pauses, breath hitching as a new thought surfaces—one last gambit that could tip the scales. The shadows in the room seem to deepen, but Arthur's resolve is ironclad. The shaking in his hand subsides, replaced by a steady pulse of determination.

"Protect her," he whispers into the silence, the words a vow that laces through each planned move like steel threads. Claire's safety is the linchpin, all else pales in comparison. For her, Arthur will face the abyss and fight to keep Victor at bay—whatever the cost may be.

Arthur's fingers linger over the last page of his frenetically drafted strategy, the web of ink still damp with urgency. But as he rereads each line, a cold realization slithers into his mind, tightening around his resolve like a vice. He can't do this alone.

He leans back in his chair, the leather creaking under the shift of his weight, and reaches for his phone. It feels heavier than usual, as if reluctant to be an accomplice to his confession of vulnerability. With each press of a button, his heart beats a syncopated rhythm of dread and hope.

"Lisa," he breathes out when her voice crackles through the speaker, the sound a lifeline thrown across the churning sea of his thoughts.

"Arthur?" Lisa's tone is soft, but it carries the strength of her professional resolve. "Are you OK? What's happened?"

His throat tightens around the words, but he pushes them out, feeling the rawness of his own voice. "I need help, Lisa. I'm up against something—I'm up against myself, and I'm afraid Victor's going to win."

There's no judgment from Lisa, only a steady presence that fills the space between them. "I can be there in fifteen minutes if you want me there," she assures him. "We'll face him together."

Her words are like a balm, calming the storm inside him enough to see through the fog of war within his mind. "Thank you, but I need to do this myself." Arthur whispers, almost too quiet for Lisa to catch.

"Stay strong, Arthur," she says before the call ends, her voice carrying the warmth of a promise. "I'll be there if you change your mind."

The phone clicks off, leaving Arthur in the relative silence of his apartment. The darkness seems less invasive now, pushed back by the glow of determination in his eyes. He stands, muscles coiled with newfound purpose, ready to weave through the labyrinth of his fractured mind one more time.

Victor won't go down without a fight, but neither will Arthur. With Lisa by his side, the shadows lurking in every corner seem less potent. He draws a deep breath, letting it fill his lungs, his chest expanding with the oxygen of resolve.

"Face the darkest self head-on," he murmurs to himself, the mantra echoing off the walls, building strength in its repetition. "Face the darkest self head-on."

Arthur knows the road ahead is fraught with peril, each step a potential plunge into chaos. But there's no turning back now. The battle lines are drawn, allies rallied, and deep within his soul, a spark ignites into flame.

This is more than a confrontation; it's a reclaiming of self, a symphony of courage in the key of defiance. Arthur, once unassuming and lost, has become the conductor of his own destiny. With his baton raised, he's ready to orchestrate the final movement in the opus of his struggle against the darkness within.

Victor's hissing voice jolts him awake. "I've done something, Arthur. Your dear sweet Claire? She's gone. I've put her somewhere you'll never find her in time to save her."

"Victor, where is she?" Arthur pleads, desperation clawing at his throat.

"I'll never tell." Victor's voice drips with mockery, echoing through the fading recesses of Arthur's mind.

Chapter 19

Arthur's knuckles whiten as they grip the frame, the dim light casting long shadows across his living room. He doesn't blink, doesn't breathe; he only stares at Claire's photograph. Her smile, once a balm to his fractured soul, now cuts deeper than any blade. It is a silent scream to save her from Victor's clutches.

"Arthur," comes a whisper, a gentle stirring in the stagnant air of resignation. Edmund materializes beside him, a wisp of memories embodied in flesh. The old man's deep-set eyes hold centuries of sorrow, yet they are unyielding beacons in the night that has enveloped Arthur's heart.

"Remember who you are," Edmund's voice wraps around him like a warm shawl on a cold night. "Remember your strength."

Beside Edmund, Samuel stands like a shadow of a man, the embodiment of Arthur's own trepidation. His frailty is palpable, his presence a mirror to the fragility lurking within Arthur's resolve.

"Your mission," Edmund continues, steady as a lighthouse in raging seas, "is a candle in this darkness. Hold it high, Arthur. For Claire."

Arthur nods, the photograph quivering in his grasp. Claire's eyes implore him, and through the veil of his fears, he sees not just her image but their shared past, the love entangled with pain, the life that hangs in the balance. He must confront Victor, not just for

Claire, but for himself—for the man he was, the man he could still become.

The silence stretches between them, binding them in shared purpose. Arthur feels it, the weight of his decision anchoring him, yet also propelling him forward. Edmund's wisdom, Samuel's quiet empathy—they are the twin pillars upon which he must build his courage.

"Time to end this," he murmurs, more to himself than to his spectral companions. A resolve, hard and sharp, carves itself into his heart. He will save Claire. He will reclaim his stolen future. There is no other path left to tread.

Shadows cling to the corners of the room like specters, whispering Arthur's doubts back to him in Victor's voice—calm, cold, relentless. They coil around his thoughts, a sinister serenade that syncs with the erratic thrumming of his heart. Arthur's eyes, once fixed on Claire's photograph, now dart around the dimly lit living room as if seeking an escape from the darkness within.

"Failure," the shadows hiss, their words slithering through his mind. "Despair."

But there is Edmund, his presence a bastion against the encroaching gloom. His reassuring words are a lifeline, a beacon in the churning sea of Arthur's fears. And Samuel, though a reflection of Arthur's own vulnerabilities, stands resolute beside him—a silent testament to shared human frailty and the strength it can foster.

"Strength," murmurs Edmund, his voice a counter-melody to Victor's discordant tune.

"Courage," echoes Samuel, a whisper barely heard above the din of Arthur's racing thoughts.

The battle rages within, a tempest unseen yet felt in every quivering sinew of Arthur's being. Fear tugs at him, but so does hope—faint, yet unyielding. It flickers, a candle in the dark, its light fragile but tenacious, nurtured by the gentle wisdom of Edmund and the quiet empathy of Samuel.

"Enough, Victor!" The word bursts from Arthur, slicing through the cacophony. He surges to his feet, fists unclenching only to drive into the fabric of his pants. Every line of his body becomes a testament to defiance, his posture straightening as if to bear the full weight of his resolve.

"Victor," he declares, voice a steely blade forged in the fires of determination, "I face you now."

In that moment, Arthur's fractured psyche stitches itself together, thread by thread, a tapestry of courage woven from the very essence of his terror. The room seems to hold its breath, the shadows drawing back as if startled by the intensity of his conviction.

"Today," he continues, each word a drumbeat, "I reclaim what's mine."

The air crackles with the power of his proclamation, the promise of a storm about to break. In the stillness that follows, Arthur's resolve does not waver. His journey forward is etched into the lines of his face, a road map charted by unwavering purpose.

Arthur paces the dim confines of his living room, each step a silent drumbeat against the floorboards. His mind, a maelstrom of thought and strategy, searches through the chaos for a plan - a lifeline to pull Claire from the depths of Victor's clutches.

"Think, Arthur," he murmurs to himself, the words barely escaping his lips.

Edmund's voice, a gentle current in the tumultuous sea of Arthur's mind, breaks through. "You have the cunning, my boy. Recall the chess games we'd play, how you cornered me time and again."

"Use that intellect," Samuel adds, his whisper soft but carrying weight. It's a ripple on still water, the touch of reassurance needed to focus Arthur's swirling thoughts.

"Distraction," Arthur says with newfound clarity. "We'll need a distraction. Something to draw Victor's attention."

"Create an illusion of sorts," Edmund suggests, nodding approvingly.

"Anonymity is your ally," Samuel chimes in, his eyes darting as though expecting shadows to leap at them. "Move unseen, unnoticed."

"Right." Arthur nods, his plan taking shape like a puzzle coming together piece by elusive piece. "Then I go in, quiet as a shadow."

"Remember, you're not alone," Edmund reminds him, the warmth in his voice a stark contrast to the cold dread lurking in Arthur's heart.

"Never alone," Samuel repeats, an echo fading into the corners of the room.

Arthur draws a deep breath, lets it out slowly, steadying the tremor in his hands. He turns toward the door, his resolve hardening with each step. The apartment door clicks shut behind him, a soft punctuation to the decision that now propels him forward.

Outside, the city thrives in its ceaseless rhythm, a living entity oblivious to the storm brewing within one man's soul. The clamor of traffic, the hum of conversation, the cacophony of urban life - it all swirls around Arthur as he moves through the streets, a ghost among the living.

His gaze cuts through the crowd, unseeing. People pass him in blurs of color and motion, their faces distorted by the speed of his passage. The city's pulse throbs underfoot, a drumbeat out of sync with his own racing heart.

The air is thick with the scent of exhaust and the promise of rain, a heavy blanket over the sensory overload. But Arthur's focus is laser-sharp, every fiber of his being strung tight with the gravity of his mission.

He navigates the concrete maze, a labyrinth designed to trap the unwary. Here, amidst the chaos, Arthur finds his clarity. His purpose fuels him, burning brighter than the neon signs that flicker overhead, casting their artificial glow on the night.

With each determined step, the turmoil within clashes with the world outside. But Arthur is steadfast, a ship cutting through the stormy sea, bound for the heart of darkness where Claire awaits - and where Victor lies in wait.

Feet pound against the sidewalk, a staccato rhythm against the din of passing cars. Arthur's breath comes in ragged gasps, misting in the cool evening air. The city blurs around him, a whirlwind of light and shadow. He weaves through the throng of pedestrians, an urgency propelling him that none can see.

Time is slipping, sand through an hourglass, each grain a second lost. Victor, The Shadow within, whispers with venomous glee, his voice an undercurrent to Arthur's frantic thoughts.

"Too late," he hisses. "You'll always be too late."

Arthur shakes his head, attempting to dislodge the doubts clawing at his resolve. But they cling like ivy, tightening with every step closer to the place where Claire's fate hangs by a thread. His heart drums a relentless cadence, echoing the fear that courses through his veins.

"Focus," he mutters to himself, words slicing through the fog of trepidation. Buildings loom overhead, silent sentinels to his inner turmoil. Streetlights flicker, casting intermittent shadows that dance menacingly on the pavement. The darkness seems alive, reaching for him, whispering promises of despair.

He feels Victor's presence swelling within, a storm cloud ready to burst. The laugh that isn't his own echoes in the recesses of his mind, cruel and mocking. With each echo, the line between them blurs, the distinction between hunter and prey wavering precariously.

"Stop," Arthur commands, the word a lifeline thrown into the churning sea of his consciousness. He will not let Victor win, not when Claire needs him most. Gritting his teeth, he pushes forward, the determination burning in his chest a beacon in the night.

Victor's shadow grows as the destination looms near—a crescendo of malice in the symphony of Arthur's splintered mind. But still, Arthur runs, driven by love, by guilt, by the need to make things right. Each stride is a battle, each breath a war cry.

"Almost there," he reassures himself, though Victor's laughter threatens to drown out his own thoughts. The building appears, an ominous silhouette against the darkening sky. It is here, at the precipice of confrontation, that Arthur must gather the shards of his courage, steeling himself for what lies ahead.

"Quiet, Victor," Arthur whispers, a silent plea for reprieve. Victor's influence recedes, but it's only the calm before the storm, the quiet taunt before the onslaught.

Arthur slows, his steps now measured, deliberate. The final approach is a tightrope walk between his own fractured being and the abyss that beckons below. As he nears the threshold, the weight of what awaits constricts around his heart, yet he moves inexorably forward, towards the reckoning, towards Claire.

Arthur's heartbeat thunders, a drum roll to the macabre dance of shadows that twist around the derelict building's facade. The place reeks of forgotten stories, windows like blind eyes staring into nothingness. Time here moves differently—slower, thicker—the air heavy with the scent of decay and the residue of fear.

He stands at the threshold, a mannequin of resolve sculpted by necessity. The night clings to him, the darkness attempting to seep through the pores of his skin, whispering Victor's name with every gust that rustles the skeletal branches overhead. A shiver courses down Arthur's spine; it's not the cold—it's anticipation, a prelude to the horrors that await.

With each step inside, the building seems to exhale, dust specks dancing in the scant light that filters through broken windows. Arthur's breath is a silver mist, his presence an intrusion on the silence that has claimed this forsaken place. The echoes of his footsteps are the only conversation, a staccato rhythm that speaks to the urgency pulsing through his veins.

The corridor stretches before him, a gaping black hole that's eager to swallow the last fragments of hope he clutches. He can feel Victor's essence woven into the very fabric of these walls, a malignant tapestry that tells tales of torment. Arthur's eyes scan the darkness, searching for the unseen, knowing he is not alone in his quest or his madness.

He moves with a caution born from both instinct and the intimate knowledge of his own fractured mind. Each shadow could be a sentinel, each creak a warning. The air is thick with the power of unspoken threats, and the weight of his purpose anchors him against the current of doubt trying to drag him under.

The corridor unfurls like a tongue of darkness, beckoning him deeper, promising secrets and sorrow entwined. Arthur's hand brushes against the peeling paint of the walls, the tactile memory of decay grounding him to the moment. His senses are sharpened to a razor's edge, slicing through the gloom as he traverses the path laid out by destiny—or perhaps by delusion.

This is no mere building; it is a labyrinth designed by a mind as twisted as his own. And somewhere within, Claire waits, her fate a flickering candle in the tempest of Arthur's resolve. He must find her, must save her, before the darkness claims them both.

Corridor narrows. Arthur's breath hitches – a sound swallowed by the oppressive silence. Ahead, a sliver of light cuts through the darkness; the doorway to Claire's prison beckons. Its frame is crooked, the door itself slightly ajar as if left carelessly open. He inches closer, each step deliberate, controlled.

Muffled sounds. Whispers? Sobs? His heart thrums a frenetic rhythm against his ribs, threatening to burst forth and announce his presence to whatever horror lies beyond. Eyes fixate on the gap in the door, imagination churning with possibilities, with nightmares.

Arthur pauses, just feet away. Sweat beads at his brow, trickles down his spine. Fear claws at him, sharp and insistent, but he swats it away like an irksome fly. He's made of sterner stuff – has to be. For Claire.

Hand trembles. Reaches. Falters. Determination wins. He nudges the door with the ghost of a touch, heart racing, blood roaring in his ears. It swings open wider, a low groan of hinges echoing like a mournful dirge.

Inside, darkness clings to every surface, shrouding the room in secrets. A hazy figure looms in the gloom, back turned, an unmistakable aura of menace radiating from its stillness. Victor. The Shadow incarnate within Arthur's fractured reality.

"Hello, Arthur."

The voice slices through the quiet, familiar and chilling in its calmness. Arthur's pulse quickens, his resolve turning to steel. He steps forward, crossing the threshold into the lion's den.

"Where is she?"

A ghostly Victor turns slowly toward the mirrors to meet Arthur's eyes, the glint of malice in his eyes a match for the cold smile playing on his lips. The fight for control of Arthur's physical body rages inside.

"Close, Arthur. Very close." The air between them crackles with tension, pregnant with unspoken threats.

Arthur's gaze flickers around the room, searching for Claire. Heart pounding. Mind racing. He can feel her – knows she's here, somewhere in the shadows, her fate hanging by a thread.

"Show me," he demands, voice steadier than he feels.

A chuckle, dark and derisive. Victor steps aside, and there, in the corner, a figure bound and slumped – Claire. Her face obscured, her stillness terrifying.

"Time to make a choice, Arthur," Victor taunts, the words a venomous whisper.

Arthur's world narrows to this moment, this decision. Save Claire or succumb to the darkness that is Victor. His hand clenches at his side, ready, resolute.

He takes a step towards her, but before he can reach her, the room plunges into blackness. An abyss opens beneath his feet, swallowing all light, all hope.

"Let the games begin."

Door slams shut behind him. Sound of a lock clicking into place. Arthur stands alone with his tormentor and the love he must save – or lose forever.

And then, nothing but the sound of his own breathing and the beating of his heart, loud in the consuming silence.

Chapter 20

D r. Turner sits alone in the muted glow of her desk lamp, the rest of the office drowned in shadows. Sheets of paper sprawl across the mahogany surface, each one a fragment of Arthur Hall's tormented psyche. She leans forward, the bridge of her glasses perched precariously on the tip of her nose as she pores over the meticulous notes and reports that chronicle the quiet man with the tumultuous mind.

Outside, the city hums with indifference, but within these four walls, the air is thick with the weight of responsibility. Dr. Turner's fingers trace the lines of text, each sentence a thread in the complex tapestry of Arthur's condition. Dissociative Identity Disorder—words that declare a battlefield within one's own flesh and blood.

Her eyes, sharp and discerning, fixate on a particular study, a therapy technique buried deep within the archives of psychiatric research, now resurrected by her unwavering resolve. It is untested, unconventional—a beacon of hope in the perpetual fog that shrouds Arthur's consciousness.

She sits back, the chair creaking under the shift of her weight, and she permits herself a moment's pause. Her thoughts are a tempest of possibilities and uncertainties, yet her determination stands as a lighthouse amidst the storm. Elaine Turner has never been one to shy away from the precipice of innovation, especially not when a patient like Arthur stands at the edge.

The clock ticks, a steady rhythm countering the chaotic pulse of doubt that threatens to rise within her. She runs a hand through her brown hair, now freed from its usual restraints, a rare concession to the late hour.

"Arthur deserves this chance," she whispers into the stillness, her voice both a vow and a battle cry. The technique could be his salvation or his undoing, but stagnation is no longer an option—not on her watch.

Dr. Turner reaches for the phone, hesitating only for a heartbeat before dialing Arthur's number. He needs to hear about this; he needs to make the choice. And whatever decision he makes, she will stand with him, guiding him through the darkness, one fragile step at a time.

The office is a shadowed cocoon as Dr. Turner leans over the scattered papers, each one bearing witness to Arthur's fractured existence. The dim glow of her desk lamp pools on the latest addition to her arsenal—a dossier outlining a therapy that whispers promises of unity where there is division.

"Integration Therapy," she murmurs, the words tasting like a secret elixir on her tongue. The technique is experimental, a dance along the razor-thin line between breakthrough and breakdown. Its potential hums through her, an electric current charged with hope. Combining exposure therapy with advanced hypnotherapy, it aims to weave the disparate threads of Arthur's psyche into a single tapestry of self.

In the quiet of the room, she imagines Arthur sitting before her, his tired eyes searching for solace in a world that doesn't understand his internal chaos. The new therapy could be the compass that guides him out of the labyrinth of his mind. It beckons with the possibility of harmony, where now there are discordant voices clamoring for dominion.

"Imagine," she speaks to the emptiness, envisioning Arthur's personas converging into a symphony rather than a cacophony, "a life where you wake up knowing who you are, every day." The benefit is clear—a sense of wholeness that Arthur has been denied, a peace that could douse the flames of conflict raging within him.

Dr. Turner envisions the man Arthur could become stable, serene, sovereign over his own thoughts and actions. No longer a vessel tossed by the stormy seas of his disorder, but the captain steering through still waters. Her heart thrums with the weight of this vision, the gravity of a soul reclaimed from the shadows.

She slides her fingers across the paper, tracing the outlines of this fragile hope—a hope that carries the scent of dawn after an endless night. Arthur's journey, fraught with turmoil, could find its respite in this uncharted territory.

"Arthur," she whispers, as though he might hear her conviction through the walls of his own mind, "there's a path through the darkness."

And in the stillness of her office, surrounded by the silent sentinels of books and case files, Dr. Elaine Turner feels the stirrings of a future where the shattered pieces of a man named Arthur Hall might finally come together to form a whole. She clings to this vision, a beacon in the psychological thriller that is their intertwined narrative—a narrative poised on the cusp of transformation.

Dr. Turner's finger halts its hopeful trajectory across the research paper, lingering on a paragraph that chills her optimism like a shadow creeping over warm sunlight. The words on the page outline the potential perils of the experimental therapy with clinical coldness—a stark contrast to the warmth with which she just envisioned Arthur's recovery. The possibility of further fracturing his already fragile psyche looms large, a specter of unintended consequences that could shatter rather than consolidate.

She lets out a measured breath, the air escaping her lips as though it carries the weight of this heavy realization. The room around her feels colder now, her office a sanctuary turned mausoleum for the hope that might soon be interred within these walls. The risks are not mere footnotes; they scream from the page, demanding attention.

"Integration or disintegration," she murmurs to herself, the words slicing through the silence of her office. It's a gamble with stakes higher than she's ever placed on the table before. To destabilize Arthur's mind is to potentially unleash chaos where there was once merely disorder, to invite a tempest that could sweep away the semblance of control he clutches in his unassuming hands.

Her eyes, so often a lighthouse for lost minds at sea, now flicker with uncertainty. What if this new approach rips open wounds too deep to mend? What if the darkness within Arthur, once disturbed, proves too vast and voracious to contain? She has always been his steadfast guide, but now she fears becoming an inadvertent agent of his undoing.

The ethical dilemma coils around her like a serpent, squeezing the certainty from her resolve. She has sworn to do no harm, yet every therapeutic venture courts harm's shadow. Dr. Turner leans back in her chair, feeling the leather contour to the tension knotted in her shoulders. Her duty to Arthur's well-being is a beacon that has guided her through many a stormy case, but never before has the path been so obscured by fog.

"Arthur deserves more," she whispers, her voice a blend of determination and dread. He is a man haunted by inner multiplicities, a labyrinthine mind where resides both his torment and his salvation. And she, with a hand poised over this Pandora's box of therapy, hesitates—not out of fear for herself, but for the man who might either emerge into light or sink deeper into the abyss.

There is no chart for these treacherous waters, no map drawn to navigate the human psyche's most hidden straits. Dr. Elaine Turner knows this, yet it is the very uncharted nature of the journey that calls to her healer's heart. But can she, in good conscience, set sail toward a horizon that promises dawn but may deliver dusk?

"Help or harm," she repeats, the decision snaking through her with all the gravity of fate. The shadows in her office seem to press closer, listening, as if the very walls are urging her to choose.

ARTHUR SITS ACROSS from Dr. Turner, his fingers laced together tightly in his lap. The room is silent except for the soft hum of the air conditioning and the distant murmur of the city beyond the window. Shadows cling to the corners of the office, as if mirroring the dark recesses of his mind.

"Arthur," Dr. Turner begins, her voice a gentle intrusion into the stillness, "I've been researching an experimental therapy that I believe has potential for your situation." She slides a folder across the desk, its contents brimming with clinical trials and case studies.

His eyes, tired and wary, flit over the documents without truly seeing them. He feels like he's standing on the precipice of an abyss, peering into an unknown that whispers promises of salvation or madness.

"The technique involves integrating your fragmented personalities," she continues, her tone meticulously balanced between hope and caution. "If successful, it could bring a sense of wholeness to your psyche, perhaps quieting the internal conflicts you've been enduring."

Arthur's breath catches. Wholeness. The word echoes in his mind like a bell tolling in a desolate church. He imagines a life where he is not constantly wrestling with the specters of his other selves, where peace is not just a fleeting visitor in his chaotic existence.

"However," Dr. Turner adds, drawing his attention back to the present, "the risks are significant. The process might destabilize your mental state even further. There's a chance it could trigger more acute dissociations."

A cold shiver runs down Arthur's spine. His hands tremble slightly, betraying the fear he fights to keep at bay. To delve into the therapy is to dance with the darkness within, to confront the fractured parts of himself he's spent a lifetime trying to silence.

"Am I... am I going to lose myself entirely?" Arthur's voice is a whisper, barely disturbing the charged air between them. His question hangs there, a fragile thread suspending him above the chasm of his doubts.

Dr. Turner leans forward, her expression earnest, her eyes radiating a conviction that seems almost tangible. "There's always a risk, Arthur. But you won't face it alone. I'll be with you every step of this journey."

He nods, though the gesture is automatic, hollow. The heaviness in his chest doesn't lift; it's anchored there by years of living in the shadowy nooks of his mind. The prospect of freedom is alluring, intoxicating even, but the price—the potential unraveling of the very fabric of his being—is terrifying.

"Take your time," Dr. Turner says softly, giving him the space to wrestle with his fears, to weigh the scales of potential against peril.

As the session draws to a close, Arthur stands, feeling like a man adrift. He thanks Dr. Turner with a polite smile that never reaches his eyes. They are pools of trepidation, reflecting a soul caught in the throes of indecision.

"Thank you, Doctor," he murmurs, his words a ghostly exhale in the dim light.

"Of course, Arthur. We'll talk again soon," she replies, her assurance lingering in the air as he steps out of the office and into the corridor, where shadows stretch long, and the flicker of fluorescent lights does little to dispel the growing dusk of his thoughts.

DAYS LATER, ARTHUR shuffles down the sterile hallway, the echo of his footfalls a staccato rhythm against the silence. Beside him, Dr. Turner matches his pace, her presence a steady beacon.

"Remember," she says, her voice a soft undercurrent against the hum of the overhead lights, "this is about taking control back. Your life, your mind, your physical body—it all belongs to you."

He looks at her, his eyes strained. The words are meant to reassure, but they're weak—like trying to patch a dam that's already breaking apart.

"Control," he repeats, tasting the word, feeling it unfamiliar and jagged on his tongue. It's a concept that dances just out of reach, a specter in the fog of his consciousness.

Dr. Turner stops by the doorway, her hand resting lightly on his arm. "I know it's daunting, Arthur. But I've seen what you're capable of—you're stronger than you give yourself credit for."

Is he? The question spirals through his mind, twining with doubts and what-ifs. Strength is knowing oneself, isn't it? And who is Arthur Hall if not a collection of strangers housed within one flesh?

"Strength isn't the absence of fear," Dr. Turner continues, as if reading his unspoken thoughts. "It's facing it head-on, even when every instinct tells you to run."

Run. The word resonates, a siren call to the parts of him that want nothing more than to flee from the dark corners of his psyche, where his other selves lurk and whisper.

"Think of it this way," she adds, her voice a firm anchor in the tumult of his fears. "This therapy could be a lighthouse guiding you through the storm. And I'll be there, right beside you."

A lighthouse. A guide. A promise of safe harbor or a warning of rocks beneath the surface? The metaphor hangs between them, and for a moment, he allows himself the luxury of hope.

But doubt is a persistent companion, a shadow that clings no matter how bright the light. What if this therapy is just another false dawn, a fleeting respite before the darkness descends once more?

"Arthur?" Her inquiry is gentle, pulling him back from the precipice of his ruminations.

He meets her gaze, and something in the earnest tilt of her brow steadies him. She believes in him—believes in the possibility of a life reclaimed from the chaos.

"Okay," he whispers, the word a fragile vessel for his tentative trust. "Let's do it."

"Good." Dr. Turner's smile is warm, an ember in the gathering gloom. "We'll take it one step at a time."

One step at a time. He holds onto those words as he crosses the threshold back into her office, a place that has become both sanctuary and battleground. And as the door clicks shut behind them, sealing away the world for now, Arthur braces himself for the journey ahead, each heartbeat a drum roll of courage and fear entwined.

Arthur's hand trembles as it hovers over the consent form, the pen an unwieldy anchor in his grasp. Ink poised to pierce paper, a commitment etched in black and white—a pledge to chase the ghost of wholeness that has eluded him for so long.

"Are you ready?" Dr. Turner asks, her voice a silken thread in the dimly lit office.

He nods, the gesture barely perceptible. The room is dense with the weight of his decision, the air thick with the scent of musty books and the faintest trace of lavender from Dr. Turner's perfume. It's grounding, and he clings to the sensory anchors, aware that they might soon be the buoys in a tempest-tossed sea.

"Remember, Arthur," she says, and he can feel the gravity of her gaze, "whatever happens, you're not alone."

That assurance is a quiet force, holding back the tide of panic rising within him. He scrawls his name across the line, the letters shaky but resolute. The pen clatters onto the desk, its job done. Arthur feels the finality of the act; there's no turning back now.

The silence that follows is suffused with the enormity of his choice. His heartbeat thunders, a cacophony against the stillness, each pulse thrumming with the potential of a life reclaimed—or a mind further fractured.

"Good," Dr. Turner says, collecting the papers with an efficiency that belies the tremor in her hands. They both feel the precipice at their feet, the abyss that awaits.

"Victor won't like this," Arthur murmurs, voicing the dread that coils in his stomach.

"Victor," she acknowledges, speaking the name as one would address a known adversary, "will have to understand that this is for your greater good."

But Victor, The Shadow, thrives in the spaces between certainties, where fear blossoms and doubt takes root. He is the question mark at the end of every hopeful statement, the lurking threat that promises chaos.

As Dr. Turner schedules their next appointment—the first step on this treacherous path—Arthur imagines Victor's icy glare, the calculating menace behind eyes that mirror his own yet reveal nothing of his soul.

"Next week, we begin," Dr. Turner confirms, snapping the agenda book shut. Her words are a gentle push forward, even as Arthur's mind teeters between hope and despair.

"Next week," he echoes, the words falling into a chasm of what-ifs.

They stand together, patient and doctor, two figures cast in the half-light of a setting sun that streams through the blinds. Dusk is settling, painting the world in shades of gray, and in the encroaching shadows, Arthur senses Victor's presence, biding his time, waiting for the perfect moment to strike.

"Take care, Arthur. We'll face whatever comes," Dr. Turner assures him, her conviction a beacon against the impending darkness.

"Thank you," he manages to say, though gratitude feels like a feeble weapon against the specter of his other self.

As he steps out into the waning light, the corridor stretches before him—a liminal space, echoing with the footsteps of decisions past and the whispers of futures uncertain. The door closes with a soft click, a period at the end of a sentence yet unfinished.

Arthur walks away, the echo of his movements a counterpoint to the silent chorus of his fragmented selves. In the recesses of his mind, he hears Victor's derisive laughter, a harbinger of the battle to come. A shiver courses through him, anticipation and uncertainty entwined like strands of DNA, inseparable and defining.

The die is cast. The stage is set. And the curtain rises on a scene fraught with peril and promise—a confrontation with The Shadow that could mend or forever mar the edges of his splintered psyche.

Chapter 21

The phone trembles in Arthur's grip, his thumb hovering over the 'call' button with a hesitant dance. It's late, shadows pooling in the corners of his sparsely furnished apartment like dark secrets. The act of reaching out churns his insides, but he presses down, and the line trills its high-pitched song of impending connection.

"Hello?," comes the soft answer on the third ring. A voice that's seen too much yet refuses to look away.

"Lisa," Arthur says after another sequence of rings, this time reaching a softer, steadying presence.

"Arthur?" Lisa's concern threads through the line, weaving a tapestry of empathy and professionalism.

"Need you both, you and Detective Lawson." he manages, his voice a strained whisper clawing past the tightness in his throat. "My place. As soon as possible." He doesn't wait for their confirmation; the click sounds louder than he intends, a full stop in the dead of night.

Minutes drag themselves out like hours, each second a separate entity that Arthur feels pass through him. And then they're there—the knock at his door, solid and demanding.

Lawson arrives first, his frame filling the doorway, a silhouette chiseled from the night itself. His piercing blue eyes scan the room before they settle on Arthur, reading every unspoken word etched into his weary face.

"Arthur," Lawson greets, voice low but carrying an undercurrent of urgency that matches the racing of Arthur's heart.

Lisa steps in behind Lawson, her presence a balm to the raw edges of the room. Her warm brown eyes seek out Arthur's, offering silent reassurance even as her brows knit together in concern.

"Talk to us, Arthur," she urges, her tone coaxing out the words he dreads to speak.

The living room is dimly lit, the light bulbs above casting more shadows than illumination. Arthur's gaze flits to the closed curtains, to the digital clock blinking an ungodly hour, to the two figures who've stepped into his fractured world ready to piece together a plan from the shards he offers.

"Thanks for coming," he starts, fingers finding solace in the frayed edges of his sleeves. His guests simply nod, their faces a pair of stoic masks carved with determination. They are here for him—for Claire—and that thought alone propels him forward into the abyss.

Arthur paces, each step a sharp echo in the dimly lit room. His voice, when it breaks the silence, is a river swollen with the rains of desperation and conviction.

"Victor has her, and every second we waste, Claire's chances of returning grow slimmer," he says, his words tumbling over each other like pebbles in an avalanche. The shadows seem to lean in closer as he speaks, as if hungry for the fear in his voice. "We're not just fighting a man; we're up against the darkest part of my own psyche. He knows what I know, fears what I fear."

Lawson stands still, a firm counterpoint to Arthur's restless energy. His eyes, narrow and intense, fixate on Arthur, absorbing the gravity of the situation through the lens of a seasoned detective. The air between them crackles with unspoken resolve.

"Arthur," Lawson responds, his voice the calm in the storm, "you have our full support. We'll confront Victor together and get Claire back." It's a simple statement, but it carries the weight of an oath, solidifying the bond of their shared mission.

The apartment feels like a stage set for a play too real, the curtains drawn against the prying eyes of the world outside. Here, they are cocooned by the urgency of their purpose, by the knowledge that the darkness they face is born from within as much as without.

Lisa steps forward, a solitary figure of serenity amidst the tumult of Arthur's living room. Her presence is a soothing balm to the crackling tension that permeates the air. The lamp light softens her features as she places a hand on Arthur's shoulder, grounding him back to the moment.

"Arthur," she says, her voice a steady stream flowing over jagged rocks, "you've always been stronger than you realize. Your resilience has brought you this far; it will carry you through this too." Her eyes, warm and earnest, lock onto his, willing him to believe her words.

Arthur's hands betray the turmoil within, a slight tremor coursing through his fingers like the aftershocks of a distant quake. He glances down at them, then back up at Lisa, finding an anchor in her calm gaze.

"Victor thinks he's buried himself away where only darkness can reach," Arthur begins, the edges of his voice frayed with unease. "But... but I know the pathways of my own mind better than anyone. Even his."

He pauses, takes a breath that seems to dredge up courage from the depths of his being. "I've pieced together the fragments, followed the breadcrumbs of memory and fear. It's led me to a place—a hideout—that only someone like Victor would consider safe."

The apartment's walls close in, cloaked in shadows that seem to absorb his every word. Arthur's gaze drifts, unfocused, as if peering into the labyrinthine corridors of his fractured psyche, searching for the thread that will lead them to Claire... and to Victor. His whisper is almost lost amid the silence that follows, heavy with the weight of what he must do.

"We'll find him there. I'm certain of it."

Shadows creep along the walls of Arthur's apartment as he stands resolute in the center of his dimly lit living room. The tension is a tangible shroud that clings to every surface, every breath. Lawson's eyes, sharp and unyielding, lock onto Arthur, igniting the space between them with urgency.

"Arthur," Lawson says, his voice low, a weapon forged from years on the force. "We need to coordinate with the police for this. It will give us the best shot at getting Claire back safely."

The words hang heavy, like an omen. The detective's posture is all business, his gaze not just suggesting but insisting on the involvement of the law.

Arthur's jaw clenches, muscles taut with a cocktail of fear and resolve. He knows Lawson is right; this isn't a chapter ripped from the paperback thrillers that line his bookshelf. Yet, surrendering full control feels akin to relinquishing a part of his soul.

"Okay," Arthur concedes, voice steady despite the storm brewing within. "Get the police involved. But I'm going in with you. Victor... he's a byproduct of my own mind's chaos—I can navigate that darkness."

Lawson studies Arthur, the gears behind those piercing blue eyes turning over each implication, each possible outcome. The detective nods, a silent pact forming between them. This operation has become a collision of two worlds: one governed by the rigid laws of justice, the other by the fluid and treacherous currents of the psyche.

"Alright," Lawson agrees, his tone leaving no room for argument. "You have insights we'll need. But remember, we're there to keep you—and Claire—out of harm's way."

Arthur's nod is almost imperceptible, his gaze fixed on some distant point only he can see. His mind teeters on the brink, peering into the abyss that is Victor's domain. In this grim tableau, Arthur stands as both the guide and the guided, his fragmented self the map they must follow into the heart of darkness.

The dim light flickers across the room, casting long shadows that dance along the walls like specters. Arthur watches, his heart a drumbeat in his chest, as Lawson steps forward, the very embodiment of control amidst chaos.

"Lisa, you'll be our anchor," Lawson's voice cuts through the tension, authoritative and unyielding. His eyes are sharp, scanning the room, taking measure of every detail. "You know Arthur's psyche better than anyone. Stay with him, keep him grounded."

Lisa nods, her presence a balm to the jittery nerves in the room. She moves closer to Arthur, her gaze locking onto his. "Arthur, I'm here," she says, her voice a gentle lull against the storm brewing inside him. "Every step of the way. We'll face the darkness together."

"Good," Lawson continues, pacing now, each step deliberate. "I'll lead the tactical side. Coordination with the police will be crucial. We need precision, no room for error." He turns, fixing Arthur with a look that's both stern and protective. "And Arthur, you're the key. You guide us through your mind's labyrinth."

Arthur feels the weight of their stares, heavy with trust and expectation. Lisa's hand finds his, a lifeline in the swirling uncertainty. Her touch is steady, reassuring.

"Remember, we're a team," Lisa's voice soothes the ragged edges of his anxiety. He focuses on the warmth of her hand, the fortifying cadence of her words. "Your strength is ours to share."

As Lawson continues to orchestrate their plan, motion and intent weaving into a tight tapestry, Arthur clings to Lisa's calm assurance. With her by his side, he dares to hope they can illuminate the dark recesses of his mind and bring Claire back from Victor's sinister grasp.

Arthur steps away from the comforting circle, his movements precise. His fingers brush over the array of tools laid out on the kitchen table—a signal jammer, a set of lock picks, lightweight Kevlar vests, and an assortment of non-lethal weaponry. Each item holds the promise of control, a way to assert power over the chaos Victor has sown.

He selects a vest first, sliding it over his head with a familiarity that belies his trembling hands. The weight settles against his chest, a tangible reminder of the risks ahead. Next, he pockets the jammer, the sleek device cold and heavy with purpose.

"Good choices," Lawson murmurs from behind him, approval lacing his words. Arthur doesn't turn; instead, he focuses on securing a tactical flashlight to his belt. He feels Lawson's gaze on him, assessing, calculating every move.

"Remember, stealth is key," Arthur reminds himself, his voice barely above a whisper. "We can't let Victor know we're coming." The thought sends a shiver down his spine, but the fear doesn't derail him. It fuels him, sharpens his resolve.

"Let's not give him the upper hand," Lawson agrees, stepping forward to inspect the equipment. His fingers hesitate over the lock picks before claiming them, tucking them into his own pocket with a nod of satisfaction.

Lisa watches, her presence a silent anchor in the room. She doesn't need tools or weapons; her strength lies in her empathy, her ability to hold them together when the fabric of reality threatens to tear apart.

"Are we ready?" she asks, her voice steady despite the tension crackling in the air.

Arthur meets her eyes, finds solace in their depths. "As ready as we'll ever be," he replies, the finality in his tone resonating through the room.

Lawson claps him on the shoulder, a gesture of solidarity that cements their unspoken pact. They will do whatever it takes to save Claire, to wrest her from the darkness that's claimed her.

"Time to go," Lawson says, and the command in his voice pulls them into action.

He leads the way, his stride confident, each step a testament to his experience. Arthur follows, the weight of the vest grounding him, the tools at his side empowering him. Lisa brings up the rear, her quiet determination a beacon in the shadowy confines of the apartment.

Together, they step through the threshold, leaving behind the safety of the known for the perilous uncertainty that awaits them outside. Arthur's heart hammers in his chest, each beat a drumbeat marching him toward an inevitable confrontation—one he must face if he's to reclaim the fragmented pieces of his psyche and save the woman he loves from the darkness that is Victor.

The night envelops them as they emerge, a trio of silhouettes etched against the flickering glow of the streetlamps. Arthur's breath steams in the chill air, mingling with the mist that creeps along the pavement, insidious tendrils seeking to entwine around his ankles. His pulse thrums in his ears, a rhythmic reminder of what's at stake.

Lawson moves ahead, his figure a steadfast beacon cutting through the fog. Each step he takes is deliberate, sending soft echoes bouncing off the walls of abandoned buildings. They're moving deeper into the urban labyrinth, into Victor's domain—the heart of the city where shadows reign supreme.

Beside Arthur, Lisa's presence is a constant warmth, her resolve radiating like a shield. She doesn't flinch at the desolation surrounding them; instead, her chin lifts, her eyes sharp and scanning for unseen threats. She's the calm amidst the storm, her composure a contrast to the turmoil that churns within Arthur.

The streets are empty, the silence oppressive, save for the sound of their footsteps—an uneven cadence that punctuates the stillness. It's a march toward destiny, one that Arthur can no longer escape. He knows that with each step forward, he's not just closing the distance to Claire but also to the darkest corners of his own mind.

Streetlights flicker as they pass, casting elongated shadows that dance mockingly at their sides. Arthur feels Victor lurking there, in the interplay of light and dark, watching, waiting, a predator amused by the prey's audacity to challenge him.

He tightens his grip on the bag slung over his shoulder, its contents a collection of hope and desperation. The tools within are more than mere objects; they are keys to unlock the prison holding Claire, and perhaps, the very shackles binding Arthur to Victor's will.

Their footsteps grow louder, more insistent, as if echoing the urgency pounding in Arthur's chest. Lawson gestures to a narrow alleyway up ahead, a shortcut known only to those who've navigated these treacherous streets before. It's a path that leads closer to the confrontation, to the inevitable face-off between Arthur and the Shadow.

Arthur swallows, the taste of fear bitter on his tongue, yet he strides forward. With each step into the darkness, his determination hardens into steel. This is the moment of truth, the point of no return. He's ready to confront the chaos, to fight for Claire's freedom—and his own.

The night hides nothing from them now; it beckons, a siren call to the depths of Arthur's fractured psyche. And together, they walk into the maw, their footsteps a solemn drumbeat fading into the abyss.

Chapter 22

Arthur's breath comes in ragged gasps, the darkness of the room clinging to him like a second skin. He feels the weight of Victor's presence lurking in the shadows, an oppressive force that tightens around his chest until each inhale is a battle. Illuminated only by the faint glow of a single bulb, the contours of the room blur and distort, as if reality itself bends under Victor's will.

Beside him, Dr. Turner's silhouette offers a stark contrast to the suffocating dark. Her voice, a steady beacon in the tumultuous sea of Arthur's mind, cuts through the silence. "You are not alone, Arthur," she reminds him, her words grounding even as his heartbeat threatens to deafen him.

"Focus on what you've achieved," she urges, her tone both gentle and insistent. "Remember your strength, the resilience that has brought you here."

Arthur nods, though the gesture feels mechanical, disconnected from the turmoil inside him. His gaze sweeps the room, searching for a sign of Victor, The Shadow that haunts his every step. But it's not sight that reveals Victor; it's the cold touch of dread that creeps along Arthur's spine, the whisper of malice that seems to echo from the walls themselves.

"Confront him," Dr. Turner says, her hand resting lightly on his shoulder—a lifeline back to the world of the living. "On your terms."

He squares his shoulders, finding fortitude in her touch. The familiarity of the office attire he wears acts as armor, a reminder of the life he fights to reclaim from Victor's chaotic grasp. Arthur closes his eyes and imagines himself standing firm, unyielding against the tide of shadow that seeks to pull him under.

"Victor," he breathes, his voice a soft but resolute declaration. "I'm here."

The silence that follows is dense, charged with expectation. Arthur stands at the precipice, the dim light casting long shadows that dance ominously around him. But he is rooted in place by Dr. Turner's unwavering support, by the knowledge that this confrontation, this moment, could mark the beginning of his emancipation from the darkness within.

Arthur clenches his fists, the faint tremble in his hands a stark contrast to the stillness that surrounds him. A shiver crawls up his spine as Victor's voice slithers into his consciousness, a serpentine hiss of malice that coils around his thoughts.

"Did you really think you could face me, Arthur?" The Shadow's words drip with disdain, echoing against the walls of his mind—a cruel reminder that the enemy he faces is one of his own making. "You're weak. You always have been."

He sucks in a deep breath, feeling the chill of the room seep into his lungs. With each inhalation, he draws strength from the very air that carries Victor's poisonous whispers. His eyes flicker open, reflecting a spark of defiance that wasn't there before.

"No," Arthur replies, his voice steadier than he feels. "I'm not weak. I am more than your lies."

The taunting laughter that answers him is devoid of humor, a cold cascade that seeks to wash away his burgeoning resolve. But Arthur stands unflinching, his inner citadel fortified by Dr. Turner's faith and his own newfound courage.

"Your attempts to control me are nothing but the death throes of your influence," Arthur counters, the words like steel beams reinforcing the structure of his identity. "I am the architect of my existence, not you."

Victor's presence looms larger, a shadow stretching across Arthur's psyche, threatening to engulf him once again. Yet, with every affirmation of his worth, every declaration of his determination, the darkness recedes incrementally, as if dispelled by the light of his conviction.

"Empty words, Arthur," Victor hisses, but there's a tremor now, a crack in the veneer of his omnipotence. "You can't renounce what you are."

"I am not defined by you," Arthur asserts, the truth of his words a beacon in the oppressive gloom. "I define myself."

This mental dialogue, this dance of dominance and defiance, spirals tighter, drawing both entities into an ever-escalating battle of wills. Arthur's heart hammers a rhythm of war drums in his chest, each beat a proclamation of his intent to emerge victorious from the shadows that have shackled him for too long.

Sweat beads on Arthur's brow, his breaths quick and shallow. The room tilts, walls breathing with the pulse of his racing heart. Shadows cling to the corners, whispering Victor's taunts, echoing through the hollows of his mind.

"Pathetic," Victor's voice slithers around him, ethereal yet suffocating. "You think you can defy me?"

Arthur's fingers curl into fists, nails biting into his palms. He focuses on the pain, a lifeline amid the chaos. Victor's influence is a tempest, relentless and fierce, but Arthur is the rock, battered yet unyielding. His thoughts fracture, scatter like shards of glass, each reflecting a fragment of his turmoil.

"Concentrate, Arthur." Dr. Turner's voice slices through the maelstrom, a beacon in the storm. She stands by him, a steady presence in the undulating darkness. "Find that place within you, the eye of the hurricane. Hold onto it."

He nods, though her words feel distant, buffered by the cacophony in his head. But he latches onto her guidance, envisioning a serene lake within his psyche, its surface undisturbed. The visualization becomes a shield, thoughts coalescing into an armor against Victor's barbs.

"Feel the ground beneath your feet," she instructs, anchoring him further. "The solidity of the earth, supporting you."

Arthur obeys, pressing his soles into the floor, grounding himself in the here and now. He imagines roots spreading from his feet, deep into the foundation of the building, tethering him to reality. Dr. Turner's presence is the sunlight nurturing his resolve, empowering him to grow beyond Victor's shadow.

"Your tricks are futile," Arthur murmurs, his voice steadier, bolstered by the image of his inner sanctuary. "I am more than your lies."

"Is that so?" Victor retorts, but the edge of invincibility has dulled. "We shall see."

Dr. Turner places a hand on Arthur's shoulder, a tangible reminder of the support he has in this tangible world. "You are not alone, Arthur. Remember that."

With each grounding technique, each visualization exercise, Arthur feels the tide turning. He is reclaiming the territory of his mind, inch by inch. He knows the battle is far from over, but for the first time, he senses the possibility of victory over the darkness that is Victor.

Arthur's pulse thunders in his ears, a relentless drumbeat as the room around him blurs and warps. Shadows stretch across the walls like grasping fingers, each one a specter of his past reaching out to claim him. His breath comes in ragged gasps, fogging the air with the heat of his panic. Memories unspool before his eyes—a carousel of moments both sweet and sour, spinning ever faster until they bleed together into an indistinct smear.

"Pathetic," Victor's voice slithers through the chaos, the sound wrapping around Arthur's thoughts like a noose. "You sift through ruins, searching for something that was never there."

Arthur clenches his fists, nails digging crescents into his palms. He commands himself to focus, to find the thread of strength amidst the detritus of his mind. The lake from his visualization quivers, disrupted by the tempest Victor conjures, but it does not vanish. It remains, a beacon of tranquility within the maelstrom.

"Strength?" Victor chuckles, the noise a jagged edge against Arthur's resolve. "What strength do you have besides the lies you tell yourself?"

"Enough," Arthur whispers, the single word a shard of glass cutting through the dense fog of doubt. He refuses to let fear take root, to let it blossom into the paralysis Victor craves. He envisions himself standing beside the undisturbed lake once more, the water clear and calm, reflecting his defiance back at him.

"Your resilience is a facade," Victor hisses, pressing closer, unseen yet palpably invasive. "A brittle shell waiting to crack."

"No," Arthur counters, the refusal ringing louder in his own ears than Victor's venomous words. "I am the architect of my thoughts, the sculptor of my reality." He imagines his hands molding the very ether of his consciousness, pushing back the encroaching darkness with sheer force of will.

"Let's see how long your little fantasy lasts," Victor taunts, but his voice has lost some of its certainty, its power waning against Arthur's burgeoning fortitude.

"Long enough," Arthur replies, his voice steady now, a lighthouse standing firm against the stormy onslaught. He feels the solidity of Dr. Turner's hand on his shoulder, grounding him. The roots that tether him to reality grow deeper, more intricate, intertwining with the fabric of his being until they are indistinguishable from one another.

"Your time is over," Arthur declares, and the shadows recoil as if struck. His heart still races, but it is no longer from fear—it beats a rhythm of triumph, a testament to the mind's ability to reclaim itself from the abyss.

Victor's menacing presence recedes, beaten back by Arthur's unwavering gaze and the silent support of an ally who believes in his strength. The victory is not absolute; the war is not won. But in this moment, Arthur stands tall amidst the wreckage of his inner world, a survivor steeled for the battles to come.

Arthur's pulse is a drumbeat in the dim room, echoing off the walls that seem to close in around him. Sweat beads along his hairline, a physical testament to the struggle raging within. Dr. Turner's voice cuts through the cacophony of his thoughts, a beacon guiding him back from the edge.

"Arthur, remember the strides you've made," she urges, her tone firm yet imbued with warmth. "You can see Victor for what he is—a distortion, a lie your mind tells itself."

He nods, feeling the weight of her words settle in his chest. They are an anchor, steadying the tumultuous sea of his emotions. He focuses on them, letting them fill the spaces Victor aims to corrupt.

"Use your insight, Arthur. Stand on the ground you have reclaimed," Dr. Turner continues, her hand a reassuring pressure on his back.

Victor's snarl reverberates in Arthur's skull, trying to claw its way into his beliefs. But Arthur's self-awareness is a shield now, tempered by months of grueling introspection and therapy. For every barb Victor throws, Arthur has a counterpoint, a truth to undermine the lies.

"Enough," Arthur says, and his voice surprises him with its resonance. It carries the weight of all he has endured, all he has learned. "I won't be swayed by your distortions anymore, Victor."

The Shadow falls silent, as if considering this new defiance. Arthur feels the shift, the balance of power teetering on a knife-edge.

"Your logic is flawed," Arthur presses on, his words gaining momentum like a boulder rolling downhill. "Your power is nothing more than smoke—intangible, fleeting. I see through it now."

Dr. Turner's presence is a quiet affirmation of his strength. Arthur draws upon it, weaving her steadfast belief into the fabric of his resolve. Victor's image flickers in the darkness of his mind, less substantial than before.

"Your existence relies on my fear," Arthur continues, each word stripping away layers of Victor's influence. "But fear is a choice—and I choose not to feed you any longer."

There's a visceral sensation, akin to shedding a skin too tight, confining. Arthur senses the tide turning, feels the surge of control returning to him. Victor, The Shadow who once loomed so large, now dwindles in the face of Arthur's reclaimed power.

Dr. Turner's smile is invisible in the gloom, but Arthur feels its effect—warmth spreading through him, a silent ovation for his courage.

"Very good, Arthur," she whispers, her voice barely audible over the still-racing beat of his heart. "Hold onto that strength."

And he does. In the dim room where battles are fought in silence, Arthur holds his ground.

The room pulses with a silent rhythm, each heartbeat a drumbeat in Arthur's ears. He stands, a solitary figure bathed in half-light, the darkness stretching around him like a tangible force. His breaths are steady, controlled—a soldier readying for the final charge.

Victor's voice, once booming and omnipresent, now falters, a crackling radio signal losing its frequency. "Arthur," he sneers, the venom diluted by desperation, "you can't escape me. I am you."

But Arthur feels the shift, the foundation of Victor's control crumbling beneath the weight of his newfound conviction. The Shadow, a mere whisper against the fortress of Arthur's will.

"Victor," Arthur replies, his voice resonating with a clarity that slices through the gloom. "You are but a chapter in my story—and it's time to turn the page."

The air thickens, charged with static as if the very molecules vibrate with the intensity of their confrontation. Arthur pictures the anchors Dr. Turner has taught him—solid and real. He visualizes a chain, each link a memory or a triumph, grounding him in the present, in the truth of his own strength.

"Remember when you thought you could break me?" Arthur taunts back, the words erupting from deep within. "I was reforging myself all along."

The Shadow recoils, a specter wavering on the edge of existence. Arthur senses the falter, the fleeting moment where dominance wanes and vulnerability bleeds through.

"Your threats are hollow," Arthur declares, the crescendo of his determination reverberating off the walls. "Your existence is at my mercy."

He imagines his words as a lance, sharp and true, piercing the heart of the darkness. The lance becomes light, blazing forth to illuminate every corner of the dimly lit room, banishing shadows, leaving nowhere for Victor to hide.

"Enough!" Arthur's shout echoes, a battle cry cutting through the remnants of fear. "I reject you, Victor. You hold no power here."

With that declaration, the illusion shatters, fragments of Victor's dominion scattering like glass across the floor of Arthur's mind. The

Shadow's form buckles, dissolving into nothing more than a wisp of smoke carried away by an unseen wind.

In the stillness that follows, Arthur stands alone, but not isolated. The presence of Dr. Turner lingers—a silent sentinel whose faith never wavered. The echo of victory hums through the room, a symphony of relief and newfound autonomy.

Arthur takes a deep breath, filling his lungs with the clean, sharp air of a battlefield won, his pulse slowing to a steady, triumphant cadence.

Arthur's chest heaves, the air crisp and electric in his lungs. The room is hushed now, the din of mental warfare fading into a tangible quietude. He stands taller than he ever has before, not in stature but in spirit. His shadow stretches across the floor, elongated and still, no longer a battleground for writhing doubts.

The clarity is startling—each thought, once a tangled thread in an intricate web of confusion, now lies orderly, comprehensible. He feels the weight of control solidify in his palms, assurance building with each steady heartbeat. The fractured pieces of his psyche, once scattered and elusive, begin to form a mosaic of self-acceptance. Arthur knows, with a marrow-deep certainty, that he has triumphed over the darkness that is Victor.

"Remarkable," Dr. Turner's voice slices through the calm, not with disturbance but with recognition. "You've shown immense bravery today, Arthur."

He turns to face her, her eyes reflecting back at him the magnitude of what has transpired. She steps forward, her professional facade softened by a genuine smile that crinkles the corners of her eyes.

"Resilience," she continues, her voice a soothing balm. "It's been inside you all along, despite the fractures, despite the shadows. Today, you've made incredible progress."

Her words are more than praise; they're a beacon, illuminating the path ahead—the path towards healing. Dr. Turner's steady gaze holds Arthur's, grounding him further in this newfound reality.

"Victor was a formidable adversary, but he was never your equal. Not truly," she says, her tone imbued with conviction. "Your mind is your own, Arthur. And it's stronger than any specter that tries to lay claim to it."

Arthur nods, absorbing her affirmation. In the silence that follows, the last vestiges of Victor's influence evaporate like mist under the burgeoning light of dawn. Arthur's journey is far from over, yet this victory marks a turning point—an undeniable stride toward wholeness.

"Thank you, Dr. Turner," Arthur whispers, his voice no longer timid but ripe with gratitude and a hint of awe at his own fortitude. "I couldn't have faced him without your guidance."

"Remember this feeling, Arthur," she advises, the depth of her experience as a psychiatrist lending weight to her counsel. "Harness it when the shadows loom again."

As they stand together in the dimly lit room, there's an unspoken acknowledgment that the road to recovery is long and winding. But today, Arthur Hall has reclaimed a piece of himself, and that is a victory to be cherished—one measured breath, one steadfast step at a time.

Arthur's hand trembles as he reaches for the glass of water on the table, the ripples distorting his reflection in the surface. He steadies himself, fingers wrapping firmly around the cool vessel. The water chills his parched throat, grounding him further in the reality of this hard-won moment. His heart still drums a relentless rhythm, but it's no longer a frantic beat—it's the triumphant march of survival.

The room feels different now, less oppressive, as if Victor's shadow has receded from the corners where it once loomed. The dim light casts long, gentle shadows that seem to nod in approval of

Arthur's feat. Even the air tastes sweeter, liberated from the taint of fear.

"Victor," Arthur whispers, testing the name that once held so much power over him. It sounds hollow now, just a string of letters devoid of command. A shiver runs down his spine, not from dread, but from the exhilaration of emancipation. He lets out a slow breath, each exhalation a release of the darkness that Victor embodied.

Dr. Turner observes him, her presence a silent pillar of support. Her eyes don't miss the subtle shift in Arthur's posture, the way his shoulders square and his chin lifts ever so slightly. She knows the war is not over, but this battle—this critical, internal standoff—is won.

Arthur meets her gaze, and in it, he finds a reflection of his own resolve. The triumph swells within him, filling the spaces that Victor once claimed as his own. It's a heady feeling, intoxicating in its potency. Relief cascades through him, washing away the remnants of the struggle that had raged inside his mind.

He is aware, however, that this is but a respite. Victor is diminished, not destroyed. But now, there is a blueprint for resistance, a template for victory that Arthur can summon when the whispers begin anew. The challenges ahead do not diminish his achievement—they fortify it.

"Thank you," he mouths silently to Dr. Turner, knowing she understands the depth of his gratitude better than words could express.

She nods, a subtle dip of her head that speaks volumes. There will be time for more words later. For now, this silence between them is rich with meaning, heavy with the gravity of what has transpired.

Arthur allows himself a final moment to savor the quiet triumph, committing the sensation to memory. Then, with a newfound determination etched into the lines of his face, he turns his attention forward. The path ahead is uncharted, fraught with shadows and doubt, but he steps into it with an unwavering conviction.

Victor, the malevolent specter of his fractured psyche, has been kept at bay. And Arthur, the unassuming man who once felt invisible even to himself, has emerged from the depths, his spirit forged in resilience.

The part of Arthur's life closes not on an end, but a beginning—the start of a journey towards wholeness, one step at a time, with Arthur Hall firmly at the helm.

Chapter 23

The door slams against the wall, its echo slicing through the oppressive silence of the dimly lit room. Arthur's heart races, a relentless drumbeat thundering in his ears as his gaze darts frantically across the shadows that claw at the edges of his vision. The scant light from a solitary bulb fights a losing battle against the darkness, casting more mysteries than illumination.

He steps forward, his breath quick and shallow, each inhale sharp as blades against his lungs. The air tastes stale, heavy with the scent of mildew and something else—something metallic and sinister. His eyes, desperate for a sign of her, finally catch a glint of copper hair, a splash of color in the monochrome gloom.

There she is. Claire.

She's bound to a chair, her slender wrists wrapped in coarse rope that bites into her skin. Her face, once the embodiment of gentle reassurance, now mirrors the terror that churns inside him. Her eyes—wide and brimming with fear—meet his. It's as though her gaze implores him, begs him to undo this nightmare.

Arthur's resolve hardens like ice within his veins. All his fragmented thoughts, the voices that usually jostle for dominance in the recesses of his mind, unite in a singular purpose. Save Claire. Protect her. Nothing else matters.

He lunges toward her, each stride eating up the distance between them. His movements are jerky, uncoordinated, propelled by an adrenaline that ignites his muscles and banishes any semblance of hesitation. The world narrows down to the space he must cross, to the woman who means more to him than the tenuous grasp he holds on his own splintered identity.

"Arthur..." Claire's voice is a whisper, a ghost of sound that somehow cuts through the cacophony of his heartbeat.

"Shh, it's okay. I'm here," he murmurs, though his voice barely sounds like his own—a strained symphony of fear and determination. He reaches her side, his trembling hands hovering over the knots that bind her, ready to tear away the ropes that imprison the only constant in his tumultuous existence.

Victor emerges like a specter from the gloom, his presence slicing through the charged atmosphere. A cruel curvature of his lips betrays amusement, a stark contrast to the gravity of the scene before him. "Oh, Arthur," he purrs, voice smooth as venom, "did you really think it would be this easy?"

The taunt is designed to wound, to burrow under Arthur's skin and unravel his focus. But Arthur, feeling a surge of protective ferocity, locks his gaze on the knots that bind Claire's wrists, his back to Victor. He will not allow this embodiment of his darkest fears to distract him from the purpose burning within.

"Your heroics are touching but futile," Victor continues, circling them like a shark scenting blood in the water. His shadow stretches across the floor, elongating into an ominous silhouette that threatens to engulf the room.

Arthur's fingers work deftly, feeling for the weakness in the bindings. The coarse rope resists, mocking his urgency with its stubborn tangle. Claire's soft whimper pulses in his eardrums, snapping his attention back with razor-sharp focus. With each passing second, his resolve solidifies; he must free her from the chair's cruel embrace.

"Isn't this familiar, Arthur?" Victor's voice slices through the air, laced with malice. "Struggling against the inevitable, always playing the savior. How quaint."

But Arthur hears none of it. His world reduces to the task at hand, to the sensation of the rope giving way beneath his persistent grip. The Shadow's voice fades into obscurity, rendered inconsequential by the need to protect, to deliver Claire from this tangible representation of his internal chaos.

With a sudden surge of motion, Victor's form blurs from the corner of Arthur's eye. The rope slackens for a fraction of a moment before chaos erupts. Victor's body slams into Arthur's side, the impact sending a jolt through his frame. Arthur's pulse hammers in his temples as he whirls to face the attack, his hands raised instinctively to defend.

"Predictable," Victor hisses, his breath a cold whisper against Arthur's ear.

Arthur shoves back with all the force his desperation lends him, the room spinning into a disorienting kaleidoscope of shadows and flickering light. Victor's grip is like iron, but Arthur refuses to be caged by the same fears that have haunted him for years. He lashes out, his fist connecting with Victor's jaw, a solid thud echoing in the confined space.

"Fight all you want," Victor snarls, wiping a trace of blood from his lip with a dark chuckle. "It only makes your defeat sweeter."

They are entangled now, a violent dance of wills, as each seeks to impose their reality upon the other. Arthur feels the fabric of his shirt tear under Victor's grasp, the sound tearing through the thick air. His own hands grapple for purchase, finding Victor's throat, squeezing with an intensity born of raw survival instinct.

Victor retaliates, knee driving up into Arthur's abdomen. A grunt escapes Arthur's lips as the air is forced from his lungs. But he does not relent; he cannot. Images of Claire, bound and frightened, flash before his eyes, fueling his resolve.

The room itself seems to recoil from the ferocity of their struggle. Objects become casualties in their war, a chair overturning, a lamp crashing to the ground with the sound of shattering glass. Each blow Arthur lands is a declaration, a refusal to surrender the territory of his mind to this usurper, this embodiment of his darkest self.

"Give in, Arthur," Victor growls, but his voice lacks its usual conviction. There's a tremor of uncertainty that wasn't there before, a crack in the façade.

Arthur hears it, seizes on it, allowing it to echo within his fractured psyche. This struggle is more than physical; it is the manifestation of Arthur's endless fight for control over his own thoughts, his own actions — against the Shadow that seeks to engulf him.

"Never," Arthur gasps out, pushing Victor back with renewed vigor. They crash against the wall, a picture frame shattering above them, shards of glass raining down like bitter snowflakes.

For a fleeting second, their eyes lock, and Arthur sees something in Victor's gaze — a reflection of his own fear, his own humanity. It is this glimpse that strengthens his arm, guides his hand, as he grasps for anything to tip the balance.

Their battle has no audience, no cheers or jeers; just two versions of the same tormented soul, locked in a relentless clash that can have only one victor. And despite the pain that racks his body and threatens to splinter his mind, Arthur fights on, because surrender is not an option when so much is at stake.

Arthur's knuckles whiten as he clutches at the air, grappling with Victor's spectral form. He staggers, his breath sharp in his chest, each gasp a battle cry from his beleaguered spirit. The room spins, a carousel of shadows and despair, but Arthur's resolve is a beacon, unwavering amidst the tempest.

"Edmund," he pleads silently, invoking the wisdom of ages past, "guide my hand, steady my heart."

A whisper, like leaves rustling in a forgotten grove, fills his senses. Edmund's voice, a gentle stream of fortitude, trickles into his consciousness. "Remember the resilience of the oak, Arthur," it soothes. "Roots deep within the earth, branches reaching for the sky."

Emboldened by the counsel of antiquity, Arthur shifts, ducking under a malicious swipe from Victor. His movements are an echo of a bygone dance, each step measured, each turn deliberate. He is not merely surviving; he is an embodiment of endurance, a testament to the enduring human spirit.

"Samuel," Arthur beckons now, seeking the quiet strength that lingers in the shadows. "Lend me your caution, your insight."

The response is a shiver down his spine, the soft touch of Samuel's presence, fragile yet fierce in its own right. "Listen to the silence between the beats of your heart," Samuel's voice trembles through him. "In that stillness, you will find your way."

Victor's laughter slices through the air, a razor against the fabric of Arthur's reality. The attacks escalate, each blow more savage than the last, a crescendo of cruelty aimed at tearing down the ramparts of Arthur's mind. But the fortress stands strong. Each cruel word, every insidious doubt cast by Victor, crashes against the bulwark of Arthur's soul and dissolves into nothing.

"Is that all you have?" Arthur taunts back, his words a mere whisper but laden with defiance. He dances away from another strike, sidestepping not just the physical threat but also the psychological barbs that come with it.

"Your tricks won't work on me anymore. I see through your lies, Victor." Arthur's gaze is steel, his posture a monument to the internal allies that uphold him.

Victor snarls, his form blurring at the edges, as if his very essence is fraying. Arthur watches, a sentinel unfazed by the barrage of desperation. He knows this dance well, the push and pull of a tormented mind, the delicate balance between chaos and control.

With every beat of his heart, with every breath that fills his lungs, Arthur Hall remains resolute, a man besieged but never broken, a vessel of many, standing united against the darkness that seeks to consume him.

The world narrows to a blade's edge, all senses honed on survival. Arthur's eyes flicker across the room, catching the glint of metal half-hidden under a tattered curtain. A letter opener—mundane yet promising. With a lunge that belies his weary state, he grasps it, feeling the cool handle press into his palm. It's a shard of reality in the nightmare.

"Come now, Arthur," Victor coos, voice dripping malice, "a scrap of steel won't save you."

But it doesn't have to save him; it just needs to buy time. Arthur angles the opener defensively, a barrier between himself and Victor's next strike. There's a sharpness in his focus, the presence of Edmund's tactical mind, Samuel's quiet strength, consolidating within him.

Victor circles, a predator scenting blood, but Arthur stands rooted, an oak amidst the storm. The Shadow lunges, a blur of darkness against the dim light, but Arthur anticipates, sidesteps, and thrusts. Metal meets flesh, a gasp is torn from Victor's lips—a sound almost foreign in its sincerity.

"Go!" Arthur commands, his voice ragged with effort as he locks eyes with Claire. Her hesitation is brief, fueled by fear and understanding. She nods, scrambling to her feet, the chair clattering to the ground behind her.

"Run, Claire," he urges again, desperation threading through his tone. Her movements are swift, spurred by adrenaline, even as her gaze lingers on Arthur, torn between escape and the pull of their shared history.

Victor recoils, clutching at the wound, his sneer twisting into a snarl. But Arthur can't afford to watch Claire's retreat—he has only seconds before The Shadow recovers.

"Arthur..." Victor's voice trails into a hiss, a serpent cornered and ready to strike.

"Enough, Victor." Arthur squares his shoulders, the letter opener held like a talisman against the encroaching dark. He is every personality at once, a mosaic of intent and resolve. His heart beats a staccato rhythm, fueling his resolve as he braces for the final stand.

Claire's silhouette vanishes into the corridor beyond, her footfalls echoing like distant thunder. Arthur pivots, breath ragged, eyes narrowing as he faces the crumpled form of Victor. The shadows seem to recoil from the tension between them, a silent witness to the impending endgame.

"Can't let you win," Arthur grinds out, each word etched with steely resolve. His fingers tighten around the makeshift weapon, the letter opener now an extension of his will to survive.

Victor stirs, a malevolent specter rising from the depths of defeat. His grin is gone, replaced by a grimace as he attempts to regain his footing, to reclaim the power slipping through his fingers like sand.

Arthur advances, muscles coiled and mind alight with one singular purpose. He stalks forward, every step measured, an echo of the predator Victor so often embodies. In this moment, Arthur is no longer the fractured man fighting for control; he is unified in his determination, his multiple selves aligning in their shared desire to protect, to overcome.

"Your time is over," Arthur declares, voice barely above a whisper yet carrying the weight of finality. He watches, calculating, as Victor lunges—a last-ditch effort fueled by desperation.

The attack is predictable, and Arthur sidesteps with a dancer's grace, the letter opener poised. He thrusts it forward just as Victor's momentum carries him past, a perfect choreography of action and reaction.

The blade finds its mark, and Victor lets out an anguished roar that seems to shake the very foundation of the room. He collapses, his body hitting the ground with a thud that reverberates through Arthur's bones.

An eerie silence descends, punctuated only by Arthur's heavy breathing. Victor lies motionless, his threat extinguished like a flame smothered by darkness itself.

Arthur stands alone, victorious yet not unscathed. The battle may be won, but the war within rages on, a constant struggle between light and shadow. For now, though, he allows himself a moment of reprieve, the knowledge that Claire is safe fueling the embers of hope in his weary heart.

Arthur's knees buckle, and he crumples onto the cold, unforgiving floor. His chest heaves, each breath a labored fight against the fatigue that threatens to claim his consciousness. Sweat beads on his forehead, mixing with the grime of battle as it traces a path down his cheek. The tremors that wrack his body speak not just of physical exertion but of an internal war waged and won.

He lies there, sprawled amongst the detritus of conflict, the silence around him a stark contrast to the cacophony that once filled the room. His eyes flutter shut, lashes casting shadows on skin pale from the strain. For a moment, in the stillness, Arthur is free—his mind untethered from Victor's insidious grip.

As his breathing steadies and his heart rate slows, Arthur pushes himself to sit upright, his back against the wall. The coolness of the plaster seeps through his shirt, grounding him to the here and now. He drags his fingers through his hair, each strand a reminder of the chaos he has survived.

The cost of victory settles upon him like a shroud; it weighs heavy on his soul. He remembers Claire's terror-filled eyes, the way her voice cracked as she pleaded for help. Those memories carve deep furrows into the landscape of his psyche, alongside countless other scars left by Victor's cruel games.

"Never again," Arthur whispers to the darkness. The promise is a vow etched in pain; a commitment made amidst the remnants of his fractured self. He knows the battle lines in his mind are drawn in shifting sands, that the enemy within can never be fully vanquished.

Resilience blooms in the depths of his resolve, a quiet determination to face whatever comes. The darkness may linger, an ever-present shadow trailing his steps, but Arthur will walk the path ahead with eyes wide open, vigilant against the return of The Shadow.

Steadily, he rises to his feet, muscles protesting the movement. A dull ache pulses at the base of his skull, a tangible echo of the struggle that has consumed him. But he stands tall, for in this moment, Arthur Hall is no mere survivor—he is a sentinel standing watch over the fragments of his own mind.

Arthur's palms press against the cold floor, his fingers curling around the grit and debris of battle. He pushes upward, the sinews in his arms coiling with effort as he rises from defeat's crouched shadow. The room tilts, a slow, nauseating spin, but he steadies himself, his breath a ragged counterpoint to the silence that envelops him.

He stands, the distance between himself and the ground lengthening until he's upright, a sentinel amidst the chaos. His gaze, unwavering, locks onto Victor's prone figure. There lies the embodiment of torment, The Shadow who has danced too long in Arthur's mind, now reduced to mere flesh and vulnerability.

The pulse in Arthur's temple throbs, a testament to the ferocity of their clash. A war rages within him still, the aftermath of such violence a tremor through each thought, each heartbeat. He can feel it—the dark tendrils of Victor's will, lurking, waiting for a fissure through which to crawl.

Victor's chest rises and falls with shallow breaths, a rhythm out of sync with the stillness that has claimed the room. Even unconscious, his presence is a blight, a stain on the air that Arthur inhales. But this victory, however transient, grants Arthur the luxury of observation without immediate fear of reprisal.

He watches, listens, feels. The quiet is deceptive, a soft blanket covering the jagged edges of his psyche. Arthur knows the truce is temporary. The scent of sweat and blood mingles with the metallic tang of fear, an olfactory reminder of the price paid for this moment of reprieve.

"Keep watch," he murmurs, the words for no one but himself, a reminder that vigilance is now his closest ally. The darkness inside him shifts, restless, a beast with many eyes all looking inward, searching for a path to resurgence. Arthur feels them move—Edmund's caution, Samuel's fortitude—they are there, too, pieces of his fragmented self-offering silent support.

The air is thick with the unspoken, the room a vault for secrets and splintered memories. Arthur understands that the war he fights is cyclical, a serpent consuming its own tail—an eternal struggle against an enemy born from his own depths.

A shiver courses down his spine, a physical whisper of what might come when Victor stirs once more. But for now, the monster's influence lies dormant, and Arthur allows himself the smallest respite. His gaze never leaves Victor's form, a silent testament to the defiance that keeps Arthur anchored.

With this day closing, Arthur's silhouette is both a monument and a warning—the contours of a man who bears the scars of his internal battleground. He breathes in the charged air, feeling the weight of his own resolve settle upon his shoulders.

He may stand victorious today, but tomorrow awaits with its unseen challenges. Arthur Hall knows the dawn will come with no promises, only the certainty that the war against his mind is far from over. And he will be ready.

Chapter 24

Arthur's eyelids flicker, the stark white walls of the room creeping into his hazy vision. Shadows seem to dance just out of sight, whispering of a darkness that clings to the edges of his consciousness. He tries to lift himself from the narrow bed, but his limbs protest, shaking with a weakness that feels foreign yet frighteningly familiar. His breaths come in short gasps, each one fighting through the lingering fog of his mind—a battleground scarred by his recent struggle with Victor.

The door opens with a muted creak, slicing through the stillness of the room. Dr. Turner steps inside, her presence a beacon of tranquility amidst the chaos that has taken root within him. Her eyes, steady and kind, meet Arthur's, and the trembling that racks his body begins to subside.

"Arthur," she says, her voice a gentle balm to his frayed nerves, "you're in a safe place now. This is a psychiatric facility designed to help you heal."

He blinks slowly, absorbing her words as she pulls up a chair beside his bed. The simple act of focusing on her face anchors him to reality, away from the precipice of fear that Victor always brings.

"Remember what happened?" Dr. Turner prompts softly. Her question is delicate, but it carries the weight of the world. Memories flood back—flashes of confrontation, fragments of rage, and the cold touch of Victor's influence all claw at his thoughts.

"You've been through a significant ordeal, but you're here now, and we are going to take care of you." Her hand rests atop his own for just a moment, grounding him.

Arthur nods, the fight with Victor still echoing in his bones, a chilling reminder of the war waged within his own mind. But here, in the company of Dr. Turner, he finds the strength to believe in a reprieve from the internal storm. For now, Victor is silent, and Arthur clings to that silence like a lifeline in the turbulent sea of his psyche.

The door creaks open, a sliver of light from the corridor slicing through the dimness of the room. Claire stands in the threshold, her silhouette hesitant, as though she might dissolve into the shadows that cling to her frame. Arthur's gaze lifts from the stark white sheets, finding her eyes, pools of turbulent emotion. She steps forward, each movement measured, a dance of doubt and determination.

"Arthur?" Her voice is a whisper, laced with cracks of vulnerability. His name on her lips feels foreign yet achingly familiar.

"Hi, Claire," he replies, his voice a soft rasp. The words hang between them, fragile threads of connection spun from heartache and hope.

She draws closer, her presence an unspoken question, her worry for him etched in the furrows of her brow. Relief breathes through the lines around her mouth, a silent testament to her fears not realized. Their shared history whispers through the air, a tapestry woven with threads of love and loss, joy and pain, now frayed at the edges.

Dr. Turner's gaze shifts from patient to partner, understanding the sacred space of reconnection that unfurls before her. She steps back, retreating to the periphery where her watchful eyes are vigilant but unobtrusive, granting them a moment veiled in privacy.

In the quiet, their eyes meet, speaking volumes in the silence. A language only they know, crafted from years of whispered confidences and screams that echoed off empty walls. Claire extends her hand, a tremble betraying the steadiness she tries to portray. Her fingertips graze Arthur's hand, the contact a balm to the raw edges of his fractured soul.

"Are you... are you okay?" she asks, her touch lingering, a physical anchor in the storm that rages within him.

"Safe," Arthur manages to utter, the word a shard of truth in the chaos. "For now."

The touch, simple and tender, becomes the eye of the hurricane, a still point in the tumultuous world Arthur inhabits. In this sterile room, with its antiseptic scent and the soft hum of machines, there lies a promise—a fleeting taste of normalcy, of care, of something that could resemble healing.

Claire's hand tightens ever so slightly around his, a lifeline thrown across the abyss that separates them. In her grasp, he finds a whisper of strength, enough to face the long path ahead, the daunting task of stitching together the fragmented pieces of himself.

And in that moment, beneath the clinical glow of fluorescent lights, amidst the echoes of a battle fought in the recesses of his mind, Arthur Hall dares to hope.

The sterile silence of the room fractures as the door creaks open, Detective James Lawson stepping through the threshold. His shadow stretches across the floor like an omen, the reality of the world beyond these walls inching closer to Arthur's cocoon of isolation.

"Arthur," Lawson begins, his voice a blend of authority and solace, "it's over. The case has been closed."

The detective's eyes, those piercing blue sentinels, fix upon Arthur with a gravity that tugs at the edges of his consciousness. They speak of sleepless nights, of relentless pursuit, but also of a shared burden now lifted.

"The perpetrator... we've apprehended him. Justice has been served for the victims."

Arthur's heart clenches, a beat skipped, then resumes its rhythm. A part of him had remained ensnared in the outside world, tangled in the loose ends of a nightmare. But here stands Lawson, the embodiment of resolution, shepherding closure to his doorstep.

"Detective," Arthur's voice emerges, a soft-spoken echo against the stark white walls. "Your dedication— I can't thank you enough." Each word is weighed, measured, teetering on the precipice of his fractured mind.

Lawson nods, his professional mask yielding to a glimpse of empathy. "It's my job, Arthur. Bringing peace to those families, ensuring the safety of our city... It's what needed to be done."

Their exchange is a dance of gratitude and reassurance, two souls momentarily entwined by the threads of justice and human compassion. In Lawson's steadfast gaze, Arthur sees a reflection of his own search for equilibrium, for the quietude that comes when the scales of justice find their balance.

"Thank you," Arthur breathes out again, the words inadequate vessels for the torrent of emotion they're meant to carry. Yet they hold a power all their own—a recognition of the humanity that persists, even amidst the darkest chapters of their lives.

Dr. Turner's heels click against the sterile linoleum as she approaches the small group gathered at the threshold of Arthur's room. Detective Lawson, his posture a testament to years of service, stands with a quiet authority beside Claire, whose hands are clasped tightly together.

"His progress is steady," Dr. Turner begins, her voice carrying the measured cadence of someone accustomed to delivering news, good or bad. "But the road to recovery is long and intertwined with challenges."

Claire nods, eyes brimming with a hope that wavers like a candle in the wind. "So, he stays here... for how long?"

"Until we're confident he can manage the complexities of his condition without risk," Dr. Turner replies, eyeing Arthur with a clinical yet caring gaze. "Further observation, therapy — it's crucial for his healing."

Lawson's blue eyes flick to Arthur, the detective's face etching a silent vow. "Whatever helps him regain control, I'm all for it."

Arthur sits motionless on the hospital bed, the voices around him distant like echoes in a cavernous void. His gaze drifts beyond the faces before him, past the walls that cage him but also protect. Memories cascade, a relentless torrent: Victor's sneer, the shadows cast by his malevolent intent, the blood-stained pieces of a fractured self.

Guilt gnaws at Arthur's insides, an insatiable beast; relief washes over him, a cleansing yet cold tide. The very air feels heavy with the weight of lives tilted askew by his inner darkness. Yet, there, nestled within the chaos, a spark of determination takes root — to bury Victor so deep that not even a whisper of his existence could escape into the world.

The murmurs of agreement from Dr. Turner, Claire, and Detective Lawson fade into the background as Arthur anchors himself to that spark. It is the beacon guiding him through the fog, the promise of a fight not only for his sanity but for redemption.

For now, Victor is a specter shackled by the light of awareness, but the battle lines within Arthur's psyche remain drawn, a map to a war that is far from over.

Arthur's breath falters, a fragile rhythm against the silence of the room. Dr. Turner's presence is a beacon, her voice threading through the stillness with practiced ease. "We're going to work through this together," she assures him, her tone soft but unyielding. "The journey ahead requires patience and courage, Arthur. Therapy, self-awareness—these are your armor. They will help keep Victor at bay."

She leans forward, glasses catching the sterile light, eyes locking onto his. "Vigilance is key. Your mind is a battleground, but you are not defenseless." Her words are a lifeline, thrown across the tumultuous sea churning within him.

Claire watches from a corner, a sentinel wrapped in quiet strength. She moves closer, her steps hesitant as if every inch towards him is a mile traversed over rugged terrain. "I'm here for you," she murmurs, her voice barely above a whisper, yet it slices through the fog enshrouding Arthur's thoughts.

Her hand hovers over his, trembling like a leaf on the verge of falling. There's a promise in her touch, an oath to wade into the mire beside him. "Even if things aren't the same between us," she continues, the battle lines of worry etched deep on her brow, "I'll support you. We'll find the healing you need... the closure we both need."

Arthur feels the ghost of their past connection in her tentative grip. It's a fractured bond, pulsing with pain and care, a complex tapestry woven from threads of shared history and shattered trust. For a moment, he allows himself to lean into the warmth of her presence, letting it seep into the crevices of his broken spirit.

Dr. Turner nods, a silent sentinel affirming Claire's declaration. In the hollows of Arthur's mind, where shadows whisper and Victor lurks, these two women stand as guardians. They are the light that Victor cannot extinguish, the anchors that might just hold Arthur steady in the face of the tempest raging inside him.

Detective Lawson stands in the doorway, his silhouette a stark contrast against the sterile brightness of the hallway. He carries the aura of finality, a chapter nearing its end, as he steps into the room where Arthur sits, enveloped in the quiet aftermath of revelation and resolve.

"Arthur," Lawson says, the name resonating with a respect hard-earned and genuine. "It's time for me to go."

Arthur lifts his gaze, eyes meeting the detective's with a clarity that feels like a victory over the chaos that once reigned within him. There's a nod, subtle yet laden with meaning. The air between them is charged with the unspoken acknowledgment of what they have endured together.

"You've shown a strength that many could only aspire to," Lawson continues, voice steady but not without warmth. "The road ahead is yours to walk, but you won't be walking it alone." He pauses, allowing the words to settle, to fortify the fragile peace that has begun to take root in Arthur's soul.

"Thank you," Arthur murmurs, his voice a soft-spoken testament to the gratitude that weaves through his fractured thoughts. There's an undercurrent of sorrow too, for all that has been lost, for the lives irrevocably altered by Victor's dark impulses. But there's hope as well, blossoming slow and tentative in the wake of destruction.

Lawson nods, a silent salute, before turning on his heel and walking out, leaving behind the echoes of a battle fought and a war still waging. His departure feels like the closing of a door, the sealing of a bond forged in the crucible of Arthur's unraveling.

Now, in the quiet that Lawson's exit ushers in, Arthur settles deeper into the chair that has become his refuge. Dr. Turner's presence is a gentle hum at the edge of his consciousness, her watchful eyes a promise of guidance through the labyrinth of his mind. Claire lingers too, her concern a tangible thing, wrapping around him like a shawl against the chill of uncertainty.

The rhythm of the psychiatric facility beats around him—a metronome of routine and recovery. Nurses pass by with soft-soled efficiency, their voices low and soothing. The faint scent of antiseptic mingles with the undercurrent of determination that permeates the walls of this sanctuary.

As minutes stretch into hours, Arthur begins to weave himself into the fabric of this new existence. Each small interaction, each measured breath, is a step away from the precipice of madness. The darkness that is Victor recedes, a specter caged by the strength of Arthur's will and the care of those who stand sentinel over his fractured self.

In this moment, there's a sense of reprieve, a breath held and then released. The storm within quiets, granting Arthur a glimpse of a future where the shadows are kept at bay, where healing is possible. For now, he is safe, cradled in the collective embrace of those who refuse to let the night claim him.

And so, the chapter concludes—not with a definitive end, but with the steady pulse of life moving forward. Arthur Hall, once adrift in the turbulent sea of his own mind, now anchors himself to the hope of calm waters, surrounded by the light of unwavering support and the promise of dawn after the longest night.

Chapter 25

A rthur sits alone, the room around him blurs into insignificance. His hands, clasped like a vice, anchor him to the present moment, yet his gaze through the window is distant, unseeing. The city sprawls before him, indifferent to the man caught in his own silent tempest.

His eyes, those tired sentinels of a weary soul, fixate on nothing and everything—the gray expanse of sky melds with the steel of his thoughts. A reflection in the glass betrays him: a face contorted by the weight of unseen burdens. Arthur's breath comes slow, each inhale laborious, each exhale carrying shards of guilt that lance his insides, leaving behind an aching hollowness.

In the quietude of Dr. Turner's office, time feels like a predator to which he has no defense. The clock ticks—a metronome to his internal struggle. The fractured pieces of Arthur Hall jostle for space within the confines of his psyche, each shard a testament to the battles fought, the losses endured.

A spasm of remorse grips him, and his features twist. Shadows play across his visage, cast by the light that fights its way through the rolling clouds outside. Arthur's mind teeters on the precipice between reality and the chasm where Victor lies in wait. He clings to this precipice with all his might, his every sinew strained against the pull of the abyss.

The temptation to let go—to fall back into the comforting darkness—is a siren call that never ceases its haunting melody. But it's a tune Arthur knows he cannot afford to heed. Each note resonates with the discord of a life interrupted, a harmony disrupted by the cacophony of a splintered mind.

In this stillness, flecked with the staccato beat of his heart, Arthur wages war with himself. The battle lines are drawn not in sand or stone but within the intangible realm of his consciousness. He is both the battlefield and the soldier, fighting a relentless enemy that wears his own face.

Guilt gnaws at him, a relentless pestilence, as he acknowledges the cost of his existence—a cost paid not in currency, but in the very fabric of his being. Regret is his shadow, ever-present, a constant reminder of the darkness that lingers just beneath his fragile veneer of control.

He tightens his grip, knuckles whitening, as if by sheer force he can hold together the fragmented puzzle of his identity. It's a desperate gesture—one born from the knowledge that the alternative is a surrender to chaos, an acceptance of the monster that stirs within. Arthur cannot—will not—allow that to happen. Not again.

Arthur's pulse hammers in his ears, a rhythmic drumming that echoes the footsteps of memory. His thoughts spiral backward, drawn to that night—the one that forever seared Victor's essence into the tapestry of his mind.

A dimly lit alley. The kind of place where hope is snuffed out beneath the heel of a boot; where shadows dance with the devil under the sickly glow of a flickering streetlight. Arthur feels the cold brick against his back, the dampness seeping through his clothes. He remembers.

There's a woman, her mascara running rivers down her cheeks, her sobs a broken melody in the silence. And then there's

Victor—The Shadow. His presence is like a shroud over the scene, heavy and suffocating. His hand is steady, gripping the knife as if it's an extension of his will.

"Please," she whispers, a single word pregnant with terror.

Victor's response is a smile, not a warm one, but a baring of teeth—an animalistic display of power. Arthur, trapped within his own mind, watches through eyes that are not his own as the blade finds its mark. Once, twice, thrice—a symphony of crimson that paints the walls, the ground, the very air with its metallic scent.

It's done. The woman crumples, a marionette with severed strings, her lifeblood draining into the cracks of the forgotten alley. Victor stands, surveying his work, the chaos he has wrought. And Arthur can only watch, a silent witness to the monster he harbors.

Back in the therapist's office, the memory recedes like a tide, leaving behind the detritus of guilt and horror. Arthur's hands unclasp, morphing into fists so tight his knuckles blaze white against the backdrop of his skin. A deep breath inflates his lungs, a desperate attempt to cleanse the residue of Victor's deeds from his soul.

He can't change the past. He can't undo the horrors that Victor, his malevolent alter, has inflicted upon the world. But he can fight. Oh, how he can fight.

"Never again," Arthur vows to the empty room, the words a silent mantra that carves itself into the marrow of his bones. Each syllable is a step away from the abyss, a declaration of war against the darkness within.

He rises, shoulders squared against the weight of his resolve. The battle is far from over, but today, he is the victor—not Victor. Today, he walks the knife-edge path of sanity, one treacherous step at a time.

The office clock ticks, a metronome to Arthur's ragged breathing. Dr. Elaine Turner watches him from her chair, the lines of worry etched softly upon her face betraying the professional calm she embodies. Her hands rest on her notepad, motionless but ready to jot down any key revelations.

"Arthur," she begins, her voice a soft lighthouse in the storm of his mind, "you've shown incredible strength today."

His eyes, still mirroring the ghostly horrors of Victor's actions, meet hers. In them, he finds an anchor, solid and unyielding.

"I must confront him," Arthur whispers, each word punctuated by a silent echo of determination. "Victor... he can't return."

"Remember what we discussed," she encourages, leaning forward slightly, bridging the gap with her presence. "The power you have over your thoughts, the control you've been cultivating—it's yours, Arthur. Your journey through this is testament to your resilience."

Her words seep into his consciousness, a balm to the raw edges of his psyche. He nods, feeling the tendrils of power that belong solely to him. It's a fledgling thing, fragile yet growing with every session, every moment of reflection. He clings to it like a shield.

"Resilience," he repeats, tasting the word, feeling it infuse him with a dose of much-needed fortitude. "I will use it to keep him at bay."

"Exactly." Dr. Turner offers a supportive smile, small but significant. "You've already made progress, more than you realize. Each day you're building a stronger defense against Victor's emergence."

Arthur absorbs her guidance, lets it settle within the chambers of his heart. The path ahead is one of shadows and uncertainty, yet now there's a flicker of light where darkness once reigned. His commitment to therapy, to delving into the labyrinth of his own mind, has become his lifeline.

"Thank you," he murmurs, the gratitude genuine, though it hardly seems enough for the salvation she offers.

"Thank yourself, Arthur. This is your victory, your battle. I'm just here to remind you of the warrior within."

He smiles, a rare and fleeting curve of the lips that vanishes as quickly as it comes. Yet, it's enough—a signpost of hope in a terrain fraught with peril. Arthur Hall, the quiet man with the fractured mind, resolves then and there to forge onward. Victor, the shadow lurking within, will find no easy passage back to the helm. Not today, not if Arthur has anything to say about it.

Arthur's fingers tap a discordant rhythm on the leather armrest, a silent echo to the thundering pulse in his veins. The clock ticks—a metronome of reality—but his mind skitters back, tugged by the ghostly hand of memory.

"Focus on your breathing," Dr. Turner had said in a session swallowed by the past. "Inhale for four counts, hold, exhale for six. It's a mooring post for your consciousness."

He'd practiced the technique under her watchful gaze, the steady rise and fall of his chest a life raft amidst stormy seas. She'd taught him to anchor himself, to be the lighthouse beckoning his alters from the foggy depths. "Visualize a place where you feel safe, Arthur. Envision it encircling you whenever you sense Victor surfacing."

The air in that memory feels crisp now, tinged with the scent of paper and ink from her books lining the walls—knowledge standing sentinel. Dr. Turner had been more than an instructor; she'd been the cartographer mapping out the uncharted territories of his inner world.

Back in the present, Arthur's breath steadies, and he nods slightly—a silent acknowledgment of her lessons bearing fruit. Each controlled exhalation is a reinforced barrier, each mindful moment a step further away from the precipice.

"Dr. Turner," he begins, voice a mere whisper against the backdrop of the office's hushed tones, "I can't... I can't thank you enough." He stops, unsure how to encapsulate the magnitude of his indebtedness into words.

She tilts her head, a lock of brown hair escaping her bun, and her eyes—those perceptive pools of compassion—lock onto his. "You don't need to thank me, Arthur. Watching you take control, witnessing your growth—that's my reward."

His throat tightens as he considers her unwavering presence, the guiding star in his darkest nights. Trust in her never wavers because she's shown him the way forward, not by pulling him along but by illuminating the path and walking beside him.

"Still," he insists, finding strength in vulnerability, "your guidance has been... indispensable."

"Then use it," she replies with gentle firmness. "Use it to build the life you want, free from Victor's chaos."

With every beat of his heart, Arthur feels the trust between them solidify. Dr. Turner is more than a therapist—healing hands sculpting the clay of his fractured psyche into something whole. She is mentor, guide, ally. And through her tutelage, Arthur has found footing on slippery slopes.

"Thank you," he repeats, this time with conviction, a buoyant affirmation that lingers in the room like a promise. He gathers himself, stands with newfound resolve, the weight of gratitude anchoring him firmly to the present.

Dr. Turner nods once, affirming their partnership in this delicate dance of healing. Her confidence in him, a beacon that disrupts the encroaching shadows.

As the clock continues its relentless march, Arthur clings to the vivid images of safety she helped him create. They are the bulwarks against the tide, the steady light keeping Victor at bay. And within those fortified walls, Arthur Hall, the quiet warrior, prepares for the battles yet to come.

Arthur's fingers trace the leather-bound journal's spine, a lifeline in the tempest of his mind. Pages whisper as they turn—empty, waiting. He breathes. In. Out. Each exhale a thread fraying, the fabric of normalcy coming undone.

"Control," he murmurs, mantra against the darkness.

The pen's tip quivers above the paper. Write it down. Make it real. Shadows flicker at the edge of vision—Victor prowling, patient. The pen touches down, a hesitant dance of ink and will.

"Today, I felt..." His words stall, truth a bitter pill on his tongue.

Normal life? Illusive. A mirage wavering over cracked psyche. Victor's laughter echoes, a distant storm rumbling. Arthur flinches. The chuckle fades, leaving silence clawing at the walls.

"Safe," he writes instead, but the letters tremble, betraying him.

He closes his eyes, seeks the stillness Dr. Turner taught him to cultivate. Meditation—a silent battleground where thoughts skirmish. He visualizes calm, a serene lake within, its surface undisturbed. But beneath, something stirs. A dark shape circling.

"Stay back," Arthur commands, voiceless. His mental fortress shudders.

Breathing deepens. Focus. He must chart the labyrinth of his own mind, map the triggers like landmines waiting to explode into chaos—into Victor. Every heartbeat a step through the maze, every breath a choice: peace or pandemonium.

"Understand," he whispers to himself, an explorer in his own twisted depths. "Learn."

Fingers tighten around the pen. Record. Analyze. Anticipate. The journal—a vessel for his fractured thoughts, a containment for Victor's malice. Words crawl across the page, slow and deliberate. A chronicle of struggle, each sentence a barrier, each paragraph a ward.

"Today, I faced fear," he writes, acknowledgment of the enemy within.

"Today, I chose me." A declaration. Defiant.

"Tomorrow, I fight again." A vow. Each word etched with determination.

Arthur blinks back the encroaching darkness, the corners of the room safe from Victor's touch—for now. His hand steadies, the narrative unfolding clearer, stronger.

"Today, I am Arthur." Only Arthur. Each letter a reinforcement of self.

"Tomorrow..." He pauses, pen poised, heart pounding. A bead of sweat trails down his temple.

"Tomorrow, I prevail." An oath cast into the abyss, challenging the Shadow lurking just out of sight.

The clock ticks on, relentless. And Arthur Hall, the fragmented warrior, bends his will against the night, penning his existence one line at a time.

Arthur's hand hesitates before it turns the final page of his journal. The air in Dr. Turner's office seems thick with the weight of unspoken words, heavy with the echoes of battles fought within the confines of his own mind. His pulse thrums a steady rhythm beneath his skin, a silent testament to the life he still claims as his own despite Victor's shadow that looms perilously close.

"Support groups," Arthur murmurs, the idea unfurling like a banner in the fog of war. He visualizes himself sitting in a circle of chairs, surrounded by others who understand the relentless tug-of-war between selves. The thought coaxes a glimmer of camaraderie from the depths of his isolation, a spark against the encroaching dusk.

"Mindfulness," he breathes out the word, letting it linger in the room, a promise to be kept. He imagines the calm that could come from such practice, the steadiness of breath and the anchoring of presence. These exercises are lifelines cast into turbulent waters, each deep inhale a step away from the precipice where Victor waits.

With these goals etched into the fabric of his resolve, Arthur feels something shift within him—a tectonic realignment of his fractured self. A sense of purpose steadies his shaking limbs, an armor forged from the very acknowledgement of his vulnerability. He is not just the vessel for a malevolent force; he is Arthur Hall, a man with the power to define his path, to reclaim his life from the chaos.

He rises from the chair, the leather releasing him with a soft whisper. The distance to the door is short, but each step carries the weight of significance. The handle is cool beneath his fingers, grounding, a threshold between the sanctuary of Dr. Turner's office and the battlefield of the world outside.

Arthur steps through, pausing for just a moment on the other side. His gaze lifts, finding the horizon through the window at the end of the hallway. There is light there, beyond the glass—a beacon amidst the shadows that have long danced around him.

His footsteps echo softly as he moves forward, the sound a gentle drumbeat to accompany the newfound lightness in his chest. With each stride, the specter of Victor recedes, pushed back by the strength of Arthur's conviction and the clarity of his goals.

The elevator dings its arrival, and Arthur enters, pressing the button for the ground floor. As the doors close, sealing him within this transient space between floors, between moments of his life, he allows himself a small, hopeful smile. Today, he has chosen his path. Tomorrow, he will walk it.

And when the doors open once more, releasing him into the bustle of the city, Arthur Hall takes a deep, centering breath and steps out. Ahead lies challenge, uncertainty, and the relentless pursuit of healing—but he faces it all with his gaze fixed ahead, ready to face whatever may come.

Chapter 26

Arthur's key turns in the lock with a soft click that seems to echo through the silent hallway. He pushes the door open and steps inside, his presence disturbing the stillness of the house like a pebble breaking a glassy pond. dust specks dance in the slats of sunlight cutting through the blinds, each one a tiny spotlight on the mundane tragedy of his life.

He closes the door behind him gently, as if afraid to wake the ghosts that surely linger in the corners. Arthur's shoes scuff against the wooden floor, the sound a heavy drumbeat to his procession of guilt. This place, once a sanctuary, now feels more like a crime scene he can't leave behind. Shadows cling to the edges of the room, harboring whispers of the past.

Moving further into the living space, his gaze is inexorably drawn to the mantelpiece. There, amidst the clutter of everyday life—bills, keys, a bowl of change—sits a framed photograph. It's him and Claire, captured in a moment of sunlight and smiles, a stark contrast to the gloom that pervades the space now.

He pauses, heart thudding erratically, as the image ignites a torrent of emotion. The happiness in that frozen moment taunts him, a cruel reminder of what has been lost. His hand lifts, almost of its own volition, trembling as it hovers just inches from the glass protecting the photograph.

For a fleeting second, he considers picking it up, feeling the coolness of the frame, allowing himself the full brunt of memories. But no, not now. He cannot trust his fingers not to crush the relic of a better time, nor his mind to withstand the flood of remorse that would surely follow.

With an effort that drains him, Arthur withdraws his hand, leaving the photograph untouched. His breath comes out in a shudder, and he turns away from the mantelpiece, the weight of unresolved history pressing down on him like a physical force.

The house holds him in a tight embrace, a shelter that is both comfort and prison. Arthur stands alone in its midst, a man fractured by his own mind, seeking solace in the silence even as it screams at him with the echoes of a life unraveling.

Arthur's steps are a muted drumbeat against the wooden floor, each one echoing the disquiet in his mind. The air feels thick with the ghost of conversations past, whispers that coil around him, tight and unyielding. Claire's voice, sharp and splintered with emotion, cuts through the stillness of the room, reverberating in his skull.

"You never see, Arthur. You never understand."

Her words from their last encounter hang in the air, an accusation that chills him to the bone. His hands curl into fists at his sides, knuckles whitening as he grapples with the memory. It's her pain that haunts him now, the hurt etched in her voice, the gulf between them widening with every spoken truth.

He must bridge that gap. He has to mend what is broken, though the path is shrouded in shadows, treacherous with hidden snares that could pull him further into the abyss. But he cannot—will not—allow their bond to fray into nothingness. This resolve anchors him, even as uncertainty whirls within like a gathering storm.

Turning away from the mantelpiece, he drifts toward the kitchen, where life's mundane evidence awaits his attention. A stack of unopened letters lies on the counter, neglected casualties of his time loss. They stand as silent sentinels, their blank faces hiding demands and consequences, reminders of a man who once had a grasp on a simpler existence.

His fingers hover over the envelopes, the paper cool and unyielding beneath his touch. Each one is a testament to a life interrupted, a narrative paused mid-sentence. There is fear in this moment, a deep-seated dread of the truths they might unveil, but he pushes past it, drawing in a breath that tastes of dust and resolve.

Peeling back the flap of the topmost letter, he steels himself against the onslaught of reality that is sure to come. The paper trembles slightly in his grip, as if it too fears what revelations may spill forth. It's a dance with the unknown, each step forward a defiance of the chaos that seeks to claim him.

In the quiet of the kitchen, with the sun throwing long shadows across the floor, Arthur Hall stands at the precipice of confrontation and catharsis. Here, in this unremarkable corner of his world, he prepares to face the aftermath of an existence fragmented by shadows that lurk within his own mind.

The shrill ring of the phone shatters the silence, a stark contrast to the stillness of the kitchen. Arthur's heart leaps, muscles tensing as he lunges for the lifeline, desperate for it to be Claire's voice that greets him on the other end.

"Arthur? Hey mate, it's Gary." The words are warm, tinged with genuine concern that grates against Arthur's raw nerves. "How are you holding up?"

Arthur's throat tightens, and he swallows hard, an automatic smile playing on his lips despite the absence of joy. "I'm managing, Gary. Thanks for checking in."

He leans against the cold granite counter top, the firm surface grounding him as he struggles to maintain the façade. His eyes dart to the unopened letters, then away—too painful a reminder of reality pressing in.

"Good, good," Gary continues, oblivious to the dance of emotions playing out across Arthur's features. "You know, we all miss you at the office."

A laugh, brittle and short-lived, escapes Arthur's lips. "I'll be back before you know it." The lie tastes of ash in his mouth, but he lets it linger there, unwilling to dispel the comfort it may bring to his friend.

"Take all the time you need," Gary insists, ever the supportive colleague. "We're just... worried, is all."

Arthur nods, even though Gary can't see the gesture—a reflex born of politeness rather than necessity. "I appreciate it. Really, I do."

"Alright then, mate. Just wanted to hear your voice, make sure everything's okay." There's a pause, a moment where Gary's intuition seems to hover at the edge of truth. "You sure you're alright?"

"Couldn't be better," Arthur lies smoothly, his voice a practiced calm that belies the storm inside. He forces a chuckle, hollow and rehearsed. "Just the usual ups and downs, you know?"

"Of course, Arthur. We all have those days." Gary's reply comes with an ease that speaks of a life unburdened by shadows. "Well, I won't keep you. Just remember we're here for you."

"Thanks, Gary." Arthur hangs up before another word can pass between them, the click of the receiver echoing like the final note of a dirge.

Alone again, Arthur stands motionless, the weight of the unspoken pressing down upon him. The darkness beckons, whispering secrets only he can hear, promises of oblivion wrapped in the guise of peace. But somewhere, beneath the cacophony of his fractured thoughts, a spark of resilience flickers, stubborn and defiant against the encroaching night.

Arthur presses the phone onto its cradle, his fingers lingering on the cool plastic with the weight of a thousand unspoken words. He releases a breath he didn't realize he was holding and turns away, seeking refuge from the relentless tide of his own deceit.

As he drifts through the silent house, his eyes catch upon a potted plant nestled in the corner. Its leaves are vibrant green, an oasis of life amidst the shadows that dance along the walls. Arthur inches closer, drawn to its quiet perseverance. He observes the way it stretches towards the meager light that filters through the curtains, resilient despite the stillness that surrounds it.

He reaches out, fingertips brushing against the smooth leaves, and in their simple endurance, he finds a silent ally. The plant is unaware of its symbolic stature in Arthur's splintered world—a beacon of growth and renewal, steadfast in the face of neglect.

In this moment, there is a soft knock at the door, a gentle intrusion slicing through the thick veil of Arthur's isolation. He hesitates, caught between desire for solitude and the yearning for a reprieve from his own mind's chaos. With a resigned sigh, he pulls himself away from the plant's comforting presence and moves to answer the call of the outside world.

Lisa Thompson stands in the threshold, her warm brown eyes immediately scanning his face for signs of the battle she knows rages within him. There's no need for pretense here; her understanding is as palpable as the air they share.

"Arthur," she greets, her voice a soothing balm to his frayed nerves.

"Lisa." His reply is subdued, the exhaustion seeping into his bones rendering any attempt at cheerfulness futile.

She steps inside, her movements confident yet considerate, as if each step is curated to not disturb the delicate balance of his mental state. They find themselves seated across from each other, two souls navigating the treacherous waters of human experience.

"Tell me about your week," Lisa prompts, her tone gentle but insistent.

Arthur's gaze flickers back to the plant, taking solace once more in its unassuming strength. "It's been... challenging," he concedes, the truth seeping out like light through cracks in a wall.

Their conversation unfolds, a tapestry woven from threads of shared experiences and mutual support. Lisa speaks little of herself, guiding Arthur through the labyrinth of his thoughts with practiced ease. Her empathy envelops the room, a blanket under which Arthur's turmoil simmers, less fierce for a time.

"Remember," she murmurs, "healing isn't linear. It's okay to feel lost sometimes."

Arthur nods, clutching onto her words as one might cling to a lifeline in stormy seas. In the quietude of her presence, the cacophony inside him quiets to a dull roar, granting him a reprieve, however fleeting, from the relentless pursuit of his own mind.

Arthur's fingers trace the lines of his own palms, a map of guilt etched into his skin. The air is heavy with confession as he sits opposite Lisa, his voice a tremulous whisper piercing the silence.

"I feel like I'm drowning in remorse," Arthur admits, his eyes unable to meet hers.

Lisa leans forward, her presence a beacon in the murky depths of Arthur's despair. "You've been through so much, Arthur. It's natural to feel overwhelmed," she says, her voice a soft current against the tide of his self-condemnation.

"But the things I've done..." His words fracture, the pieces reflecting the brokenness he feels within.

"Your condition... it doesn't define you," Lisa counters, her gaze steady and sure. "You are more than the sum of your actions, more than the chaos of different identities."

He breathes out slowly, allowing her affirmation to seep into his pores. In her eyes, he finds the mirror of his potential, not just the shadow of his past.

The sudden chime of the doorbell slices through their connection. Arthur's pulse quickens, each beat a drum roll of anticipation. He stands, muscles tensing with uncertainty. As he approaches the door and pulls it open, there stands Claire, her figure a haunting reminder of both love and loss.

"Arthur..." Her voice falters, revealing the tightrope of emotions on which she balances.

"Hi, Claire." He searches her face, finding the flicker of hope that fights to shine through the cloud of apprehension.

Claire steps inside, a tentative guest in a home that once knew her touch well. Arthur feels the weight of possibility resting precariously on his shoulders, aware that this moment could be the fulcrum on which their future teeters.

Arthur settles onto the couch, his movements rigid, like a marionette steered by unseen hands. The space between them is an ocean of silence, each ripple a word left unsaid. Claire sits across from him, her posture straight, yet not unwelcoming.

"Arthur," she begins, her voice threading through the tension. "I don't know where we start."

"Neither do I," he admits, his own speech a whisper against the vastness of their shared pain. Shadows dance on the walls as if reflecting the turmoil within.

Claire's eyes trace the lines of his face, seeking the man she once knew. "You look tired," she says, a simple observation that carries the weight of a thousand sleepless nights.

He nods, feeling the fatigue in his bones. "It's been...hard to find rest." Each word is a stone thrown into the stillness, creating ripples that cannot be undone.

"Me too," she confesses, her fingers twisting in her lap. "I lie awake, wondering what's real and what's another of your... shadows."

Arthur flinches at the mention of his other selves, the barrier between them reinforced by his condition. He struggles to maintain control, to keep the fractured parts of his psyche from emerging.

"Can you forgive me?" he asks, his heart a drumbeat of hope and dread.

Claire's response is slow, measured like the ticking of a clock in an empty room. "I want to understand, Arthur. But I can't promise forgiveness right now."

He nods, accepting her words as one accepts the cold truth of winter.

They sit in silence, the air around them thick with unasked questions. Eventually, Arthur musters the courage to bridge the distance. He extends a hand, palm open, an offering as vulnerable as his battered spirit.

Claire stares at his hand, conflict warring in her gaze. She hesitates, caught in the web of their past, every thread a memory laced with joy and sorrow. Slowly, tentatively, she places her hand in his, her slender fingers entwining with his.

In the contact, there's a spark, faint but undeniable. A glimmer of hope ignites in her eyes, a silent acknowledgment of the man beneath the disorder, the heart that beats steadily amidst the chaos of his mind.

Their hands locked together, they allow themselves this moment of connection, two souls adrift reaching for the possibility of healing in the quiet storm of their lives.

Arthur stands, the distance between him and Claire a chasm of shared history. His breath catches as he takes a tentative step forward, each movement an echo of years weighed down by secrets and silence. The air is thick with the residue of confessions, the space around them vibrating with words left unsaid.

"Arthur?" Claire's voice slices through the fog of his apprehension, a beacon calling him back to the present.

He looks at her, really looks at her. She is the still point in his ever-turning world, her presence a balm to the chaos that roils beneath his skin. There's a question in her eyes, one that doesn't need words, and it tugs at something deep within him—a longing for understanding, for absolution.

"Can we..." Her voice trails off, but Arthur understands. It's not just about forgiveness or the past; it's about now, about what comes next.

Slowly, he closes the gap, his movements deliberate, mindful of the fragility of the moment. Claire watches him, her body rigid with anticipation and something that resembles hope. When he's close enough to see the flecks of green in her brown eyes, Arthur stops, his hands hovering in the space between them.

"May I?" The question is a whisper, barely audible over the thundering of his heart.

Claire nods, a silent permission that speaks volumes.

With a tremor betraying the turmoil inside him, Arthur wraps his arms around Claire. She stiffens for a heartbeat, then melts into him, her own arms encircling his waist. They stand there, locked in an embrace that is both an end and a beginning.

Their bodies tremble, a shared shiver that runs through them like a current. It's relief, it's fear, it's the raw edge of everything they've been through and everything they have yet to face. But in this moment, they are together, two halves of a fractured whole finding comfort in the mere act of holding and being held.

The room seems to hold its breath, the shadows cast by the fading light stretching across the floor like silent witnesses to their reconciliation. Time itself pauses, giving them this interlude, this chance to cling to the fragile thread of connection that has somehow remained unbroken through the storm.

As they pull back slightly, their eyes meet. No words pass between them, but there is an understanding, a recognition of the journey ahead. It will be arduous, a path riddled with doubts and fears, but for the first time in a long while, there is a glimmer of hope.

They stay wrapped in each other's arms, the embrace a quiet declaration of their commitment to try, to heal, to move forward together. And as the chapter closes on their trembling figures, there is a sense that the true work of mending what has been torn asunder is only just beginning.

Chapter 27

Arthur's fingers tap an anxious rhythm on the leather armrest, a soft staccato in the silence of Dr. Turner's office. The room feels like a cage made of bookshelves and diplomas, trapping him with his own fractured thoughts. He glances at the clock; each tick is a heartbeat, a reminder that time marches on while he wrestles with the shadows within.

The door opens with a hush, breaking the cycle of Arthur's tremors. Dr. Turner steps in, the light from the corridor spilling over her like a spotlight on the stage of his recovery. Her eyes, warm pools of understanding, scan his form with a doctor's precision.

"Arthur," she begins, her voice a blend of professional concern and genuine care. "How have you been feeling since we last spoke?"

The words hang in the air, heavier than the thick tomes lining the walls. Arthur swallows hard, his throat tight with the effort to speak truths he'd rather leave unvoiced.

"It's been... difficult," he admits, his gaze drifting away as if the words are too burdensome to look in the eye. "I'm here, I'm trying, but it's like standing on the edge of a cliff. And beneath me... Victor waits, I can feel him watching, waiting."

Dr. Turner nods, her expression unchanging, a rock amidst the stormy sea of his confession. She invites him to continue, her notepad resting idly in her lap, a silent witness to his struggle against the darkness that shares his name.

Breath by labored breath, Arthur excavates the weight of his fears, his words etching a raw landscape of his psyche. "Every morning is a battle," he confesses, the tremble in his voice betraying the steely resolve of a man who's walked through internal hell and still clings to hope. "I'm committed to this—to unraveling the knots Victor tied inside my head."

His fingers interlace, squeezing in a silent plea for strength. He speaks of Victor as one might speak of a tempest—destructive, unpredictable, and terrifyingly near. "I won't let him back out," Arthur asserts, the determination crackling like a live wire within the vulnerable timbre of his speech. "I can't."

Dr. Turner leans forward, her presence a beacon in the gloom of Arthur's confessions. With each nod, she stitches encouragement into the seams of his tattered will. "You've shown incredible courage, Arthur," she says, her voice a soothing balm that tempers the rawness of his admission. "Victor hasn't had a foothold in months, and that's a testament to your dedication."

She pauses, allowing the gravity of her words to sink in, to fortify the ramparts of Arthur's resolve.

"But the journey isn't over," Dr. Turner continues, her tone soft yet firm, a gentle but unyielding reminder. "We need to keep working together, to stay vigilant, so you can continue to live without his shadow over you."

Arthur absorbs her words, letting them settle deep within, where the darkness of Victor stirs, ever waiting. The promise of control, of keeping Victor at bay, it's a lifeline thrown into the roiling sea of his fractured mind.

"Thank you," he whispers, a simple phrase heavy with gratitude for the woman who stands sentinel at the gates of his sanity. Dr. Turner offers a smile, small but potent, carrying the weight of shared battles and victories hard-won.

Their session wanes, but the fight endures, Arthur's next steps echoing the quiet, fierce determination that fills the room—an anthem against the silence that follows.

The windowpane is a cold, unyielding barrier under Arthur's touch. Outside, the world is a blur of autumnal decay, leaves surrendering to gravity's pull, the sky a brooding overcast. His breath fogs up the glass, reality smudging at the edges as his mind spirals back to Victor's realm—where shadows reign and screams are muffled.

A shudder ripples through him, a silent wave crashing against the shore of his consciousness. In his mind's eye, he sees Victor's handiwork: the chaos wrought with a smile, the violence draped in velvet darkness. Each memory unfurls like a twisted lullaby, singing of control lost, of a monster wearing his face.

"Arthur," Dr. Turner's voice slices through the fog, a beacon calling him home. Her hand rests lightly on his shoulder, grounding, real. "Let's come back to here and now. Can you feel the chair beneath you? The weight of your body grounded to it?"

He nods, the motion jerky, an automaton waking from slumber. His gaze snaps to hers, eyes wide, searching for the anchor she offers.

"Good. Now take a deep breath with me." She inhales deliberately, her chest rising, a visual cue he mirrors. "Hold it... and let it go slowly. Feel the air passing your lips, the tension leaving your body."

Exhale by exhale, the room solidifies around him, the specters of his other self dissolving into the soft hum of the office—a symphony of normalcy. Dr. Turner's presence is a steady pulse beside him, her voice a lifeline tethering him to the present.

"Remember, Arthur, Victor is a part of you that we understand better now." Dr. Turner's words weave strength into his resolve. "You have the power to keep the darkness at bay. You have done it before; you can do it again."

FRACTURED REFLECTIONS 283

Arthur closes his eyes, letting her confidence seep into his pores, feeling it bolster the ramparts of his will. He is here, not in the abyss. He is Arthur, not the shadow. He clings to this truth, a mantra against the night that threatens to engulf him.

Arthur's lungs fill with the sterile chill of the office air, each breath a silent pledge of his resolve. The shadows lurking in the periphery of his vision retreat as he locks eyes with Dr. Turner, finding an anchor in the storm. His voice, usually a faint whisper lost to the winds of his own mind, gathers strength from necessity.

"Dr. Turner," he begins, the words thick with emotion, "I can't... I don't have the words to thank you enough. You've been more than a guide; you've been the light leading me out of a very dark place." His hands, once trembling, now rest calmly on his knees, the physical manifestation of his internal battle waning.

The doctor regards him with a gaze that is both piercing and warm, her eyes reflecting the depth of her commitment.

"Arthur, it's you who has done the hard work. Your courage is what allows you to face these challenges head-on," she responds, her voice a soft but firm declaration. "But know this: I am here for you, every step of the way."

She leans forward slightly, bridging the gap between professional and confidant. "Taking care of yourself is not just important—it's essential. And reaching out for help does not signify weakness but rather the strength to fight another day."

Arthur absorbs her words like a parched earth soaks up rain, letting them nourish the seeds of hope planted within his troubled psyche. Her unwavering support is a beacon, guiding him through the fog of uncertainty that wraps his mind.

"Thank you, Dr. Turner. Thank you for believing in me when I couldn't," Arthur whispers, the weight of his gratitude heavy in his chest. The burden he carries feels lighter for the moment, shared between patient and healer, a sacred bond forged in the crucible of his fractured existence.

The clock on the wall ticks its final tick in the hour of confession, and Arthur feels time's invisible hand pushing him towards the door. The room, once a crucible for his fears, now feels like a parting friend. Relief washes over him, a soothing balm on the open wounds of his mind. Yet beneath it, trepidation coils like a serpent, whispering reminders of the darkness that lurks within, ever ready to emerge from the depths.

"Dr. Turner," he begins, his voice carrying the weight of battles fought and those yet to come. "I can't say that Victor won't try to return, but even with my seriously fractured reflections, I'm ready to fight him with everything in me."

Dr. Turner nods, her eyes a testament to her belief in his strength. "You're not alone in this fight, Arthur. Remember that."

He stands up, a motion that carries him into a future uncertain yet full of promise. His legs feel like they're made of both lead and air as he crosses the small office that has become a sanctuary of sorts. Reaching out, he offers a handshake—a gesture of thanks—only to find himself pulled into an unexpected, brief embrace.

"Thank you," he murmurs into her shoulder, the words muffled but saturated with sincerity.

"Take care, Arthur," Dr. Turner replies softly, stepping back to give him space. Her eyes, sharp and kind, hold his for a moment longer. "Keep fighting."

With a last nod to Dr. Turner, Arthur passes through the door, the threshold between vulnerability and the vast world beyond. The chapter of his life written in these walls ends, and a new one beckons—a narrative he vows to pen with hands steady and heart resolute, free from the influence of The Shadow known as Victor Hall.

As he steps out into the corridor, the familiar landscape of the psychiatrist's office recedes behind him. With each step, he feels Victor's shadow stretch thinner, a dark echo dissolving in the light of his determination. The glimmer of hope in his eyes is tempered by the knowledge of the internal vigil he must keep. But today, hope flickers stronger, fanned by the winds of change and the support of an unwavering ally.

Arthur emerges from the shadowed alcove of Dr. Turner's building, stepping into the cacophony of the city's heartbeat. Skyscrapers claw at the overcast sky above, their glass and steel surfaces reflecting a world that moves in relentless streams of color and noise. The sun, obscured by a gathering of ominous clouds, offers no warmth to the bustling streets below.

He breathes deeply, the cool air sharp in his lungs. His shoes click against the concrete with purpose, each step a silent drumbeat in a personal march against the chaos that threatens to engulf him from within. The throng of people swells around him, a tide of anonymous faces and lives intersecting with his own—a blur he filters through a lens of watchful determination.

Eyes flicker left and right, scanning for shadows that linger too long, for movements too deliberate. He searches not for threats of flesh and bone but for the spectral hint of Victor, ever poised to pounce from the dark corners of his mind. The city's din fades to a distant hum as Arthur's internal vigil consumes his senses.

With every step, he rehearses the mantras Dr. Turner taught him, the words like talismans against the encroaching dusk of his psyche. His jaw sets firmly, muscles tensing with the effort of maintaining the fragile equilibrium between himself and the entity that shares his existence.

As he weaves through the crowd, his figure becomes just another part of the urban tapestry, unremarkable and unseen. But beneath the veneer of normalcy, the battle lines are drawn. The darkness within shifts restlessly, a serpent coiling in the recesses of his consciousness. It is a reminder that Victor, though subdued, is never truly vanquished.

A bus rumbles past, its exhaust fumes a momentary shroud that engulfs Arthur in a ghostly haze. For an instant, the world dims, and he feels Victor's cold whisper snake through his thoughts. A shiver runs down his spine but dissolves into resolve as quickly as it came.

"Stay present," Arthur whispers to himself, a lifeline amidst the dissonance of life around him.

The crowd swallows him, his solitary form assimilated into the mass of humanity. And yet, there is a singularity to his journey—an isolated path he treads alone, marked by the stringent self-awareness he must uphold.

As Arthur Hall disappears into the fabric of the city, the chapter closes with a pulse of foreboding. The readers are left to ponder the unseen struggle that continues to rage within this quiet man—a struggle against the darkness known as Victor Hall, against the very fractures of his soul.

The world moves on, indifferent, while Arthur walks the tightrope of his own existence, where one misstep could unleash the tempest lurking in the silence.

Don't miss out!

Visit the website below and you can sign up to receive emails whenever Bekka Scott publishes a new book. There's no charge and no obligation.

https://books2read.com/r/B-A-UBPLC-LCDCF

BOOKS 2 READ

Connecting independent readers to independent writers.

Did you love *Fractured Reflections*? Then you should read *Beneath the Ashes*[1] by Bekka Scott!

Beneath the Ashes

Emma Dawson thought she had her life figured out. A loving mother, a devoted wife—until the day she discovered that everything was built on a lie. Her husband, the man she trusted with her heart, wasn't who he claimed to be. When Detective Ross reveals that the charming Carlos was actually someone else, a ruthless man with a deadly past, Emma's world shatters. But Carlos's deception is only the beginning.

Emma isn't the only one hiding secrets. Her mother, Martha, and her son, Jaxon, are tangled in their own web of darkness. That fateful night when Carlos vanished—they know the truth, the gruesome

---

1. https://books2read.com/u/3198Vr

2. https://books2read.com/u/3198Vr

actions they took to protect Emma from a monster. And Emma? She harbors a secret so dark, its revelation could destroy them all.

As the police close in on Carlos, the Dawson family must confront their own buried sins. How far will they go to protect each other? In a world where every truth comes with a cost, and every secret could be their undoing, the lines between victim and villain blur.

Read more at https://authorbekkascott.com/.

Also by Bekka Scott

Fractured Reflections
Reflejos Fracturados
Bajo las Cenizas
Beneath the Ashes

Watch for more at https://authorbekkascott.com/.

About the Author

Bekka Scott is married to her high school crush, mother to three daughters and a bonus daughter, and Nana to ten grandmonsters.

She has two dogs, Sally Barbara Jean, Walter Mitty, and a cat, Sammich. In addition to writing, she has been a crocheter since the age of three.

You can find her on Instgram, Facebook, X, Tiktok, Linkedin and Goodreads.

Her author website is here: https://authorbekkascott.com/ Follow for new releases and updates.

Thank you for reading.

Read more at https://authorbekkascott.com/.

9 798227 502087